*[Pag 157]*

"Ann Bonny and Mary Read convicted of Piracy Novr. 28th. 1720 at a Court of Vice Admiralty held at St. Jago de la Vega in ye Island of Jamaica." B. Cole dated. 1724

B. Cole sculp.

MARY READ:
PIRATE WENCH

by
Frank Shay

SICPRESS 2013
METHUEN, MASS.

Frank Shay's *Mary Read: The Pirate Wench* was originally published in 1934 Ives Washburn in New York..

To:
Frances Edith Foley
With Love

TABLE OF CONTENTS

Author's Preface

The heroine of this book of adventure on the Western Seas is Mary Read, who lived and died in the manner pictured here. Serving first as an officer under many famous buccaneers, she later commanded her own vessel, and led her men in boarding fat Spanish galleons and in the rape of New Orleans. Death came to her in a manner befitting her career. So much as is known of her life is embodied in this tale of her scouring the seas.

I wish to take this opportunity to acknowledge the valuable aid and research of E. Irvine Haines, historian of the period.

F.S.

Cast of Characters

THE PEOPLE

Mary Read

Boatswain Jones

Edwin Brangwin, the Governor's Son

Anne Bonney

Mrs. Anne Fulworth

Calico Jack Rackham

Governor Woodes Rogers

INCIDENTAL PEOPLE

Moll Read

John Martell

Captain Skinner

Howell Davis

Charles Bellamy, the socialistic pirate

Stede Bonnet, the hen-pecked pirate

William Fly, the prize-fighter

Charles Vane

Edward Low, the meanest pirate

William Lewis

Edward Teach, alias Blackbeard

Edward England

Kit Winter, the admiral

Captain Sawney, the "governor"

George Lowther

Bartholomew Roberts

Frank Spriggs

Dick Turnley

Will Cunningham, first to refuse the King's Pardon

Jim Fife, the first to accept the King's Pardon

Captain Yeates

    and Others

Book One - On The Account

I

The low-ceilinged, long room of The Saylor's True Friende was warm and bright against the black coldness of the November night. Outside the winds blew across the quays of Bristol Town, rattling windows and doors; inside the swarming patrons, shouting and laughing, were fortifying themselves against the short cold trip that would divide them, even to their loyalties, between the two ships standing out in the roadstead. Before dawn they would catch the flood that would carry them to their separate ways.

In one corner of the room sat the august Captain Skinner, master of the Cadagon, snow, out of this very Bristol, with a miscellaneous cargo for trading along the Guinea Coasts and in the Bahamas. If he found those things which he sought he would continue to Charleston, to New York and Boston before turning his ship homeward. About him were grouped his men, two with coddling wenches on their knees, the rest content to coddle their jorums of hot rum. In another corner was Master John Martell of The King's Fancy, brigantine, out of Cardiff. There were more wenches among his company and the men were drinking brandies, Genevas and tots of straight rum, for money was freer among Martell's raffish company.

The staff of the tavern handled the huge throng expertly. Mine host, who answered to the name of Marcus Cribb, presided behind the long oaken counter, passing mugs, tankards and glasses to Moll Read and to her son, Buttons, a stripling of sixteen, whose already roughened hands show he is no stranger to hard work. The lad is straight and fair, his hair caught behind his ears in a tiny pigtail, his cotton shirt buttoned tight to the neck. His breeches and woollen stockings though well worn show that he takes some pride in his personal appearance. At every opportunity he listens to the talk of strange places and stranger people.

The ships' masters were completing their companies and, with the exception of the staff of the tavern, all but one man there had been signed. Skinner's papers lay on the table in front of him, but Martell's were brought out only when a man was ready to sign or put his mark to the articles. To all outward appearances both voyages were on honourable and legal intent, but Martell's price was higher and the first requisite for membership was the possession of a cutlass, one or more pistols and a stout right arm. In days now gone Martell had been a pirate; that was known, but only those who signed his papers could tell that once again he was on the account. Good Captain Skinner's name was above reproach, as every Bristol man well knew.

Pirates ashore? Pirates ashore and rubbing elbows with the very men who with the turn of the tide or shift in the winds might become their next prey? Bad times were upon Old England, and it was only fair that Bristol folk should be alive to their opportunities. King George the First, disliking his chilly realm, and likewise the people whose language he did not speak and whose politics he did not understand, had left for his beloved Hanover, for his full-breasted mistresses and his own people. He had placed the Prince of Wales at the head of the country, temporarily of course, and that worthy, bitterly disliking his father's policies, was busily changing them to suit his own fancy. There was confusion in Britain; no one knew who was master but all were willing to play one against t'other, if there were a profit to it.

"Last chance," announced Master Skinner. "I have room for but two more men. You there, Jorgen, how now? You be a good hand an' you know my snow an' you have the purchase. Or do you sail wi' yon picaroon?"

The man addressed leaned back and waved a happy hand. He was fair drunk or he would have been on his feet, hat in hand, and clutching his forelock.

"Nay, Master Skinner. I vowed a wench to stop over a bit an' I be a man o' my word, as well you know. Nor do I go with yon buccaroon. I may yet change my mind and board the Cadogan before she takes the tide."

Moll Read, mistress of the tavern and of mine host, edged her boy towards Master Skinner.

"Oooee, marster," she cooed. "'Ere's the lad for 'ee. A strong bully, a-feared o' none. Wot'll you gi'e for 'im?"

"Give, Moll, wench? I'm no master that needs to give a bounty to make up his company. I leave that to 'Is Majesty, King George, be he First or Second, and to yon Martell, the picaroon. He might give a pretty penny to fill out his company."

"Martell's arsking fifty guineas," announced an unknown.

Hard times indeed in Old Bristol. Bristol Town's a sailor's town and Bristol women are sailors' women. Time was, before the German took the throne, that would be in Good Queen Anne's reign, that a master must needs put out good gold in advance to win a sailor's services. Now they required their companies to share the dangers of a little freebooting on the side. Skinner, for instance, taking ten guineas from each of twenty-five men and as much as his officers could afford, would place a like total with theirs and use it all in a special trading account. In such a voyage as he now planned the amount would be trebled or even quadrupled and each man would get his fair share. He made his crew partners, at the same time sealing their lips if in his trading he exceeded the bounds of lawful trade. Too, he secured their services without further wage, save the shilling a day they would get from the Admiralty. To make the offer more attractive each man was permitted to trade on his own provided he shared his gains with his master.

"Mister Skinner," called a loud voice from Martell's table. "Mister Skinner, by what token do ye call me pirate?"

The patrons looking in the direction of the speaker saw that it was John Martell himself.

"Ho! Who dares say ye be no pirate? A pirate confessed ye be an' yer head's where it is only because 'Is Majesty's sarvants are a stinking lot of cringing knaves without courage to tighten the rope. If you had your deserts we'd be dropping a cheer as we passed you in chains."

"I've a mind to——" began John Martell.

"Only honest seafarers have minds to do the right thing. Ye no dare to call the watch nor the aldermen either."

The disputants made no attempt to advance upon each other; only Moll Read was active.

"'Ere's a mon for 'ee, Martell, that'll surprise 'ee. Take 'im for ten pound."

"Nay, wench, I'm 'aving a word with Mister Skinner."

But the pirate's opponent had sat down and he was without words. He was not a Bristolman and he was in Bristol only on tolerance. One overt act and the hand of every man, even to the Bristolmen in his own company, would be raised against him. Wisely he took advantage of Moll Read's interruption and resumed his own seat.

"Five, then, an' he's yours for all time. I want 'im out o' the hoose before the sun rises, I'm that sick o' his blokey face."

"Nay, Moll, I pay for no hand. I'll take 'im on for 'alf a share at twenty guineas. It's a bargain an' I do it only for you."

Moll screamed: "But I'm sellin' the fool, d'ye understand?"

"No trade," said the pirate with finality. "I like the lad's looks an' I need such a boy for my cabin. Aye, Moll, m'own, on second thought I'll take 'im for nothin' an' let 'im earn what he can sarving the company."

"Oooee," cooed Moll, "an' will the good marster gi'e me two golden guineas to seal the bargain?"

"Aye, Moll, when The King's Fancy returns to this blighted port. Ha! ha! ha! Keep your devil's brat; he looks like hell's own spit and blood." He rose to his feet. "Be getting along, my bullies, we'll complete our company at Cardiff."

Moll Read screamed another curse upon the master, his vessel and its voyage.

"It'll be strange work that I'll put that lad to before another day's done. I should a done it the week past, more to my own profit." To the lad she hissed, "Make a ship, bastard, elst I'll expose 'ee."

The watch entered at this moment and, striking his staff to the floor to gain attention, cried:

"Twelve is the hour and God's peace be on Old Bristol. To your wessels or to your homes. 'Tis the King's law."

He took up his solemn position near the door and waited as the men filed out, first Martell's company and then Master Skinner's. The wenches hurried off into the night.

Moll Read and mine host left by a back door and only the lad Moll had called Buttons Read and the half-drunken sailor were left.

"Do you go to your lodging, mon?" demanded the watch of the sailor.

"Aye, I'm there. I'm stopping here the night, if it please you, the watch. Is it not so, lad?"

"'Tis so, master," said the youth. "Your bed's above the stairs." He then went about his task of putting out the lanterns that hung about the room.

The watch, convinced that all was in order, went out into the night and to his rounds.

When all the lights but the one above the bar had been extinguished and the lad was waiting the sailor's departure, that worthy demanded another drink. He rose to his feet, it could be seen he was no more drunk than when he entered, and came to the oaken bar.

"A stiff jorum, make it, lad. It's cold the night an' I've to make my way to the High Street."

"Your bed's aloft," the lad began.

The sailor winked broadly.

"Aye, a shilling wasted but there's many a 'alf-empty bed in Bristol that needs warmin' and fillin'."

The lad who a few minutes before had seemed to be but a riverside lout was now all attention.

"You're of Master Skinner's company, I trow. Yet you took lodging here and your vessel leaves before dawn."

"Aye, an' much may happen before dawn. There's five hours that can stand a bit o' improvin'. Why do you stick to this tavern? I heard Moll trying to join you up to either company. Moll has many times the ten guineas Master Skinner asks."

"I'm not ready yet," answered the lad. "My ship'll be a fast one, one that I may be proud to name mine own. One that will go to the Indies, mayhap to Tasman's land and Cathay and Cipango. A privateer or a letter of marque, should my King need me."

"The King's shillin' is poor pay an' a marster must look sharp about 'im to 'old 'is men. Skinner's an honest man, by any way you look on't. But he's not above turnin' an 'appy penny or two by loadin' slaves at some port 'e drifts into. 'Oo's to say 'e's wrong to turn misfortune to an 'andy profit? Take last voyage: we stowed forty blacks in the lazareet an' sailed as proud's you please into Charlestown Harbour, right under the nose o' the King's Governor, if you please, and sold 'em at fifty guineas the 'ead. That's not piracy, nor privateerin' either. Privateerin's but a step to piracy and it's another to Tyburn Hill or Wapping's Execution. Win your beard first, m'lad, afore you tempt the gibbet."

"I'll cheat the gallows—"

"The boast of every rogue, yet most o' them swing afore they've learned to live." The sailor flushed his throat from his tankard.

"Tell me sum'mat more o' Boston Town, marster," pleaded the boy, his arms on the bar.

"It's a bonnie town, a bit o' old Bristol. Indeed, to many it be Bristol beyond the seas and there's many a comely wench there awaiting a likely lad to tell her downright his business with her. 'Zounds, they've a game they call bundling, but your ears are too soft to hear o' it."

The lad blushed.

"Aye," laughed the sailor. "You must have a wench tell you how 'tis played or not learn it at all. There's yet time to join wi' Skinner. Say the word!"

"I'll not say it. My ship's not yet built."

"There'll be a handy profit this time. With a good trading and fair winds there should be ten times ten guineas for each and all."

"To my thinking 'tis no better than piracy," said the lad. "Why not go all the way and join Master Maxell's company?"

"A curse upon the man an' 'is vessel! A-robbin' 'onest British ships an' a-defyin' good King Jarge. I'm no blackbird, m'lad, but only a British s'iling man lookin' to turn an extry penny."

The sailor threw a well-filled purse upon the bar.

"Be having your score from that, lad, an' I'll be about my business." He applied himself to his tankard.

The boy's eyes glistened at the sight of the stout purse and his ears thrilled to the clink of gold coins. His manner changed at once and his eyes, laughing into those of the patron, did not follow his hands as they became engaged beneath the bar.

"Let me be 'freshing up your rum, marster, while you tell me more." The youth was about strange business and needed his eyes as well as his hands. The sailor took a final gulp from his tankard and set it down.

"You must be all o' sixteen, fellow, and weigh upwards o' ten stone, an' it's time for ye to be out o' this swyvin' and crimpin' 'ole. It has a foul name. Tell you what I'll do: I'll go settle wi' yon wench and return here and take you to the Cadogan. What say? I like your trim, lad."

"I'm not wi' the ten guineas, master," answered the youth as he returned the tankard to the drinker. His voice trembled a bit, not in fear of what he had put in the sailor's mug, but that he had bungled. The man was fair game and had Moll Read glimpsed the purse on the bar she would have been doing the same thing. He was sure he had not bungled, he had watched Moll often enough since he had returned from Flanders and Holland.

He had come back to Bristol Town and asked the whereabouts of Moll Read and he had known where to ask and where not to mention her name. So Buttons had hurried to The Saylor's True Friende expecting to be recognized at once. Hopefully he had gone to the tables served by Moll and ordered a tot of rum. And, instead of a greeting, he had been insulted. Because of his youth and apparent insolvency his score had been demanded before he was permitted to put hand to tankard.

He had tossed his purse upon the table and Moll had as quickly changed her manner.

"Ooee, a fine lad," she had cooed, "an' it's a better tot he deserves wi' so much gilt i' his pocket." She had forthwith returned to the bar and drawn him a special dram, "'The Landlord's Own', m'hearty!" and placed it before him with a smirk. The Landlord's Own had proved too much for the lad, and whilst he had lain drugged Moll had filched his purse, unknowing that her victim was her own flesh and blood.

Later on learning his identity, she had taken the incident as a huge joke, had told of her error with great gusto, yet had done nothing towards making amends for it.

If he had his purse now, with its contents, he might hope to buy a station on the Cadogan. But Moll was in no mood for restitution. She'd far rather crimp her own than pay one red farthing towards forwarding his desires.

Now, if the sailor would but drink quickly, he'd still have time for the Cadogan. To make conversation he said:

"I think, marster, I'll go you the Cadogan."

"Aye, that's the gillie. An' I don't mind tellin' you that were it not for the luck o' the last voyage I'd no be able to pay my purchase. But there's fourteen guineas to that pouch an' I'll ha'e me time this night an' sail wi' the tide i' the dawn. Ha'e your duffle but ready an' I'll stop by for 'ee." He placed the tankard to his lips and drank long and deep.

"But," said the lad, "Master Skinner is in bad name along the quays. I heared tell he's a marooner."

"The story's a true one a' that. There's a fine line atween looking for the main chance and goin' on the account and Master Skinner's one who can draw that line. His swivel's never been pointed at any Briton an' never will, if I know my master. It was but last year when one of his company, a Cornishman whose name I no longer recall, lined up nine or ten others with him and demanded the Master go on the account. Master Skinner heared them out and called for a show o' hands. Ten wanted to go pirating and fifteen wanted to see Old Bristol again. So Master Skinner placed the ten in a longboat with one day's provisions and sent them to an island in the Bahamas. There they be to this day, or their bones. There's no fooling with Master Skinner."

"But that shows he be a firm man and one cannot but admire such. I ask only that my first marster be a true man and a brave one."

"Be having your score from that pouch, lad." The sailor took another decisive swig from his tankard and wiped his lips on his sleeve. As he restored the purse to his pocket, it seemed for the moment as if he were about to leave.

"Be in no haste, marster."

"Aye, but there's a wench awaiting me on the High Street and we'll be breakin' bread within half an hour and the laws of good King George in twice that time."

The lad's heart jumped as he saw the man smother a yawn.

"Do you mind if I take my tankard to yon bench?"

The youth smiled his acquiescence. How long, he wondered, would it take the drug to act? And how long would it remain effective? Long enough for him

15

to possess himself of the fat purse. Beyond that he had no plans. He knew, if he thought about it at all, he would have to bolt or else face a charge of robbery; there was none other present who might be made a scapegoat. The sailor found the bench and threw himself down heavily without further attention to his tankard. Slowly his head slumped to his chest and then came a snore, deep and resonant, followed by a complete relaxing of his body.

Silently and with almost catlike cunning the boy came from behind the bar. For a moment he listened at the door that gave on the landlord's room in the rear and then, satisfied that he would not be interrupted from that quarter, continued towards his quarry. For an instant he stood above the sailor and then deliberately kicked one of the outstretched feet to see if any degree of consciousness remained. A grunt was his only answer. Quickly he reached into the pocket containing the purse and his fingers closed around the leathern pouch; cautiously he withdrew them but his inexpert hand was betrayed by nervousness, and when success was all but his he must needs drop it clanking to the floor. As he hurriedly sought to repossess it, he saw the sailor had opened one eye and before he could straighten up the man was upon him.

"How now, my young gossoon? Running a-tick, be you? And no new offender, an old hand, I'll warrant."

The lad easily avoided the clutching hands and stowed the purse in his shirt front.

"Hold now, I say! Let me have my hands on you!" shouted the still groggy man.

The lad's sole thought was to keep out of the way of those tarry, ham-like fists swinging in every direction; one blow of either would have laid him cold upon the floor. He danced about avoiding every attempt to lay hold of him until, unwittingly, he found himself properly cornered. Spreading his arms wide, the big sailor started closing in, and it was only chance that the boy ducked beneath and made a clear escape.

"How now, my bully! I've a trick worth two o' that!"

Once more he closed in on the youth, cornering him this time away from the bar and door and crouching low to prevent another dodge; the boy swung with all his might to the jaw and the heavy sailor went over backwards, losing his balance and stumbling to the floor. The youth let out a strange laugh, a laugh from the belly, and one tinged with neither fear nor relief, but rather triumph. His opponent got slowly to his feet, deciding to make it a real battle, and was met with a rain of blows to the face and body, any two of which should have stopped him in his tracks.

"'Zounds! A fair pair of hands you carry in your pocket. But I'll lead you to the watch yet, my bully."

The boy knew his opponent was slowed considerably by the drug; his only escape from the tarry fists lay in constant action, leaping and feinting, placing a blow wherever he found an opening.

"Stay, now, be still," pleaded the sailor. "Let me but blow you down and have in the watch."

But the boy was not staying to be blowed down. He was intent upon getting near the lantern hanging above the bar; if he could but knock it down he might escape in the darkness. With his body he feinted as if to make for the door then ducked to the opposite direction, but the sailor was not fooled, not completely. As he weaved from one side to the other one of his hairy hands fell afoul the lad's shoulder; fear added agility to the thief's movements and he tore himself from the menacing hand and fell back against the wall, leaving half his shirt in his opponent's clutch. Quickly he tried to cover his breast with his hands but there was too much of the shirt gone and the well-rounded breast lay revealed.

"Hola, by my trow! A wench! A woman!" The heavy mouth went agape, the eyes stared first with unbelief, then with delight. Placing his hands on his hips, the sailor threw back his head and gave voice to a loud and lusty laugh.

"Aye, my own. 'Twas a fine bit of flogging you were in for, I trow, but it's to be a different kind of flogging you'll be getting now. Come, lass, my purse and then to our business. I'll ha'e my way before I call the watch, do mysel' a bonny turn." He held out his hand for the purse and added a single word: "Come!"

The girl, blushing, seeking to cover her breast with the remaining fragment of her shirt, saw the sailor coming toward her and sought to hug the wall. As he neared her she lowered her head and, using the wall as a springboard, hurled herself against his midriff. The hard head caught him in the high stomach and he went down gasping for breath. He saw the youth's shadow pass over his body and then heard the crash of a lantern and hurried footsteps in the dark. A door opened and slammed before he could get his wind back and rise to his feet.

The sailor set up a great hue and cry that brought Moll Read and mine host carrying fresh lanterns, brought the watch and all within sound of his voice. The watch stamped his staff upon the ground and called for silence and the great booby tried to tell of the lad who was no boy but a wench, a cutpurse, if you know, who had made off with his pouch after beating him. The watch listened intently and asked if it was a man or a woman who had beat him and stolen his clink; the sailor said it was neither, but a boy who was to go to sea and whose torn shirt had revealed her a woman. Was it mine host, here, or Moll Read, there, and speak truly? 'Twas neither but a lad who had become a woman, and the watch laughed and so did the crowd. The watch again stamped his staff and demanded silence; then he winked an eye at the proprietor, saying as he turned to go:

"It's a vile brew you sell here. Better be getting back to your berth, sailorman, an' sleep on't. Good night, landlord."

Then he went off into the night and Moll Read and mine host slammed the door in the face of the sailor who had tried to bring disrepute on their honoured tavern.

II

The young cutpurse, her swag safely stowed in her breeches pocket, had snatched a fresh shirt, a leathern jacket and heavy greatcoat from a peg in the passageway and hurried out into the night. On tiptoe she had circled the tavern and taken up a position from which she might observe events without being detected. She had seen the watch come up, followed by idlers, had heard a few words as the door opened and closed, and had seen the watch take his departure and the door slammed in the sailor's face. She knew that no pursuit was contemplated and that the only persons she had to fear were the sailor and her mother. Moll Read would not have tolerated any such invasion of her prerogatives and would have demanded the swag down to the last farthing.

Danger lay in other places. She now had money to purchase a station on Master Skinner's Cadogan, the needed ten guineas to take her on the slave trading venture to Sierra Leone, but should her victim turn up on board her shift would be a short one. If she remained ashore in that fear, the sailor might see her and in pressing his charge make known her true sex to the people of Bristol Town. She thought of Master Martell's sloop, lying out in Bristol Channel, ready to sail on a venture that would not bear too close scrutiny. Had not the sailor said that lacking his purse he would have to ask the occasion of Master Martell? There was danger at every point.

Indecision and the cold night air made her pull her greatcoat closer about her body. The sailor was still standing before the tavern door, muttering imprecations upon the house and its landlord and vowing vengeance. The girl felt she could not move until she had learned his destination or at least the direction he would take. Manifestly, his indecision was as great as her own.

With a final curse for the door he turned and went towards the High Street. As soon as his footsteps had died away, the cutpurse turned in the opposite direction but paused, after a few steps, to let out a hearty laugh. Who was the wench on the High Street who would entertain a penniless sailorman and to what would her honeyed greeting change when she learned her visitor had already been ta'en by a lad who was none other than a wench?

18

The thief resumed her journey toward the jetty; mayhap she'd learn from a passing sailorman where she might find a berth. Ships stood in the Severn, single riding lights bobbing with the tide. Old Bristol had become a great port since the Navigation Act of Good Queen Anne. Bristol ships and Bristol lads were familiar to every port o' call and a sailorman with a fat purse could easily find a berth, aye and choose his own master.

Arriving at the jetty she paused a moment to take stock of her chances. From the distance she could hear the sailor again hurling imprecations at the door of The Saylor's True Friende and the raucous voice of Moll Read in answer, threatening to call the watch if he continued to annoy honest folk. The sailor, she was sure, had been to see his wench and his frame of mind had not been improved by her reception; soon he would be returning to the jetty. As his footsteps came closer, the young thief looked about her for a place to hide. An upturned smallboat belonging to one of the ships in the roadstead lay but a few paces away. Pitching it over on one side, the girl crawled under and let it roll back. Here she was safe for the moment and could see what happened. The sailor, she judged he was her man by his footsteps, came down the jetty, still muttering and cursing and stamping his feet in a great rage. Her heart stopped as he paused beside the smallboat to kick it but then he quieted down and sat himself on the upturned bottom.

He sat thus for the better part of fifteen minutes, from time to time breaking out noisily and indignantly against the treatment he had receiv'd and vowing vengeance. The girl underneath gradually recovered her poise as she realized her victim was ignorant of her proximity. The night was a cold one, but she was used to the rigours of outdoor life and could spend the night where she was without great discomfort. Before long she heard other footsteps coming down the jetty. The newcomer came directly towards the boat under which she was hiding.

"Aye, Master Skinner," said the sailor, rising to his feet. "It's a misfortune I've had, master."

"How, now, Jorgen? A misfortune, eh?"

"Aye, master. At The Saylor's True Friende, the tavern beyond, if you will. A cutpurse fouled my tankard, and made off with my pouch."

"'Tis a misfortune, Jorgen, an' my heart to you. Are you joinin' the Cadogan snow?"

"I would, master, but my purchase was in my purse an' 'tis gone!"

"Then, my man, you're out! You are a fair hand and I'll ha'e to look sharp to find another as good. 'Tis bad at this late hour."

[1] Snow: a large two-masted vessel with a short mizzen mast which was removable. She, the snow, could make fair headway under a trysail.

"But, marster, could I but go wi' the Cadogan an' let my purchase be ta'en by three from the return?" There was a whine in the sailor's plea.

"No. Not at all. What if there be no return? Who's to pay then?" Captain Skinner's voice was harsh and indicated no yielding.

"Please to you, marster." The sailor sank to his knees, his voice rising shrilly.

"Nay, an' that's all," thundered the captain. "'Ere's a shillin' for you, an' get you gone before I call the watch. Off wi' you!"

The sailor got to his feet and accepted the captain's shilling and scuttled off; he had had enough of the watch for one night. When he was alone, the captain sat down on the boat and called for the boatswain who should have been on duty beside it.

"Aye, 'e's another I'll be losin' if 'e's no more wits about 'im than that other."

"Ho, boatswain," he shouted and almost leaped into the Severn when he heard the answer come from beneath him.

"Here, marster," and the boat was tilted to permit a young fellow to emerge. Still on his hands and knees, he continued, "Your mon's drunk an' he told me off to 'wait you, marster."

"'Nother? Take me to the Cadogan snow an' be quick. If they be not there at sailing, we sail wi'out 'em."

"Aye, marster, so I told 'im. 'E said for me to go i' 'is place. 'E was a-spendin' of his purchase money an' I have mine."

There was a pause.

"Make a light," ordered the captain, "that I may see who I speak."

"Nay, marster, I 'ave no light."

"Well, let's have this smallboat i' the water and time enough on the Cadogan snow."

Together they put their hands to the smallboat and in a moment both lowered themselves from the jetty. The youth took the single pair of oars and put his weight against them, sturdily pulling for dear life. Out into the stream shot the boat, the captain shouting directions from the stern. When he had her going as he wanted her, the captain said:

"Your name, lad? Your name and where do you hail?"

"Buttons, worship. Buttons Read, son of Simon Read of good memory."

"Aye, I remember Simon well, a good man, a true one he was, too. An' you be 'is spit, eh? You pull a steady oar. I'll not say the word till I get you under lantern light."

For ten minutes the youth pulled on the oars, never looking about to see the direction, leaving all to the captain. The smallboat grated along the side of the Cadogan and Skinner ordered the lad to make it fast.

Later, on deck and in the glare of a riding light, Skinner looked at his latest recruit.

"Let me feel your muscle. I need none but a strong lad."

The girl flexed her forearm to meet the captain's demands and she helped his decision by pulling the stolen purse from her pocket and jingling it to show she had the purchase money.

"Aye, a sturdy lad and a good sailor, too, I'll trow. If you truly be Simon Read's lad, consider yourself engaged."

"A mercy on you, marster," passing him her purse. "Take what you will."

"Where's your chest, Buttons?" asked Captain Skinner.

"On my back, marster. If you go south to the Guinea Coast, I'll have no need for more."

"Nor will you, but we may go to Tasman's land before we see Bristol Town again."

Buttons did not know it, but this remark was made for the benefit of one lurking in the shadow behind the poop.

"Then I'll make my purchase as we go, marster."

"Look sharp, there, Howell Davis," shouted the Captain to the one in the shadow. "Go below an' remain quiet!"

The man in the shadow disappeared.

"Think twice, lad, those two left behind may be the lucky ones. This cruise may yet end on a length of tarry rope."

"I'll cheat the gallows, marster."

"Aye, if you be Simon Read's spit, you will that. Go below and be quiet."

III

Buttons went below to the forecastle and as she entered a voice greeted her.

"Sime Read's lad, eh?"

"Aye, mate, 'is own spit and blood. An' who be you?"

21

"Howell Davis, o' Milford Haven. I be second to command. Should any mishap occur to that cuckold above I'd be marster o' the snow. It's a word to you, lad, to 'ware your course. Do I make myself clear, son o' Sime Read?"

"Aye, sir, that you do."

Buttons selected a bunk far from the companionway. Her secret was still her own and with her greatcoat she prepared for sleep. All about her were snoring men, her mates as long as her sex remained undiscovered, but men who upon learning the truth would fall upon her like ravening wolves. She had heard of Howell Davis, the Blackbird of Milford Haven; a dark character feared by all who had had dealings with him yet a good trader and a fearless mate, he was a strict disciplinarian and one needed by Captain Skinner in his dealings with slave merchants.

Even though she had had a hard day and was not afraid of her situation, Buttons found sleep difficult to achieve. She had been far and seen much in her seventeen years, but this was her first voyage as a sailor. Of her own early life she remembered little, but her mother, Moll Read, had been a mouthy piece and able to keep no secrets. What she did know of her early life, when she thought of it, was in the words of her mother, ribald and raucous. She did not like to think of her mother; always since she had been aware she had feared the woman and she knew the woman feared her. From whose loins she had sprung was a mystery to all but Moll and she could be counted on not to tell the truth. That her father had been a seaman was evident. Simon Read, whose name she bore, was a privateer when he took Moll to his mother's cot back of Bristol and said she was his bride. Moll was with child and if Simon was ready to admit it was his, that was enough for the parent. Whilst Simon was still in port a son was born to him and he had bestowed his own name upon the young squaller and then had gone off to sea, admonishing his parent that he had done well by her and expected her to do well by his. Simon's first venture was interrupted by a Spanish ball that carried him overboard and the battle was too fast and furious to permit a search for the pieces.

Moll's grief was short-lived. Within a few months she was again with child. Fearing her mother-in-law's wrath she took what money she had with her son and had journeyed to France. There, as Moll tells it, a daughter who was to be named Mary was born and there it was young Simon was buried. Moll had wished it the other way about, as she often said, but wishes were not always won.

When her money gave out Moll found that France and Flanders were not highly remunerative fields for her line of endeavour and thought to try London. Engaging a passage across the Channel was a coy business and the light and airy widow waited long before she found a master gullible enough to let her share his couch. From birth Mary had worn her dead half-brother's clothes and Moll now found it to her advantage to pass as the mother of a lad rather than the protector of a girl child.

London, too, proved a bad field even for a comely widow and, after several threats to drop the daughter into the Thames so that her harlot's progress might not be impeded, Moll learned that the lot of those without children was no better. Even the finest of the courtesans was compelled to stoop to petty thievery to eke out a living and it was indeed petty thievery. The professionals were highly organized and were not at all abashed at turning an interloper over to the watch and then appearing before the magistrate to make complaint, thereby leading a Thieves' Parade to Newgate Prison. Moll quickly learned that if she was to survive she must beat the professionals at their own game and open up a new field of knavery.

Into this world she introduced her daughter whom she had nicknamed Buttons, making the child an accomplice and doing very well by herself until by her endeavours she had changed the fashions of the nobs and swells. It is not a long story.

It was custom's fancy for the ladies to pile their coiffures high upon their heads, decorating these creations with semi-precious jewels, expensive ribbons and even spending great sums upon the wigs themselves. The dandies were no less vain and met their ladies' modes with jewelled hats and expensive perukes and periwigs. These were high above the reach of the average thief and it was only because of her superior imagination that Moll Read was enabled to prey on them. Secreting her child in a huge basket she lifted the wicker to her head and carefully balancing it walked the streets. At a given signal the child would lift the cover and snatch whatever came to her hand, quickly lowering the lid and remaining quiet. This act, of course, required much practice and could succeed only when done with great speed. Brooches and decorations, wigs, hats and shawls all disappeared into Moll Read's capacious basket and, as the child became more agile and adept, the two were able to go further afield, even to the exclusive Mall.

Soon other thieves purloined the idea and the wary Londoner learned to put little of value upon his head; when necessity compelled him to appear upon the streets in full hair dress, he tied it there with a scarf.

New vigilance on the part of the gulled and competition from those who had adopted her methods forced Moll Read to take up other callings. These were numerous and faulty and none of them brought her the thieves' acclaim and all were but steps toward Newgate and Tyburn. Moll's associates had taught her the necessity of working close to those who could not, for reasons best known to themselves, call the guard; a bit of blackmail was harmful to no one, they argued, and quite profitable to one with imagination. Unfortunately, Moll Read had no knowledge of the misdeeds of the wealthy and was compelled to work

23

closer to home. Indeed, the only person she knew with money was her mother-in-law and in her straits she remembered that her late husband had consigned her and her child to his parent's mercies. With what was left from her thievings she engaged passage on the Bristol coach for herself and three-year-old son.

The old lady gazed upon the child and said:

"He's a fine lad, the spit o' his father. I'll ta'e 'im and rear 'im as m'own, but I'll ha'e no trollop in my cot. Leave the lad nigh me an' I'll gi'e 'im of my own bread and bed. Aye, that I will."

Moll Read would have none of that; there would be nothing in it but grief for her. Tearfully she refused to be parted from her own dear son; if she was not welcome, it could only mean he was not wanted either.

"Go to your trade," stormed the old woman, "but leave Simon's lad to me."

"Nay, mither, I'll not be parted from mine own son."

The old woman was firm until she saw her grandchild being led from the house; then she had both of them back. If Moll would keep her skirts straight and bring no ill fame on the name of Read she should have two crowns a week against the lad's support. Moll tried to wheedle a whole guinea and even came down to two and one, but ten shillings was as high as the old 'un would go and she had to be content with the modest living it would provide. She took a small house on a quiet street and Buttons played with the boys of the neighbourhood. It was several years before Buttons learned the difference between boys and girls; during this period all she knew was that some children wore breeches and some skirties and she was one of the former.

Buttons, as she lay warm in her bunk, thought of these things in her own way and did not let the raucous and ribald manner of Moll enter her reminiscences. It was only ten days gone that she had heard the first of these events recited to the landlord. Moll had gone on to tell of how when Buttons was nine the grandmother had died and the two crowns ceased to come and she had sold her daughter to a French lady as a house-boy. There had been a pause in the telling for the grand laugh of how the French lady had taken it when she learned of the deception, but Buttons could have told them, then and there, that before discovery had come she had deserted her menial post and had joined the army as a powder boy.

Moll Read's story of deception and deceit ended there. Buttons knew that if she were to remain at The Saylor's True Friende Moll would not hesitate to sell her again, either as a boy or girl, to whoever offered the highest price. Indeed, the mother had suggested that the deception was no longer necessary and that Buttons might take her rightful place among the belles of Bristol Town.

"An' a girl 'ere's no worse off than those in Lunnon," she had averred. Indeed, thought Buttons, she was better, by far.

Buttons smiled to herself in the dark of her bunk. Little enough did her mother know of her life after she had left the service of the French lady. For two years the girl had served without distinction with the soldiers of the Crown, accepted as a male and fighting as such. Her comrade had been a youth of eighteen, a comely lad who had taken her fancy and with whom she had shared her blankets. Each night they lay in each other's arms for warmth and camaraderie and all had been well until he had discovered her sex. He was delighted to know he might ameliorate the rigours of the campaign with a mistress, but Buttons would have none of it; marriage it would be or nothing. Her comrade, now deeply in love with her, could deny her nothing and together they appeared before the commandant and asked for permission to marry.

There was great merriment as word quickly spread about the camp that two of the King's men were determined to marry and many came to see the curious couple. Later it occurred to the commandant to inform his wife of the phenomenon and this good woman undertook a little investigation of her own. For purposes of record Buttons was required to resume her right name and to promise to wear feminine apparel at the ceremony; a promise that was broken later when Mary with her lad appeared before the chaplain in nothing but her breeks and jerkin. The commander's gifts were honourable discharges from the service and the initiative in forming a purse to be given the happy couple on which to begin their lives. So generous were their comrades, every friend they had being in the army, that they decided to open a tavern solely for soldiers. The Three Horseshoes they called it and located it at Breda, where it was to stand for over two hundred years, ever a monument to the thirst of military men.

To the young husband the whole affair was a lark and he tended bar while Mary, still in men's clothes since the mystery of bustles and skirts was too great for her, waited on the tables. There was much coarse jesting at the expense of the young proprietor and many attempts by love-hungry soldiers to seduce the young wife. She quickly learned to defend herself with her fists, and many a comrade with decorations for valour found himself lying in a corner of the tavern, while a deft hand removed his score from his pocket.

The tavern was a success from the start and in every way. The couple prospered in love and finance, but the young landlord could not forgo the idea that his duties were a continuation of the wedding party. Toasts he drank with each patron besides taking great joy in watching his wife protect her honour. The strain was too much for his frail years and he succumbed, happily it is said, in his bed beside his wife within six months of the marriage. Mary Read had been made bride and widow in her sixteenth year. She buried her husband in the cemetery outside Breda and started back to Bristol Town to see her mother.

At Calais, whilst awaiting the Channel boat that was to take her to England, she listened to a recruiting speech made by a sergeant of cavalry and, liking his looks and the thought of travelling a-horseback with him, she had enlisted. It had been the sergeant she had liked and not the living with her horse; after a few months she had deserted and resumed her journey Bristolward, the same Bristol from which she was now retreating. She had come with fewer than twenty golden guineas from the proceeds of the sale of The Three Horse-shoes, only to be robbed of them by her own mother.

IV

Three days later the Cadogan, outward bound for Sierra Leone and the Guineas, stood off the Scillys. A trim, sleek vessel, white from the shrouds to the water-line, she took the winds gracefully, scudding along like a clean piece of paper before the Southern trades. In her hold she carried a general cargo, manufactured metal wares, woollens, boots and shoes, china from the kilns of Staffordshire, hoops for casks and other goods of interest and necessity to the colonists of the far-flung empire. She was an easy-riding ship, the pride of her master's eye and the only rift was that she was over-manned. Fifteen men could have measured her in any weather but there were that many and ten more, so that Buttons was assigned to the cabin when such a captain rated no such factotum in the usual course.

Buttons' duties were anything but onerous; she had much time on her hands and spent the better part of it playing cards and throwing dice with the men in the forecastle and the aftercastle. Master Skinner had taken his toll from the stolen purse and with the few coins left she was able to wager small sums against needed clothing and equipment. She was no gull at games of chance and her winnings included an extra pair of boots, breeches and stockings, shirts, blankets and mufflers and a chest to stow them in. She was accepted by the crew, easily and completely, sharing their lives and their rough, masculine intimacies. She experienced no great difficulty in concealing her sex from them; most sailors slept in their clothes, removing only their boots and greatcoats and, save in the tropics, keeping well covered at all times. There was a degree of privacy for the individual, a small lazaretto being set aside for the usual ablutions and, far forward, the head.

As the vessel bore southward and the winds became warmer the crew stowed their heavy outer clothing and went about in shirts and breeches, barelegged or in wide, breechy pantaloons. Buttons kept her shirt buttoned to the neck, a device regarded by the others merely as a personal idiosyncrasy. For sixteen years she had worn male attire and it had become as natural for her as for her brother seamen; a woman's garments would have been her undoing.

In her role of cabin-boy Buttons had access not only to the sailors' quarters forward and after, but to the master's cabin and the mate's house, and she early became aware of the formation of certain lines of loyalties. Howell Davis dominated the forecastle and had, secretly, forbade his men having any truck with the afterwatch, Captain Skinner's, of which Buttons was nominally a member. The two officers seldom met on deck; when they did they did not speak save in the line of duty. It was rumoured among the crew that Davis' share in the venture equalled that of the master.

That more was amiss than over-manning would not be apparent to the former powder-boy of the King's Forces in Flanders. There were two swivels, one forward and the other aft, and regular drills were held each morning and afternoon, "for purpose of defence." These small cannon, so mounted that either of them might be trained upon any possible target, might indicate that the voyage was not to be an entirely peaceable one. It took but a single well-directed ball to bring the largest merchantman back on his heels, but Captain Skinner was to trade in dangerous waters, and both he and his chief officer conducted their drills along defensive lines. Buttons, idling before the companionway, could see that Howell Davis' gun was pointed at the captain's cabin as often as at an imaginary enemy. Indeed, when the piece was not in use, it was invariably found to be trained upon the master's quarters.

Once, in an unguarded moment, Captain Skinner said to his cabin-boy:

"Ah, Buttons, m'lad, all's not well aboard the Cadogan. If ye hear aught spoken against your master, do you tell me. Hear ye?"

"Aye, master, that I will."

As far as Buttons could determine there had been no other ears present at the time, yet within the hour, having business in the forecastle, she had passed Howell Davis and heard him hiss in her ear:

"Sime Read's spit's a pimp, I trow."

"Pimp? Nay, Master Howell, a loyal man."

"An' to whom? To 'is father's memory? Or to that pantaloon who calls 'isself captain?"

Buttons had hurried on with her task without answering. She did not care for Howell Davis and if asked, at the moment, whose cause she would espouse in case a decision was demanded would have promptly answered that she had but one master and he was also the Cadogan's.

In the aftercastle there seemed to be less whispering, less hugging the shadows and a more outspoken honesty among that watch. One sailorman had summed up the attitude of his fellows:

"The master's a righteous man and a brave one. Where 'e goes, there go I."

The vessel passed Funchal early in January, but did not put in for water or news, continuing on to the more favourable Las Palmas, in the Canaries. Here the ship hove to and the master called for his smallboat and quartermasters to take him ashore. Another ship's boat was to take in the casks for fresh water. As the master went to the rail he summoned Buttons.

"Arm thyself, lad, and stand fast. Let no man enter my cabin whilst I'm away. No man, whatever his rank or his business."

"Aye, marster," saluted the girl.

Captain Skinner lowered himself into his boat and his crew of four bullies quickly pulled for the shore. As the second boat left with the casks Buttons saw Howell Davis order one of the starboard smallboats to be made ready for his own use, and before the master reached the shore four other bullies were pulling the mate towards Las Palmas, but to another point. Buttons stood guard for two hours before she saw the mate's boat returning and another before the captain's left the shore.

"Send Master Davis to me," bellowed Skinner as he came on deck. The chief officer sauntered up and stood before his master.

"Winter, the pirate, is in these waters, Howell Davis. The scoundrel's ta'en several ships. Do you ken that?"

"Now that you've told me," drawled Davis.

"One report has it he's gone south, another westerly," went on the captain.

"Aye, an' which do you ken? If I know the man I'd say he's gone westerly, the better the hunting," said the mate.

"An' you know him well enough, I'll warrant." He looked levelly and directly into the eyes of the second in command. "I shall continue to the Guineas."

Howell Davis' glance did not waver.

"Aye, master. You did not plan—otherwise. You do not wish to pass Rum Cay again, I take it, master." His voice dropped to almost a whisper: "There were ten men, master, ten who may now be ghosts, living or dead."

"Have done! Enough o' that," growled Skinner. "The Cadogan goes to my pleasure."

"Aye, sir, that I know full well."

"An' for reasons best known to mysel', I'll set her course for the Guineas. Call your watch!"

There was a sinister smile about the hard lips of Howell Davis as he turned to call his men. He gave his commands in a manner satisfactory to the most exacting master, and before night fell Las Palmas was far astern.

What either of the officers had heard ashore was not made known to the cabin-boy. Captain Skinner showed he did not like the news he had had ashore, nor did Howell Davis dislike his information. That the infamous Winter was in these waters meant more to Davis than it did to Skinner seemed apparent. The men in the forecastle received a double rum ration that night and on the following morning Captain Skinner ordered the drills at the swivel guns to be resumed. This time, however, he divided his own watch into two gun crews and ordered Howell Davis to do likewise. If fear of treason dictated this move he did not say it, leaving the impression that one watch might work the ship while the other defended it. If Howell Davis had any misgivings about the master's designs he said nothing and continued his duties with his usual efficiency.

Late in February they dropped anchor off Moyamba, off the Guinea coast, under the protecting wings of a bark flying the Royal Ensign, an eight-gun vessel obviously placed for the protection of all British traders. Captain Skinner ran up his own ensign and called across the water for the latest news. Almost immediately a smallboat put out from the warship and rowed towards the Cadogan, seemingly a gesture of courtesy. Captain Skinner, in his best silk breeches and a small sword at his side, went to the rail to greet his visitor. Buttons, standing discreetly behind her master, observed that every one of the stranger's eight guns was manned and that the men on deck all carried muskets.

As the smallboat came within speaking distance the eight-gun bark quickly hauled down the Royal Ensign and ran up in its stead the dreaded Black Peter, the skull and cross-bones in red on a black field. A shot was fired across the Cadogan's deck to enforce the new ensign's mandate.

"Man the swivels, afterwatch!" cried the master. "Load and prepare to fire." After a moment's pause, he ordered, "Fire!" But no shots answered the pirate's shot. Buttons ran from her post at the aftergun to announce to her master:

"The swivels are spiked, marster."

"Place Howell Davis under arrest," began the Captain, but his order was cut short by one from the smallboat.

"Snow Cadogan! Stand and deliver!"

Skinner lifted his two hands high above his head to show he was unarmed and planned no further defence of his ship. The smallboat brushed the side of the snow and the officer and six men leaped to the Cadogan's waist. The pirate officer barked a single order:

"Below, men, and search."

Turning to Skinner he said:

"Who are you and what do you carry, mister?"

Captain Skinner gave his name and stated his cargo, adding that he was here for a bit of trading on his way to Boston Town where he was engaged to carry masts for His Majesty's Navy.

"You be Captain Winter, I take it," said Skinner.

"Nay, mister. England's my name, i' the sarvice of Captain Winter. I was told there was one Howell Davis, a Welshman, in your company."

Howell Davis stepped forward.

"I be he," he announced, proudly.

"Captain Winter bespoke my mercy for you, but I do not care for your face," said England. "To your station."

"Master Davis is a traitor and under arrest," said Skinner. "For spiking yon swivels."

"I would a word wi' you, master," said Davis to the pirate. Howell Davis spoke in whispers to Captain England, who, from time to time, nodded his acquiesence. When Davis had finished the pirate said:

"Nor do I care more for your voice, now, fellow. To your station and take your chances wi' the rest."

Howel Davis seemed to be on the point of sinking to his knees to plead his cause, but thought the better of it and obeyed the order.

Captain Skinner stood alone and unregarded with only Buttons at his side. One of the pirate's men came up to the master and thrust a hairy face into that of the captain.

"How, now, mister! Do you not recognize me? An' Jeems 'ere, an' Toby there. Aye, that you do, I can see. Eh, Toby, 'ere's our artful marster who marooned us on Rum Cay. What serves us must sarve im. Eh, Jeems?" He spat full and plentiful into Skinner's face.

"'Ere, now, none o' that!" called Edward England.

"'E's our pleasure, marster. 'E did us a turn last year an' now's come ours. Eh, mates?"

"'Ear! 'Ear!" called both. Then all three fell upon their former captain and bore him to the deck, pummelling him and rending his clothes.

"'Ere, now," said the first speaker. "Let's have 'im right. To the capstan, mates!"

In a moment they had dragged the unfortunate man to the windlass and triced him to it. One of the men who had gone below to search came on deck with his arms filled with bottles of rum. These he passed to the three who were tormenting and humiliating the Cadogan's master.

"Back to the bark an' bring the others," ordered the spokesman. "This is their fun as 'tis ours."

One man detached himself from the mêlée and went to the smallboat.

"Out o' the way, lad," said the bottle bearer to Buttons, "an' mind your 'ands."

Buttons would have liked to help her master, but as none of the men of her own watch lifted their hands she could not do otherwise than follow their example. Howell Davis' watch stood apart, as if detached from the whole spectacle.

The men about the Captain broached several bottles and passed them around. The pirates lost interest in everything save the rum, and their captain, in and out of the master's cabin, was busily completing his survey of the prize.

"Aye, Skinner, and how to you. How's Bristol Town and Moll Read? Would you like a dram o' your own fine rum?"

Shortly thereafter the smallboat returned with the other men who had been marooned on Rum Cay and more bottles were brought up and passed about. Each of the newcomers passed Skinner offering him some new indignity and injury. The crew of the Cadogan were now sharply divided into two camps, the one laughing uproariously at the antics of their captors, the other sullenly defiant and helpless. The latter knew only too well that at the first sign of resistance their heads would pay the cost and they obeyed on the double every order uttered by any pirate.

Captain England ordered the crew of the Cadogan to assemble on the poop just as one of Skinner's tormentors hurled an empty bottle at the unfortunate man's head, hitting him above the eyes. Buttons hesitated a moment and found herself urged along by a kick from one of the pirate crew. When the crew was mustered aft England looked them over carefully, studying their faces and physique, and examining the garments they wore. He looked so long and intently at the cabin-boy that Buttons, for the first time, feared that her sex would be discovered and the thought sent a cold chill over her. But the inspection ended without further comment.

"Now, m'hearties," said England. "I'll have you know with whom you're dealing. I am Captain Edward England, in the sarvice of the dread Captain Winter. We are on the account and in yon bark lies the booty o' many a proud ship. Who amongst you wants to join our company? It's an easy way an' there's no standing watch, no labouring when you do not feel for it. There is rum for all and in great plenty. Come, m'hearties, decide quickly."

One man stepped forward. He was Howell Davis, of Milford Haven. A look of distaste and displeasure passed over the pirate's face, but his voice did not betray him.

"Aye, the first," shouted England with the forced enthusiasm of a recruiting sergeant. "Who'll follow this brave man? I make him captain of this sloop and the very next shall be the mate. Come, quick, hearties."

One by one the men of Howell Davis's watch stepped up beside the head of their crew.

"Twelve in all. We need three more," announced England.

At this point the attention of all was drawn to the plight of Captain Skinner by a scream. His tormentors were now breaking the empty bottles before they hurled them at him and his face was already bleeding from a dozen gashes. One pirate was drunkenly chanting:

"If I swing by a string

I will hear the bells ring,

An' that will be the end o' poor Tommy."

Buttons had heard Moll Read sing it often, the song of the thieves of London. She was sure that were Moll here on the Cadogan's deck she would become one of the cut-throat crew.

Now the pirates about the captain were on their feet, circling about the almost unconscious master, throwing rum into his wounds and tearing aside his shirt to make a larger target for their missiles. Above the din they made Buttons could hear Skinner's groans and screams of pain.

"We are," went on England boastfully, "on the grand account. With these two ships and all you brave bullies we go to take the Don, a Spanish ship. On the Don are many beautiful wenches, Spanish ladies the like o' which would not talk to you men, and these brave lads who have already joined shall have first choice. Come, decide quickly. A warm Spanish lady for each man o' you. Plenty o' fine Spanish wines and brandies to quicken your pulses, and rum, too, for them as likes it."

England, for a moment, watched his men torturing the master. Sotto voce, he muttered: "Aye, there go the fine breeches and the sword that I'd picked for mysel'."

Buttons shivered again at the thought of the Spanish women who would be thrown to these fellows and of her own fate at their hands should her sex be revealed. No, she would not risk discovery by joining them. Far better to be marooned and to take her chances with the men she knew. She was, she knew, the match of any man aboard the Cadogan so she would cast her lot with them.

The men torturing her captain had now joined hands and were dancing a saraband about their almost unconscious victim, singing a bawdy street song. One called for music and forgot it the next breath, others cried for rum and these did not forget.

"Have done, down there," shouted England. "Do you hear?"

"Aye, marster." The singing and dancing were silenced and the men applied themselves to their bottles.

"Fine clothes and much gold shall be ours. When we take a rich ship anything you see is to be yours, even to the captain's breeches or his shirt. Take what you will and all gold doubloons are to be divided, so and so, according to station. Eh, you there, lad. Come join us and the youngest virgin shall be yours, the finest breeches and silken shirts. Hey, now, what say?"

But Buttons' eyes were on her former master. She saw the pirates put their heads together and talk in tones too low to be heard. Then one of them detached himself from the crowd and went to the captive.

"'E was a good marster, 'e was, for all 'is bad ways, and I'll not see him done wrong. 'E's entitled to an 'onerable death and I propose to give it him." The speaker drew a pistol from his belt and examined the priming and set a match to it. Then, quite deliberately he took hold of the captain's nose and lifted it high until the torn and bleeding mouth gaped awide. Then he shoved the pistol as far into the captain's throat as it would go and awaited its firing. When his task was finished he turned to his mates and said:

"Aye, 'e was a good marster according to 'is lights and 'e dies like the brave man 'e was." A loud cheer greeted his announcement.

There was a retching sensation in Mary Read's stomach, the first she could recall; she was cold and sweaty behind her knees and she wished she were back in Bristol Town, even though it meant Moll Read's questionable protection. She had seen violent death often enough, but nothing approaching the barbarity of these pirates. A thousand maroonings would she choose before she would join with them.

Captain England turned from the gruesome spectacle with a laugh.

"That, m'hearties, is how we treat with traitors."

The pirates who had tortured Captain Skinner now turned to other interests and Buttons saw one of the Bristol men who had steadfastly refused to join the corsairs pulled down from the poop and stripped of his clothes. Clothes, she learned, were in demand among the picaroons and considered a part of the prize. The naked man hurried to hide behind the shadows and the pirates, sensing more fun, were after him and belabouring his hide with their cutlasses.

Howell Davis, now designated captain of the Cadogan, stood beside England, who turned on him.

"I tell you, Davis, I've no stomach for a man who'll not fight for his vessel, come what may. But Captain Winter knows you for the traitor you are and I can only obey my master's orders. You have but twelve men to sail the sloop, can you manage?"

"With such a twelve I can," answered Howell Davis.

"Last chance," announced Edward England, "to join with my brave lads. Last chance!"

But no other Bristol man, none from the afterwatch, came forward and in a burst of temper the pirate chief shouted:

"Very well. Every one of you strip to the buff; my men need your garments."

An anguished look crossed Mary Read's face. It was only by keeping hold of herself that she was able to save herself from fainting.

BOOK TWO - KING'S PARDON

I

Mary watched her shipmates of the Cadogan as they began removing their clothes. A blush crept to her cheeks and her heart sickened with a great fear as she began unbuttoning her jerkin. Indeed, one of the pirates from the Sparrowhawk was already before her, one hand grasping the hem, ready to claim it for himself. Abruptly she pushed the man aside and placed herself before Captain England.

"I'd like to join you on second thought, marster, but I want no part of yon yellow bastard, Howell Davis by name. I'd like to go along wi' you in the Sparrowhawk." She had some difficulty in keeping her voice from betraying her sex.

"Ah," laughed England, regarding Buttons appraisingly, "a lad o' fine bottom. Nor would I consent to serve under one who stinks as he does. Get your chest, lad, and wait me near the cockboat." Turning to the new master of the Cadogan, he went on: "More's the pity you could not hold the loyalty o' such a lad, Davis."

"A snipe, and useless among birds of prey," said Davis.

England watched the crew gingerly removing their clothes.

"What do you do with these others?" he asked.

"I be o' two minds, mister. The first be to silence for ever their tongues lest they return to Bristol and inform against me. The other be to sarve them as Skinner sarved his men, maroon them. What think you?"

"I think as Captain Winter directs, as any loyal man would. To my mind these twelve who refuse to go on the account with you are too valuable to be wasted either in death or marooning. Captain Winter did not speak his mind about manning the Cadogan snow and I may not be exceeding my orders if I place on your decks the very men that Skinner marooned. Aye, 'tis a good idea. You saw how they did for him? Aye, I shall do it, damme! It will sarve you as a constant reminder o' the way o' traitors and hold you to the mark o' honour. Those of your watch will man the snow with the lads from Rum Cay."

The pirate chief turned to the naked men and summoned them before him. Each of them, seeking to cover his exposure with his hands, obeyed with alacrity.

"Here's another chance for you men. I do not question whether you act from unwillingness to go on the account wi' us or from your dislike of Mister Howell Davis. That be your own thought and no man can take it from you. Let it be known that, speaking as I am for the gallant Captain Winter, none shall pay wi' his blood; the worst that can befall you will be marooning and at as convenient a place as our activities will permit. If any of you wish to follow the brave lad nigh the cockboat and join us i' the Sparrowhawk he may enter the company wi' a full share and receive his clothes and gear. Now, what say you, my merries?"

Three men reconsidered and held up their hands. The others, ten in all, held to their purpose, preferring to be marooned on a lonely shore without clothes to cover them or food for their bellies, strangers on a more strange strand. But these were Bristol men and Bristol men were of their own minds. And they were true.

Howell Davis' hand went to his newly acquired cutlass and he made as if to unsheath it and lay about among these men who held to their own opinion. Edward England smiled at him mockingly; it seemed to those who watched the two men that the pirate wished Howell Davis might commit an overt act so that he might rid the sea of him.

The three who had reconsidered were getting into their clothes and the ten nude men were ordered to uncover the hatches and prepare to tranship the goods wanted for the Sparrowhawk, to lower and man the smallboats. Already their shoulders were beginning to show the effects of the Guinea Coast sun and England hoped its rays would compel some of them to change their stout minds.

Buttons got her first lesson in piracy then and there. An impulse to aid in uncovering the hatches was met by a sharp command to stand aside. Then it was explained to her that while prisoners were on board all menial tasks were done by them, that those who elected to throw their lot with the pirates were spared all unnecessary labour.

Two of the pirates were told off to sew the remains of Captain Skinner in sailcloth and to bury them with whatever ceremony they thought fit.

England carried on his inspection of the cargo of the snow and those articles he needed or could find use for were sent on deck; cases and casks of wines and liquors, clothing, boots and shoes and much of the Staffordshire ware. Then, selecting two men from his own crew, the pirate went to the former master's cabin and looted it of everything of value. Skinner's little leathern case, copper-bound and brass-locked, containing his purchase money was among the things he took. An hour later England stood on the quarterdeck with Howell Davis.

"Make up your company, Davis, and have them sign the articles. Your share of the loot will be carried to Captain Winter. There are enough goods on board for you and your crew. At dawn to-morrow ship your anchor and make for Mariaguana, in the Bahamas, and report to Captain Winter. I'll expect you there when I arrive; I go by another route. That is all, sir."

Howell Davis saluted and saw his superior to the cockboat. Edward England, whether from contempt or a mere lack of interest, did not look back after giving the order to cast off.

Buttons' first taste of piracy seemed scarcely as terrible as she had imagined. Save for the murder of Captain Skinner, which had little or nothing to do with the actual act of piracy, she had seen no violence save the stripping of the members of the company. Edward England was, by her way of taking stock, a far better man than Howell Davis and she felt she might find him an even better master than Skinner. She saw that he was observing her closely.

"I'd make ye my cabin-boy but you seem bully enough to go on your own and I have a boy to do for me. What manner o' man is this Howell Davis? Know you him well?"

"Nay, marster; but that we were shipmates I'd not know him at all. An unsavoury fellow to my mind, sir."

"I saw to that. Well, he's his orders and if he fails to report to Captain Winter, it's none o' my concern. You will go in the first watch. Know you the cutlass?"

"Nay, marster, only the sabre. But with that my right arm is a true one."

The bark was a large, commodious vessel and, like all her kind, heavily overmanned. Buttons was consigned to the forward castle where she found the bunks wide and comfortable with the booty from many vessels. Seeking one still unoccupied, she was informed that the crew slept two to a bunk and that she would have to share with one of the older men.

"What! Better far a marooning than to lay the night through with one o' you."

"'Tis bonny i' these waters, lad, the nights be that chill."

"I lay on the deckhead then," decided Buttons. "Methinks you want for a touch o' water." She wrinkled her nose in distaste. At that moment a young fellow of twenty entered, a blond chap of cleanly habits who seemed to find as much to dislike in the forecastle as she. Buttons appraised him by and large and said, "I might share a bunk with yon lad."

The young fellow looked at her closely. Then, pointing his finger, he said:

"Yon bunk's mine. Stow your gear, lad."

"What's your name, mate?"

"Jones, and none other. Seaman Jones. An' yours?"

"Buttons Read, the bloody spit o' Sime Read, a man for men and beyond the ken o' these."

Buttons stowed her stuff, roughly tossing it into the bunk, and then swaggered out on deck. She wanted to seek another place to lay her head before Jones could discover her imposition. The naked men from the Cadogan were busily scrubbing the decks, urged on by pricks from the boatswain's cutlass. All about her was an air of expectancy; men lolled about the deck looking hungrily at the quarterdeck and cabin. Then the boatswain forgot his charges and blew a shrill blast on his pipe, summoning all hands to the mainmast. Captain England, supported by three other officers, appeared on the quarterdeck and held up his hand for silence.

"Four new men to our goodly company. One has been sent to the forward watch, the other three to the after. As soon as the prize is distributed they will report to the mate and sign the articles. The prize, Cadogan snow, out of Bristol, taken this morning, yielded but a small quanto of rum and wines and some eleven hundred guineas. One half to our gallant master and his humble servants, the balance share and share alike to one and all you brave lads. Five golden guineas and a fine bottle o' rum for each."

The men formed in line and accepted their share of the prize, jingling the gold coins in their hands and holding the rum against the sun to determine its quality and strength.

In the forecastle Buttons sold her rum to another for a guinea and then brought out her dice. The stakes were larger than she was accustomed to playing for but this was due to the lack of small coins among the crew. She won steadily, forgetting the noon meal in her ardour for gaming and pausing only to take a swig of the bombo that was being passed about.

At the evening meal she remembered she had not located a place on deck for sleeping and went about seeking it at once. But on the Guinea Coast the night descends like a blanket and the deck was dark. Then her boatswain ordered her on watch. Though she was tired from the day's excitements, Buttons was glad to accept the duty. When she came forward at midnight her bunkmate went on and, for the first night at least, her problem was solved.

But not entirely. She threw herself on the bunk and fell asleep almost at once. When she awoke her bunkmate was already off duty and was snoring his head off beside her. Buttons managed to get in a few more winks before it was time to rise. To her great pleasure and relief she found that Jones suspected nothing, but she resolved to find that spot on deck before another night.

II

Buttons was early ordered to the crow's nest, high above the crosstrees of the topgallant, to scrutinize the horizon. To the east was green Africa; after that only the Cadogan snow broke the slender threadlike line over which came prey and danger alike to such as she now was. A bright lookout was kept on any ship but the man in the pirate's crow's nest was picked for alertness and clarity of vision. And the long glass Buttons held in her hand could send that horizon far distant or bring it close. She swept it again and again with her glass and then put it up.

Below her on the deck men were struggling with the anchors. In a minute they would be flocking to the rigging, all about her, above and below. Across the narrow strip of water she saw Howell Davis on his quarterdeck and wondered, curiously, how long he would tread it. She heard England's order to unclew the sails and make fast and ten minutes later the Sparrowhawk was running before the wind, on a course south by west, the little sunburnt town of Moyamba dropping quickly behind. Soon the town itself was out of sight; soon, too, the Cadogan was hull down on the horizon, following truly the course set for it by Captain England.

At noon Buttons gave up her post to her bunkmate, a little saddened that he went on duty as she came off, but happy in knowing that by such an arrangement she could have the bunk safely to herself. She went below to get her pannikin and then to the galley for her food, a composition of dried meat, beans and grain, all cooked together, and a handful of hard ship-biscuit. She ate the unsavoury mess, liking the pirate life less than ever. Seeing her dislike for the food, one of her mates assured her that in the evening they would have a rare treat of conkie, a soup made of conch clams.

Two whole days' journey down the African coast the Sparrowhawk hove to and the prisoners were ordered to the boats to be marooned on the shore. Captain England gave them one more chance to join up but none accepted the offer and Buttons, watching them from her station aloft, knew that if it had not been necessary to expose her body, she would now be with them. Five prisoners and four pirates to each boat, a few bottles of water and a bag of ship-biscuit. It was only half a league to the shore but the pirates would go no further than necessary; the prisoners could swim the rest of the way. The spot had been picked for its loneliness.

The two smallboats made off, the prisoners rowing themselves to their doom. The green foliage indicated some sort of life on the shore, but whether it was friendly or hostile none could say. Buttons with her eye fastened to her glass watched her old shipmates on to their marooning. She raked the shore and saw copper-coloured natives peering from out the rank growth. When it was apparent where the boats would land, these natives came out from their hiding-places and advanced towards the surf. Twenty paces from the shore the pirates compelled their prisoners to leap overboard and there was a great laugh from the men on deck as the naked men struggled to keep upright in the heavy surf. One sun-reddened wretch lost his footing and only through the aid of a companion was able to reach the shore, there to face a fate as little known as the one he escaped. But when the marooned men's bodies began appearing above the water the natives ran back to the bush.

One alone, a fat bulky wench of chocolate colour, danced up and down, running first to the left and then to the right, as if selecting a choice victim; finally she grabbed the first she could, bundled the fellow's arms to his sides, and ran the half-exhausted wretch into the bush. The captured man let out a shriek but his mates did nothing but huddle in a dismal group just above the tide line, not knowing what danger they had most to fear.

As soon as the two smallboats returned, the Sparrowhawk got under way again but when Buttons was relieved she noted that the course had been changed and they were now travelling due west. On deck she learned this was the Sparrowhawk's usual course. She was too small a ship to attempt attacks on convoyed merchants or upon the plate fleet, but there were many merchants too miserly to share the cost of a convoy who sent the vessels along a southern course, outside the haunts of the West Indian pirates. These were usually Portuguese Jews and those Spanish merchants whose trade was with Peru and Chile on the West Coast. It was far cheaper to send the vessels about the Cape than to tranship the cargoes at Darien and reload them on other vessels on the eastern side of the Isthmus. A mean trade both for the merchant or the pirate, but of late years the renewed activities of the buccaroons had driven many reputable merchants to adopt this plan. Their vessels could keep far south until they got clear of the seaways and then set a swift course for Spain. Much plate and many ingots were coming from Peru by this route.

Under Edward England Buttons was an indifferent pirate. She gave her master her loyalty and performed her duties acceptably but her heart was not in the work, especially when the Sparrowhawk would swoop down upon some second-rater who dared not fire a shot in reply. The pirates' first ship was a Frenchman, the Bonne Femme, out of Bordeaux, returning from a successful smuggling venture along the West Coast of South America. She had sold her cargo and was bringing back quite a haul in plate and ingot, both in pesos and marcas. She had also some quinine and spices.

"The good woman turned out to be a filthy bitch," said Buttons. "The least the master could do would be to fight for his vessel and cargo, but not that Frenchman."

They took next a Portuguese merchant who was returning from a fruitless voyage to the Argentine and Brazil. His stock, designed for sale to the Indians, was of such low grade that even the pirates would have none of it. If they had not been so far from land they would have set the crew adrift in their own smallboats and fired the vessel and its cargo of tawdriness but, as it was, they contented themselves with the small amount of money the captain had taken and let them go.

Buttons found that her watch and that of Jones did not always follow each other; sometimes Jones went to the guns and another lookout was sent aloft. Increasingly often they slept the night through together and so compared notes of their past lives. It was hard for Buttons' companion to believe that his young bunkmate at seventeen had seen so much of the world, had been in battles, run a tavern and engaged in so many other activities as well as enlisting in a pirate crew. He himself had served from fourteen as a cabin-boy and had lately been taken by Captain Winter and sent to the Sparrowhawk. His former master had taught him the elements of navigation and he was continuing his studies under Edward England in the hope of bettering himself.

Jones confided to Buttons that he was happier manning a carronade than at the wheel and was considering giving up his nautical career in favour of one more militant. Buttons liked to hear him talk and often to keep him at it she would oppose his abandoning his original plan to be a master. At times she would be lulled to sleep by the hoarse monotone of his voice whereupon, annoyed, he would fetch her a slap on the rump and turn over and go to sleep himself.

Buttons soon learned, solely through her own observation, that the crew of the pirate ship were hardly better than their prey. In a word, they were mostly second- and third-rate men, loafers and cheap adventurers who sought wealth and ease in the pirate's life but were unwilling to assume many of the risks.

She did not believe that Edward England was fooled. In fact, she was sure that if he had had greater confidence in his men's courage he would have gone after bigger prizes, taking the greater risks involved knowing that, come what might, his crew was behind him to the death.

This year, 1717, was a bad one for the pirates of the Caribbees. A determined effort was being made by the nations of Europe to put down freebooting and only England was failing in her effort. Men-of-war ranged the seas destroying buccaneers' vessels and hideaways. The story was told of one pirate who had preempted an island of the Bahamas, a small cay, as a cache, leaving but two lonely men on guard. The captain of a French warship, learning of the hidden stores and seeing the two men, had assumed the place to be a strongpoint and fired broadside after broadside upon it, reducing the stores to ashes and pulpwood. After the bombardment a strong landing party had been sent to take the place, or what was left of it. After much skirmishing they found the badly scared guards whom they took prisoner with a great show of force. Such an incident might provoke laughter but it also showed the pirates what they had to fear.

Again, the great merchants had grown wary and ships and vessels containing goods of great value were sent out only under heavily armed convoys. For over fifty years Spain had suffered at the hands of the Brethren of the Coast and she had learned the lesson that she had to protect herself, that protests to other chanceries were of little or no avail. Piracy had indeed fallen upon bad days and men like Christopher Winter, realizing that quantity must make up for lack of quality, had ceased destroying their prizes; they had begun the practice of recruiting from among their victims and of sending the captured ships out on the account. Edward England had been a pirate for but a few months when he had seized the Cadogan, as had Buttons' bunkmate, Jones. Howell Davis, long desirous of becoming a runagate, had at last gotten his chance.

Mary Read was showing little aptitude for the career into which she had been pressed. She cared not for the life, the danger did not excite her and, if she must get her livelihood by her wits, she still had her dice.

For three weeks the Sparrowhawk stuck to her westward course, her eight guns masked and her crew lounging about the decks. Even with her shrouded guns she presented a malevolent appearance and no one was deceived by her seemingly aimless curiosity; no ship on an honourable voyage would be ready to leave her course to get a view of a passer-by as was the Sparrowhawk. Only the lookouts were always on the alert; with powerful glasses they raked each newcomer fore and aft before deciding whether she was quarry or armed foe.

The stentorian summons of the bugle awakened the entire crew on a dawn in the third week; there followed a wild ringing of the ship's bell and megaphoned commands from the quarterdeck. Tumbling out on deck Buttons guessed what had happened at a glance.

The Sparrowhawk had stumbled on an armed Spanish merchantman, one she would have avoided in the usual course of events. The Spaniard, too, would have avoided the pirate if he had known his true colours in time. The captain of each ship, surprised at the predicament in which he found himself, had an impulse to show the other his heels; then each decided to fight it out. The Spaniard carried four more guns than the Sparrowhawk, a crew only slightly smaller and had something to fight for. But Edward England had his first opportunity to show what he could do and he was first with his orders.

"Cannoneers to your stations. Load cannons, starboard. Musketeers aloft, boarders stand by with grapples. Starboard cannon, aim. Broadside!"

The four little guns of the Sparrowhawk's starboard belched forth their messages.

"Hard over, starboard, wheel!" commanded England. "Reload, starboard! Musketeers, fire! Starboard cannons, aim, broadside!"

The riflemen aloft had begun taking toll of the Spaniard's deck but he had come about and only two of the pirate's balls raked his deck while his cannoneers sent six balls across the deck of the Sparrowhawk. From her place beside one of the port guns, the one manned by Jones, Buttons saw the boatswain of her watch carried away. But the Sparrowhawk, too, was coming about; the next order brought the larboard guns into play and all four shots took effect on the Don. Edward England pushed the quartermaster away from the wheel and, placing both hands on the spokes, brought the pirate up under the starboard bows of the Spaniard. Calling an order to the larboard gunners for another broadside, he ordered:

"Boarders, grapple! Musket men to the decks. Prepare to board."

Jones' gun was useless at such close quarters; with Buttons he joined the boarders who were swarming aboard the merchantman, cutlasses in hands. But before they could use them the Don's flag was brought down.

There was little joy aboard the Sparrowhawk in her victory. The Don carried quite a stock of bullion and plate aboard, consigned to a Cadiz banker, but little else of value; the rum was hardly enough to wet the pirates' whistles, each man being compelled to take his away watered in his pannikin. Two days were spent stripping her; her twelve cannon were stowed in the hold, together with such sails as could be used on the Sparrowhawk, her armoury was raided and her powder and shot removed. Left with enough sail to keep her course and barely enough food to keep her crew alive, she was turned adrift, to report to Spain that the pirates were now working southward.

When the Sparrowhawk was ready to resume her voyage, it was found that six pirates had been killed and four wounded. Jones, for exceptional bravery, was promoted to boatswain and moved forward to a cabin of his own.

Buttons at last had her bunk entirely to herself and, strangely enough, liked it no better; indeed, she liked it less. Jones had been good company and she had liked hearing him talk about his future plans.

At the division of the spoils each man of the crew got forty-two pesos of gold and thirty marcas of silver ... which, when they got to their rendezvous, would keep them in rum and women for about a week.

Meeting Boatswain Jones on deck, very self-conscious of his new rank, Buttons said:

"Aye, Jones, me lad."

"You'll sir me in the future."

"So! Getting too big for your breeks, I wot."

"A cat'll teach you respect for your betters."

"It was boatswain you were made, not master. I'll pay me respects to those who win it. Jones you are to me, and Jones you remain. An' how do you like it, my brisk and sprightly lad?"

"I care little enough for it and I may yet have you on the quarterdeck."

"Fast does it because I may not be here when you get to it."

"What do you mean?"

"I'll talk to thee again when thy head has returned to its old size." Buttons turned abruptly and started for her bunk. She found herself stopped by a hand on her shoulder; as she turned to face Jones her hand fell to her cutlass.

"How now!" she cried.

But neither was willing to carry matters to extremes; after an instant Jones dropped his hand and Buttons turned away.

After that she did not hesitate to fox Jones whenever she got a chance. She guessed that the lad found his new duties onerous in that they left him little time for studying navigation or his gun practice. Coming upon him later the same day, she cried again:

"How now, master boatswain? How do you like matters?"

Jones looked at the lad hard as if trying to find the mockery he expected, but he did not permit himself to smile.

Buttons leaned against the rail and said:

"What manner o' man be you, Jones?" and then let out one of her deep belly laughs.

"What do you mean?" he asked darkly.

"How long have we been together on this vessel?"

"I've no head for figures, not that kind."

"Well, I'll tell you. Five weeks, man. Five weeks, day and night, and I ask ye again: What manner of man be ye?"

A stupid look came to Jones' features and this gave way to a frown.

"By my bollys, I think you're fox't, you be clear daft! Now give over and get to your duties. Aloft or below. Look sharp."

"If you'd use you nollie, you'd know I'm never drunk."

"Get to your station!" he commanded.

"Aye, boatswain lad, but I'm needin' a good man to tell me it." With another laugh Buttons turned away and strolled toward the forecastle.

She knew she could rib the stupid Jones for as long as she wished but that wasn't what she wanted. What she did want was her companion of the days and nights before the Sparrowhawk had attacked the Don. Buttons couldn't come right out and tell him she was a woman; to her way of thinking, that would never do. But if he were to discover it for himself, she would know how to handle the situation, she was sure.

It was rumoured on board the vessel that the Sparrowhawk would reach the rendezvous at Mariaguana within three weeks, after coasting up along the Windward and Leeward Islands and stopping for news at the Spanish Isle or not, as England might decide. If for any reason the rendezvous had been changed Captain Winter would send a ship to meet them, but it would only be by clinging to the coast they could be assured of meeting the messenger.

But to Buttons three weeks seemed a long time. In the nights she had spent alone she had decided to desert the Sparrowhawk at the first likely looking port of call. Piracy was a misbegotten game and a much overrated manner of getting wealth; she cared little for the life and her one desire now was to have the slow-witted Jones to talk over her plans with during the watches of the night.

Some time after the capture of the Don Edward England and his crew were called upon to play unwittingly the part of Samaritans. An English schooner had been blown southward from its course and had been set upon by a Spaniard. The smaller boat, without cannons and with only a few muskets in the forward and afterhouse, had almost outwitted the larger vessel, had avoided its carronading by perfect seamanship, but had been unable to prevent the Spaniards from boarding her. Locked in the forecastle and afterhouse the resolute captain and his little crew had put up such a stout defence, firing their muskets through the windows, that the foe had been ingloriously driven off. Three Spaniards lay dead on her decks testifying to English courage and marksmanship. Being in a position to take advantage of the wind, the master of the schooner had been able to get away before the Spaniard could pick up his smallboats.

But the Lady Betsy was already doomed; when Edward England sighted her she was being kept afloat only by the work of all hands at the pumps. The pirate captain brought the Sparrowhawk smartly about and with the aid of grapnels was able to keep the little vessel floating until he had brought the six members of the crew and the three passengers aboard. Then by quick work he transferred the schooner's cargo to his own vessel; it comprised a goodly quantity of New England rum and some manufactured goods. The captured men were given an opportunity to join the pirates and in their anxiety to avenge the cowardly attack on their vessel gladly accepted the chance; two of the passengers also joined on condition that Edward England would promise to attack the Spanish ship. The third was a missionary on his way to a little outpost on the Island of Trinidad. The dominie had courage and was willing to fight, but asked that his cloth be respected.

Among men of the ilk of England's crew there are two kinds; those who have an abiding faith in religion but who, so to speak, have laid it aside for the time being, and those who are lacking in all respect for the church.

With the permission of the Sparrowhawk's company the master and mate of the foundering schooner were added to the quarterdeck crew with a right to one and a half shares; the men and the two passengers were assigned to the crew. The minister was given a release which in case of capture would indicate to the authorities that he had been impressed against his will.

Buttons, lolling near the quarterdeck, heard the discussion between the master of the schooner and Edward England.

"You will, of course, land my cargo at an English port," said the skipper of the Lady Betsy.

"I fear not, mister. The only ports open to us are not the kind you seek. We've a rendezvous at Mariaguana and that's where we are bound."

"You've rescued my passengers and my crew but that hardly gives you the right to take my cargo, sir."

"Your cargo would be at the bottom of the sea were it not for me. My men need your rum and to-night it will be served out to them. Two things be needed on a vessel such as this: rum for the crew and careening for the ship. This vessel's been to sea too long to be fast and her bottom is as foul as a Spaniard's heart. You'll share in your own cargo."

"You go, you say, to Mariaguana, in the Bahamas?"

"Aye, but only to meet my master, Captain Winter. Then I expect we'll sail for New Providence."

The little skipper thought for a moment.

"May I remove my name from your articles, sir?"

"You may not. What has happened to change your mind?"

"I'd rather not tell you, sir."

"Very well, but you'll sink, swim or hang with the rest of us."

The man chewed his moustachios for a moment and then said:

"When will my goods be divided? When we get to port?"

46

"Nay, man. At least not all. Some is due my men right now and will be given them this very night. What is left will be taken to Fort Nassau and sold to their credit."

"Ha! I suppose then only my rum will be consumed. Very well. I still wish to withdraw my name from your articles."

"If I knew your good reason, I might consent."

"I will have to think this o'er," said the doughty little skipper.

Buttons wished to learn more, there seemed to be a weighty reason behind the little man's request, but just then the boatswain's pipe called the pirates to the mainmast. Nothing from the cargo of the Lady Betsy was of interest to them save the rum; that would be distributed to them at nightfall, each man to receive but a single bottle, as the ship could not afford to lay to while the men sobered.

When the rum was received Buttons had a thought to sell hers to some fellow with money yet, more than she desired the money, she wished to give the new boatswain a token of her, well, call it her respect. She took her bottle to his cabin but noted that his own lay on the bunk untouched.

"Has thy head shrunk, fool?" she asked. "Or does it still need a bit of bleeding?"

"It's but a few hours since I ordered you to your station! Get hence."

"Aye, but I've brought you good news. One bottle o' rum's not enough to get a head such as yours, fox't, so I've brought mine for you. Take it to bed wi' you, m'hearty."

"I'll have none o' your rum. I like not my new position, Buttons lad, an' I would cadgilly return to yon forecastle, that I would."

"How now? What's amiss?"

"I miss you, lad, and your merry chatter."

He laid a hand on Buttons' shoulder. The girl in the boy's clothes did not shrink from the touch; indeed, a more sensitive fellow than Jones might have felt the slight pressure her body gave back to his hand.

"Aye, go on, man. Go on!"

"Do you ken now, were I to get bloody well fox't, do you think the master would send me back to yon gadlings? To my old bunk?"

"There'd be nowt in that, my lad," said Buttons in a low voice.

She was wishing that she could tell Jones the truth about herself; she must be strong and yet she could not be strong. She did not want to be strong, she wanted to be weak, a woman dependent upon a man. In her effort to throw off the spell of the moment she cried:

"Be a mon, Jones. Drink your fill o' the rum and you'll be that much better."

"Drink'll not do," he cried, as if trying to blast his real need into her young mind.

Buttons had lived long enough, had seen too much not to understand the man's need. And her own. Softly she said to him:

"What manner o' man be you, Jones?"

"Aye! What's that?"

"You heard what I asked. Or did you not?" She made sure the cabin door was closed.

"You mean what?"

"Just what I asked you. What manner of mon be you? What manner o' mon could lay beside a wench for six weeks and not know of it?"

"Wench? Where at? You, Buttons lad, a wench?" He grasped her shoulders. "Nay, fool me not, lad. I'm in no mind for it."

"How came I aboard? When your lads took the snow I refused to join wi' you until came the command to strip. Recall that? Then I joined wi' ye to save my maidenly modesty." She gave one of her long laughs. "What must I do to prove mysel' no liar?"

"Enough," cried Jones. "I'll have ye to-night!" He caught her in his arms and pressed a heavy kiss upon her lips. "Aye, this very night."

Buttons suffered him to fondle her body and to find her lips again and again. Then she put him away.

"Nay, I said I was a woman but I'm no wench. Time enough when we get to port and there's a dominie to say the words."

"Nay, I'll not wait, Buttons. Give over." Again he sought to take her in his arms.

"Stand off, lad. My word's the last. Ye'll wait until there's a preacher or you'll not get that you seek. You might call a girl by her given name. Mary'll do."

But Jones was not to be put off. What he could not get by cajolery he would take by force, a true pirate. He closed in on Buttons only to find his head thrown back by a blow on the chin and then brought down again by another in his wind. He was sorely tempted to strike her back but better reason prevailed; even his dumb wits told him that was no manner of courtship.

"You must have a parson?" he asked when he got his wind back.

"Aye, 'tis well you know it. A worthy parson at that."

"There's such on board," he said. "One o' to-day's prize is a parson. I'll get him here."

"Wait a bit. How do you know he's a parson? Where's his kirk? Where's his vestments? Whose word am I to take that he is a true one and that I'm not to be harried?"

"He had the Book, the Bible, wi' him when he came on board. Held it close to his chest, he did."

"Aye, I recall that. But there's much to talk about afore you go to summon him. Let's put our nollies together."

In whispers the two talked for above a quarter hour and then Jones went in search of the dominie. In a few minutes he returned with the man and explained, in Mary's presence, just what was wanted of him. The minister could only protest.

"I'm very much afraid, my children, that you are making a mock of my cloth. I assure it will be best to wait until we get into port where this child may don the proper habiliments of her sex."

"Must I lay wi' you to prove I'm a woman?" Buttons demanded angrily. "Get on wi' your ritual."

"Now, now, lass, if lass you really be. I must take counsel with my Master that I may not be led astray."

"None o' that. We want no part of Edward England in this, if he's the man you mean. Nor of that funny little fellow who goes about chewing his whiskers, the captain of the Lady Betsy."

"I mean neither of those, child. I'm speaking of my Master, the Lord God."

For a moment the missionary stood with bowed head and then, turning a sad smile upon the two young people, said:

"Very well. I'll marry ye."

And forthwith was performed one of the most curious marriage services ever seen or heard on land or sea.

"An' keep your mouth sealed. Do you mind?" Jones laid a hand to his pistol.

"Aye, brother," answered the sad-faced dominie. "Ne'er fear! I'm not so proud of my part in this travesty."

As he started to leave Buttons said to her newly acquired spouse:

"The fee, you fool, his fee. 'Twould be a grievous thing to forget his fee."

Jones gave him two of the guineas taken from the Cadogan and the Church left in peace.

"Now I must be getting back to my station. I've had no other orders, master."

"Nay, we are through with those orders. Here you stay by order of none other than Captain England's self."

"What? Does he know?" cried the bride.

"Not from these lips. When I went to get the dominie I asked the master might I make you boatswain's mate and he said aye. Here ye abide wi' me from now on."

III

Marriage may not have served to make a better pirate of Buttons, but it did help to ameliorate her lot as well as that of Boatswain Jones. As Jones' mate she no longer acted as lookout; her only duties in fact were to serve her immediate master and these she performed capably and well. She had much time to herself but never for a single moment did she permit herself to go out of character. Was there a game of dice in the forecastle? She was one of the throwers. Were they gaming at cards in the afterhouse or in the steerage? If she was not yet a player, she would be when the stakes got big enough or the play faster.

Much of her time was spent lolling below the quarterdeck, for from there she often heard much of the conversation above her. And there were other places where she heard other conversation, too. For instance, on the third day of her bridal, she was dozing beneath the port cockboat when she became aware of voices nearby. They were those of the officers and the crew of the Lady Betsy. It was the dominie's voice that awakened her.

"If it's a plot, I'll want none of it," the man of the cloth had said.

"Aye, I doubt if ye'd be worth much to us," said the little skipper. "Keep your mouth shut, sir. And be going about your godly duties, whate'er they be on this ungodly vessel."

The dominie took the hint and left.

"Woodes Rogers coming wi' the King's Pardon is our chance," the other voice went on. "I take it these pyrates have not yet had the news. I take it he may have already arrived and there's our opportunity. As we go into New Providence the six of us can take over the vessel and deliver it and its crew to the proper officials. Are ye wi' me?

"Each one of us is well-armed, thanks to Captain England, and each of us knows more of New Providence than he does. That's enough. As we go into the harbour whatever ensign they'll show on this vessel must come down and the white flag must go up. Then when the officers of the R'yal Navy come on board we'll take credit for the capture. Again I ask: Are ye wi' me to a mon?"

The answers were whispered but one said:

"They'll learn at Mariaguana."

"An' mayhap they won't. I know as you do that there's revolt in Winter's ranks. On the Cadogan the crew, as rotten a gang of pyrates as ever beat up the seas, revolted and put their master, a blackgurd named Howell Davis, in irons and delivered him to the governor of Barbadoes. You know that, all o' ye. An' ye know now that the snow is again an honourable vessel and is being returned to Bristol to 'er rightful owners. Howell Davis is one o' Winter's men and so is Master England, o' this vessel. What happens when England's crew learn His Majesty's sending a free pardon to all pyrates who'll accept it and give up their buccaneering ways? They'll revolt, won't they? They'll return to the path o' honour, that's just what they'll do. The only ones we have to take care of are those on the quarterdeck. Once we get them where we want them a few words to the men of the crew will do the trick.

"Now give that your best minds. It's our plan and it'll work. Go to your stations and keep your mouths sealed, for I'll brand you a King's Traitor if you but breathe a word."

Buttons did not leave her hiding-place for some time after the conspirators had dispersed. And then she made no effort to see Captain England to acquaint him with what was afoot; nor did she tell her husband at once. The conspirators had two weeks in which to complete their plans and Buttons had the same time in which to decide what she would do.

If it were true that Captain Woodes Rogers was coming from England to the Bahamas with the King's Pardon for all repentant pirates, there might be trouble certainly. Buttons didn't want to lose her husband and she didn't want to stay on the account. What she wanted most of all was to go ashore and settle down and be a genuine housewife, taking care of husband and home and children if such there were. She might, she thought, like the Bahamas; she had heard the soil was fruitful and that there were no cold, foul winters as in England. Too, land was cheap in addition to being fertile. She had over a hundred guineas in prize money and more was due her on the sales to be made in port.

Watching her husband at his duties in the waist of the ship, Buttons wondered momentarily whether she would have been happier remaining on the Cadogan and returning to Bristol. That city was behind her and life, whatever it held for her, lay in the New World. Jones was a happy part of this future, a very necessary element, who must be won over to her plans. A day or so later she mentioned her idea to him, casually.

"A farm? By my bollys, are ye daft? What's come o'er ye, woman?"

"Aye, a farm, lad, and ne'er mind your bowels. A wee farm. We've enough between us to go until we get our hands in."

"Pushin' a shovel in the earth! Not for me, lass. No, not for Jones."

A few more bits of information had come Buttons' way.

"But they're tellin' me that all who take the King's Pardon will get twenty acres, save those who are married and they'll get forty," she said. "We could take ours near the sea, not that we'll need much from it, but because it'll be good to know it's there."

"Nay, I say. I'll have none of it. A sailor I am and a sailor I stay. Be off with you. I have me duties."

"What's a fisherman but a sailor? Looky here, my good man, list well to me. Above two hundred guineas we have atween us an' for twenty of them we can get a couple of blackamoors to do for us. Slaves they call them and they'll do the muck for ye. Think it o'er."

"Aye, and I'm thinking that your nollie's turned. Too, I'm thinkin' o' this thing you called the King's Pardon. What of it?"

"Hain't ye heared? There's a Captain Woodes Rogers, now on his way from the old country, to offer all pirates their honourable places if they'll but quit their pirating ways."

"Beshrewe me, wench. Where did you learn o' this?"

"That's my business. And be quiet with that wenching o' yours. Do you want the vessel to know?"

Jones grabbed her right hand and began twisting it.

"Tell me afore I cripple you."

"Have done, Jones! Hear ye! Give over!"

But the husband would not and Buttons, following the twisting, came up behind him and with her free fist caught him on the ear with such painful force that his hold on her wrist was broken.

"What manner o' woman be you?" he exclaimed, rubbing his ear. "I've a mind to give you a taste of the cat."

"Do, lad. And discover to the rest that I be a woman. Then let them laugh at their bully boatswain. 'Tis no manner for a young groom to treat his bride."

"Bride? Demon, I calls you. For half a crown I'd send you back to the forecastle, wife or no wife."

"Do, man. An' I'll take the King's Pardon on my own."

Buttons did not return to the forecastle, but remained in her double capacity as the boatswain's mate. Her love for her slow-witted spouse just about matched his for her and she did not, save in moments of passion, look upon a possible parting with horror. She was determined to take the pardon and hoped Jones would take it with her. Later, the same day, when his wrath had subsided, Jones asked Buttons where she had learned of King George's dispensation. She told him what she had heard while drowsing under the cockboat, whereupon he was all for dragging her at once to Captain England.

"Wait, man, wait. There be no hurry. It's another ten days to Mariaguana and there I'm sure we'll get news. But wait. The fellows can do no less than hang themselves. Or do you fear them?"

"Nay, lass, but——"

"Cease, fool, calling me lass. I'm a lass to you only and I'd keep it that way. Go on."

"I don't trust any man in the crew. It's been, to their minds, a poor venture, and Captain England and his master, Winter, take too heavy a share of the purchases. They'll list to those others who'll fill their ears. What then? The men on the quarterdeck are all they have to fear: one story for the men, another for the officials on land. I say, I must tell Master England."

"Tell him, if you will, but tell him cadgilly. If it's put to me, I'll lie you down and if you go too far, I'll tell England I'm no lad, lest your fool tongue does it for me. Tell the master you've heard rumours but go no further. Tell him you heared them wi' your own foolish ears, but leave mine out of it."

"Beshrewe me, Buttons, I think you're one of the conspirators."

"Think as you like, fool, but leave me out of it."

"I must put my mind to this."

Buttons let out one of her hoarse laughs.

"Then they need have no fear. By the time you've made up your mind we'll all be ta'en."

Jones aimed a kick at her buttocks which she easily avoided. Buttons wished he would treat her like that on deck, rather than endanger her position by calling her a lass.

Captain England was but little impressed by the news that the men he had rescued from Davy Jones' locker were planning to betray him; he laughed down the suggestion that he and his officers could be taken by any such device. What did strike him down was the news that Howell Davis had lost his ship and was now lodged in gaol at Port Royal.

"My log will vindicate me before Captain Winter, but I fear his wrath. I knew Howell Davis for a craven and I should have taken it into consideration. But those others, those who would take my vessel from me are wasting their time."

If Captain England had more to say, it was interrupted by a cry from the lookout to the deck that was carried on by the entire crew.

"Land ho! On the larboard bow. Land ho!"

All hands rushed to the rail and began speculating on what island it was they saw. It was Bridgetown, the outermost of the Windward Isles, and the pirates knew that from now on to their destination they would never be long out of sight of land. They knew, too, that failing to meet one of Captain Winter's vessels, they would anchor off Mariaguana within a few days now. Forty-two days it had taken them from the Guinea Coast, quick time for almost any vessel, but a phenomenal speed for one such as the Sparrowkawk. Rum was passed about to the crew and there was a great clamouring among the men to be placed on the water details, a heavy, thankless job of rowing the tanks to shore and filling them and bringing them back to the ship. Heavy work, indeed, and little to the pirate's liking. But the land was the lure. Anything could happen on land and going ashore was, as it still is, the best part of the sailor's lot.

The conversation on deck became animated; men discussed what they would do once at New Providence, even at Mariaguana, for that lonely port harboured taverns and women. The women were not so much; for the most part half-breed offspring of the wenches on the other islands who had been sold into slavery and who had later rebelled at the domination of their white blood by their black. They combined the defects of both races yet, for sailors ashore with money in their pockets, they would do to wash clothing as well as to cater to sterner needs. In the ports the women had little shacks to themselves before which they stood dressed in long, open-fronted gowns resembling Mother Hubbards. To a likely looking billylegs they would exhibit their charms at the same time pointing to the ever-present wash-tub. Some of the women had husbands who distilled rum back in the brush and who found it convenient to remain there while a vessel was in port. Such was Mariaguana, such indeed were most of the ports of the Windward and Leeward Islands in those days.

Buttons Read looked with quiet disdain upon these little islands, the same that had taken away the breath of the Great Admiral. Unlike Columbus she was no discoverer; but she did have much in common with many of those who had followed in the first man's wake, the conquerors. Even her unpractised eye could tell her that most of these islands were valueless; for all their rank and riotous verdure, they were too unlike the quiet hills of Devon and Somerset. Buttons was a true Englishwoman in liking controlled loveliness.

Leaning on the rail, she listened to the ribald jests of her fellows as they told each other of their previous conquests ashore and talked of rum and women, two of life's elements that were seemingly inseparable in their minds. There was a yellow girl here, she heard, a Spaniard there; all about her were men who declared that only black women knew the art of love, that the darker the meat the richer the quality; still others desired the fire of the Frenchwomen. Buttons' problem was not theirs. She would go ashore, she hoped, with her husband; would she then adopt the habiliments of her sex or would she continue to pose as a man? If she were to go alone, she was certain she would continue in her present role; the islands provided but one job for women and she had no mind to take it.

Could she, who had done no elemental labour in her life, subsist on the land? Would her hundred guineas build her a little cot that would house her and warm her? She would like to be near the sea; one born in Bristol always had the sea in his ears.

"Aye, you booby, let chance direct you. There's always a tavern for you to serve," she muttered finally.

Buttons made no attempt to go ashore until the Sparrowhawk anchored off La Desirade, a long island off the coast of Grande Terre. This, she learned, was a favourite rendezvous for French pirates, the Fraternité de la Mer of history. Here she went with Boatswain Jones, not, she told him, to keep him away from the Frenchwomen, but because she wanted to try her legs.

"Aye," he said stupidly. "I've no relish for them. You're more to me taste, lass."

"None o' that, hear. I'm going to see if the land's solid enough for my feet."

But Jones ashore was a sailor ashore and he wanted his fun, preferably with Buttons, but a Buttons with skirts on. When he began to forget her garb she admonished him with her fists, calling him low names in her hoarse voice to put him in his place.

"Enough of that. Save it for our cabin, lad. I've a mind for a pint o' ale. What say you to that?"

"Ale, lad! This is a French port and I've a mind for stronger tipple. Rum for me and I'll wager it will be your call, too."

There were other Britishers in the tavern and from them Jones and Buttons learned that the ship from which they'd come was hurrying to New Providence to be in on the pardon.

"Piracy's dead and smugglin's not worth the candle. It's the plough for me. Twenty acres I'll have and I shall pick me a nice plot with a cow, some pigs and a garden, and for money I shall plant the new fruit called pineapples. It'll be a bonny life. If I can find me a wench, I'll be well set for the future and the devil take those who say me wrong."

"Hear?" whispered Buttons to Jones. "There's a man after my own desire. Piracy's dead, says he, and from the takings on this cruise, I take it he's right. What then? Accept the King's Pardon and make the best of it."

"Shut up your mouth!" cried her husband. "I'll take the sea. Say, man, what does the King offer besides a wee farm? Does he offer me a vessel to sail the seas? There'll be a might of ships left in the harbour when all these tailors and drapers take up the pick. Are the vessels to be left to rot in the sands? Or will King George send me to sea in one of them, in all honour?"

"I don't know 'Is Majesty, but I doubt he's such a fool as to send a pirate out in a vessel where he'll be likely to forget his vows."

"Then I'll have none of King George nor of his pardon nor any part o' him. Wench, another tankard." Turning to Buttons he continued, "That's your answer for all time unless I decide to follow Captain England."

Jones was decidedly drunk before it came time to return to the Sparrowhawk, very drunk and overly amorous. To avoid his advances, Buttons left him to his own devices and sought amusement by herself. Further along the waterfront she found another tavern and, entering it, ordered a bombo, a refreshing mixture of lime juice, sugar cane rum and a little sugar. Two wenches were attending the tavern alone and one of them showed a disposition to smile upon the young sailor ashore. Buttons laughingly repelled the woman's advances, declaring she had a wife in New Providence. The Frenchwoman retired, but after a time returned and smilingly offered Buttons a small nip of brandy, murmuring:

"Avec mes compliments."

Buttons thanked her, smiling, and was about to drink. Then suddenly the face of Moll Read seemed to rise before her eyes. She slapped her thigh a resounding blow, laughing long and loud.

"Hey, wench, come you here. Have a seat, lass, I like your cut," she cried.

Buttons toyed with the tot of brandy while the wench made her way to the table; then she pulled her down beside her.

"Yer a likely wench," she said in English, "an' me an' you could 'ave a bit of high fun. Hey, now! What say?"

The Frenchwoman professed to understand no English, but the languages of the sexes is the language of the world and Buttons soon had her attention and interest. Her arm was about the woman's neck and she had made as if to kiss her when suddenly the tavern wench found her neck held in a vicelike grip and her head pried upward so that her mouth opened awide for breathing. With her other hand Buttons took the brandy and poured it down the woman's gullet, holding her grip until a convulsive gulp told her the liquor had been swallowed.

"A fine, warming drink, my bonny, and it'll do you good. Fancy trying an old trick like that on a young chap like me! Hold still, you trollop, I want to see the potion work."

Satisfied that no amount of retching would emit the drink, she let the woman's head down, but kept hold of her waist.

"A bonny fine piece you are, you are," she smiled. "One who could give a better man than me a fine tussle, I'll be bound. Sit still. Sit still and take your medicine like a lady." Buttons watched the woman narrowly. "Come now, be still. I'm studying to be a leech."

The tavern wench's gasping ceased and Buttons roughed her up a bit, never for a moment releasing hold of the ample waist. Within a few minutes she knew that her suspicions were justified; the woman yawned agape and the lad let go of her.

"How now? What sort of wench would you make? To go a-nodding in a man's arms! I'll have none o' you." Buttons stood up and, looking down at the now bleary-eyed wench, fetched her a slap across the cheeks. "Awake, so you may see your gull walk out on ye. Adieu, and pleasant dreams."

At the door she stopped and, looking back, let out one of her prodigious laughs.

IV

The Sparrowhawk did not linger long at La Desirade; the call had been made simply to give the men a break from the monotony of ship life and it had served its purpose. But to Edward England it had meant more than that for it was there he had gotten more convincing news of the impending disaster. For hours he would stand beside the man at the wheel or on the quarterdeck with his chief officer, silent and lost in thought. On the second day out he called the former captain of the Lady Betsy and brusquely ordered him to take his chest and gear to the forecastle; the former mate was to go to the afterhouse. Then he called Buttons to his cabin and commanded her to be always on the alert, to listen to all that was said and whispered on deck and to report to him.

"Aye, master, but to what shall I listen? To those who are willing to accept the King's Pardon or to those who will have none of it? After all, I am no snitch-tongue."

"Nay, lad, I'll not ask you to betray your mates and I fear no man on board. I want to know the drift of their talk, what they desire, for I will have to report to my own master when I meet him. Knowing his great soul, I can say he will not stand in the way of any man who wishes to turn from piracy. My course is marked out for me, for where Captain Winter goes, there shall I go, too."

Buttons understood; in her heart she felt a little ashamed that she, too, could not blindly follow a brave master and in that same heart no question of England's great courage had ever risen.

"That's all, Buttons. Tell me only what you hear, forgetting all partisanship and smaller loyalties."

"Aye, master." The youth saluted and returned to the main deck.

Buttons heard much on both sides. Some were all for taking the oath and returning to their homes with whatever they could salvage; some recalled stories of buried treasure and thought they would accept the pardon and then go in search; others, and Buttons was compelled to admit with a little shame, the stronger, the more resolute declared they'd have no part of any oath save that of the pirates and would rather die than be beholden to King George, "be he George the First or George the Next." These latter, however, were in the minority. Buttons would have liked to join them for she always responded to great courage in men, hating only the weak with a venom that was in itself a strength. In her mind she manned a small ship with Captain England as master, Jones as chief mate, herself as boatswain and the thirty leal men in the Sparrowhawk as crew. Given four guns and a snow or a sloop she felt sure they might conquer the seas. By craft as well as courage, by attacking the enemy in the weakest spot and by throwing caution to the winds, such a ship with such a crew would be wellnigh invincible.

Buttons laughed loud and long. As she had told Jones a hundred times, she was through with being on the account.

Such a ship and such a crew, she thought, might sail up and down the seven seas for seven years and never make a purchase.

Aye, piracy was dead. The Spaniards were storing their gold in inland vaults, refusing to risk it to capture. Merchants, unwilling to pay the high insurance rates, were holding their ships in port while their representatives stood in the various chancelleries of Europe demanding that the buccaneers be put down for all time. France had listened and then acted because the French merchants were stronger than the corsairs; England was acting because the Whigs were now in power and they gained their strength from the trading and commercial classes as well as the aristocracy. Aye, piracy was dead and the wiser would realize it first. Buttons was not stupid.

The day before the Sparrowhawk was due at Mariaguana Captain England called Buttons to his cabin.

"Aye, Buttons lad, what have you learned?"

Buttons told him that all but thirty of his men intended to accept the dispensation and the boatswain's mate would be among those who would go ashore.

"Nor do I blame you, lad. There may be some pickings left, but by the time you're a man there'll have been an end to us oldsters. Go ashore, pick out a good, sound wench and take the King's acreage. With the extension of His Majesty's power, these islands will be the land of the future. 'Tis better land than you'll find in all of England and money is free. God care for you, lad, and think of us olders who could not quit."

Later, in her own cabin, Buttons said to her husband.

"You're still pig-headed, I see. The master said as I should take the pardon and that goes for you, too. Do you come with me or do you stay?"

"You know my mind, wench, and I won't be harried."

"There's nought in all your nollie to be worth the harrying."

"Have done, I say. I love the sea more than I'd love any wench and that's that."

A mocking smile spread over Buttons' face.

"I know it, cheild, and a woman might look about when she's ashore for a more halesome man, one that might master her. Hey, now!"

"Have done, I say, or I'll give thee a thwack——"

"Aye, that you would, were you man enough. Have you the occasion, man? The deck's clear and you may call for fists or cutlasses. I don't fancy wasting powder and shot on you."

Her closed fists on her hips, Buttons awaited his answer boldly.

"To your station!" he shouted in anger. "I'll have you catted at the mast."

"I'm at my station, mullet-head. Nor do I care much for it. To-morrow we meet with Mariaguana and there'll be little sleeping this night. I might spend it at my old post i' the crow's nest."

"Spend it in hell for all I care," shouted the now thoroughly aroused Jones.

"Hardly in hell," laughed the girl. "There's a brisk and sprightly lad on duty up there who might like my company."

Jones was on her in a bound and bore her to the floor of the little cabin. While he was on top of her he managed to pummel her face and body, but she was the stronger and, twisting quickly, she found herself superior. What this loving wife did to her unloving husband may be left to the imagination; suffice it to say she spent the first part of the night on deck nursing her bruises and the latter part with her head on his shoulder. In the few hours before dawn she was sure she would not be able to tear herself from him, but would follow him to the end of the seas, pirate or not. It was still the dark of night.

V

The cry of "Land ho!" from the man on watch came with the sun. Those who were not already on deck hurried out with such speed that they were there before the look-out could give the point.

"Three points to the starboard. Land aho!"

Mariaguana is an outer-guard of the south-eastern group of the Bahamas possessing a series of fine harbours along its southern shore. Except for a small settlement taking its name from the island it was practically uninhabited and, at that time, not definitely assigned to the protection of any European power. Its population of a hundred or so, black and white, included Spanish, French, English and a few Dutch. Only when the pirates used it as a rendezvous did it come to life; with the arrival of the eight ships comprising Captain Winter's fleet it was looking forward now to prosperous days. The Admiral's flagship was the Rising Eagle, a bark of sixteen guns, and from its mainmast flew the signal for all captains to report on board at once.

"Prepare to lower the larboard and starboard longboats," ordered England. "Boatswain, pipe the entire crew to the mainmast. All hands, I said!"

There was a rush for the better positions and, when all were assembled, Captain England said:

"Men of mine, pirates all, brothers of the coast, list to me. I am called to report to my master, the gallant Captain Winter, and I haste to obey his summons. That there is news of interest to all of you I know. That important decisions are to be reached I can assure you. I, as well as you, have an idea it will deal with our future, whether we are to continue on the account or to accept the Royal Pardon. That you men are of two minds is no news to any of you. When we drop our anchors, the boats will be lowered. I do not wish to question the loyalties of any of you. Those who wish to quit will send six men to the larboard longboat; those who wish to continue as we are will place themselves in the starboard boat. To show I am no partisan I shall pick four men to take me to the Rising Eagle in a smallboat. I'll want for my own crew Boatswain Jones and the boatswain's mate Read and Seamen Bull and Mervey. I alone will go aboard the flagship and the rest of you will stand by until I give the signal to come on deck. That is all. To your stations. Top men aloft! Loose anchors. Prepare to cast larboard and starboard anchors. Top men attention. Reef sails. Beware loose ends."

The great sheetings were brought in, and aloft only the skeleton of the Sparrowkawk was visible.

From forward came the cry, "Starboard anchor ready, sir!" followed at once by a similar cry from the larboard side.

"Leadsman, attention! Prepare to sound! Heave the leads!"

"No bottom," sang out a voice.

"Sound astern! Helm to the leeward."

"No bottom!" came from the after-rail.

"Hold your helm true. Now, luff a bit. 'Vast, there!"

"Sixteen fathoms," came from the prow. A minute later it was repeated from the stern. Again laconic numbers were shouted and repeated.

"Twelve!"

"Ten!"

"Nine!"

"Seven!"

"Clear larboard and starboard anchors."

"Topmen, attention! Clew sails! Reef! Strike!"

"Anchor-men, attention! Cast anchors, larboard and starboard."

There was a perceptible slowing of the heavy vessel, a creaking of ropes against braces; men were straining at the capstan, others were running to and fro making gear fast; within five minutes the great vessel was calm, at anchor, and, dismissing the crew, at peace.

"Well done, men," called Edward England from the quarterdeck. "Man the longboats!" As if at a prearranged signal, six men fell over to the starboard boat and six others went to the larboard. When they were in their places, the master sang out, "Lower away!" The two boats disappeared from the sight of those on deck.

"There will be no shore leave until I return. Ready, crew!" Captain England came down the steps from the quarterdeck and without further formality leaped into the cockboat and was followed by his chosen crew.

Captain England kept his thoughts to himself on the journey to the Rising Eagle, sitting aft in the little boat while Buttons, pulling on an oar, tried to read his mind. There was a resolute set to his jaw and she was certain that whatever convictions he had, he would readily set them aside to follow his master. Buttons had seen such loyalty, but never experienced it. Whatever the game brought forth, her mind was already made up and there was no question of loyalty save to her own self.

Captain England went up the rope ladder to the deck of the flagship, his voice was heard greeting his commander and then all was silence. Giving some thought to her surroundings, Buttons saw other smallboats coming up from other ships and the two longboats from the Sparrowhawk feathering their oars as they were held against the tide. Men ranged the rails of the Rising Eagle shouting comments to those in the boats. How had they done? Aye, it was poor all over these days! A pox for King George! A pox for his reeve that bore his pardon.

"Have you a bit of rum for us?" asked Seaman Bull. "We're as dry as our breeks!"

"Have you your score?" came down in answer.

"Divil a penny," said Bull.

"Then you shall have none."

Buttons suddenly decided the tedium of waiting might be relieved by a tot and she drew a small coin from her pocket.

"An angel, a siller angel for two bottles o' straight rum. No water, mind you!"

"Come on board. 'Tis done," said the man.

"Nay, my man, my master says me not. You might bring it here."

"Aye, I'm the fool, hey? An' have you cast off?"

The controversy was amicably settled by the man coming down with the bottles in his pocket and getting his coin when it was decided the beverage had not been diluted.

An hour later Captain England came to the deck and summoned them all to come aboard.

"Make yourselves comfortable, my lads. The captain will have a word to say to you in a few minutes."

Buttons learned on the flagship that Captain Winter's own men had had a run of bad luck as far as takings were concerned. They had intercepted a Yankee rum ship but a week back and that staple was now their chief stock in trade; they were glad to exchange it for whatever coins they could muster from their guests, for most of them were planning to quit the sea and money was an absolute necessity on shore. Buttons' practical eye saw that they were doing a very excellent business indeed.

The boatswain of the Rising Eagle was called to the cabin and in a minute returned to pipe all hands down. When all was quiet, the eight pirate captains filed out and took their places along the quarterdeck. Then Captain Winter stepped forward to the rail; he was as ferocious a looking man as Buttons had ever seen, with a great bulbous nose, heavy blue jowls, and reddish, watering eyes. He rubbed the back of a hairy hand across his lips and cleared his throat.

"Men of my fleet," his voice was like his person, "we have come together not to determine our future course but to learn what you are to do. Captain England has told me that some of his men still wish to go on the account, not many but enough to spoil our plans. In my crews there are upwards of six hundred men, and I want to disarm every man and every vessel and to sail into New Providence and beg the King's Pardon. We have sinned, I now realize, we have sinned greatly, and our only reward is death. This is our opportunity once again to lead sober and industrious, honest and Christian lives. I have ordered my captains to return to their vessels and to disarm every man, to disarm each his vessel and to bring the arms and cannon, together with all shot and powder, into Mariaguana where it will be sold. We will reduce our stores to the bare necessities to take us to our new port where we will bend the knee to King George and ask his forgiveness for our transgressions. Those are my orders. Let them be put into effect."

From a capacious pocket he drew a black bottle and placing it to his lips, drank long and deeply. There was a murmur of dissent rippling through his audience that became a shout of disapproval before he had replaced the bottle. A man from one of the other ships rose and shook his fist at Winter.

"I know you for a fraud, Captain Winter, and I'll do no such thing. I shall stay on the account, aye, and I'll call upon your very men to join with me. Your plan is a very jolly one. Forsooth! We are to deposit our goods on yon shore, are we, and ye are to sell it to the highest bidder and then ye will sail into New Providence with all the siller and gilt and live in grand style. How now, Captain Winter? How now, when I say we will have none of your filthy plans nor will we take your dirty orders?"

"Have done!" shouted Winter. "Or I'll place you in irons."

"Nay to that, marster. You've not irons enough to place men o' my kidney in constraint. I say to you men who think as I do that a fair and equable division will be made in goods and ships. On my wessel, The Royal William, are forty such, and I ask you men who think as I do to call off the number of men on each wessel and sing it out. That'll be our answer to Captain Kit Winter. Sing out loudly, men!"

"Thirty-four on the Sparrowhawk" announced Boatswain Jones. "Not counting the crew of the Lady Betsy."

Others called out their quotas and it was found that of the six hundred more than a third, or to be exact, two hundred and ten men were still loyal Brethren of the Coast.

"Now, Master Winter, we will take us three ships, together with stores and guns and we will say farewell and good luck to you. But not until we have our division of the prize money. Hark to that, Kit Winter, and what say you?"

Captain Christopher Winter was for the moment inarticulate. From a single sloop, manned by a dozen hands, he had built up his famous flotilla and he called every splinter in it his own. Over a thousand men had paid with their lives for this position he held and their bodies were now at the bottom of the sea. He was a man high in the councils at New Providence and his position there, so long as he minded the laws, was strong and secure. He turned to his captains and, controlling his wrath, spoke to them in whispers. That they were not in entire agreement with their admiral was evident. One, Captain Will Cunningham, refused his commands, folding his arms across his chest and shaking his head.

"That's our captain, boys! Huzza for Captain Will Cunningham!" The original protestant shouted the words and many voices took it up. "Go to it, Will! Good lad, Captain Will! Will's our man!" The cries were heard on all hands.

Cunningham came to the rail and held up a hand for silence.

"I am of your mind," he said quietly, "and if you will return to your ships I think I can bring our great captain to terms. But whatever you do, men, do not leave your ships lest they show you their heels while you are away.

"They say piracy's dead and mayhap they're right. Certain it is that piracy in these waters is at a low ebb. If you ask me to be your captain, I shall feel duty bound to lead you into more prosperous waters. Return to your stations, appoint one man from each ship to keep in touch with me. Whatever plan is devised, I shall send you the intelligence."

But the Admiral of the Fleet was not yet ready to accept any terms but his own. He wanted the insurgents, mutineers he called them, to observe the articles they had signed which assured him and his flagship one-half of all purchases, the prize ship itself to become part of his fleet. Buttons as a member of England's crew had to await his return, so she sidled up to hear as much of the discussion as she could. The eight men on the quarterdeck were chiefly concerned in holding the admiral's tongue in check. One, a Captain Jennings, a Welshman who shared Winter's views, seemed more effective than the rest, and he was finally elected presiding officer of a meeting to be held then and there; being an equable man, he proposed that the sharing of the booty be done before the capitulation of the fleet took place. To all but Winter this seemed the most sensible course and it was agreed upon then and there. The admiral, voted down, had a single shot left; he insisted that they move on to New Providence at least before the distribution was made. This plan was scotched by Captain Dennis McCarthy, the lowest in grade and master of the only sloop, who was unwilling to accept the King's Pardon solely because of his Irish blood.

"Sure, now, Captain Winter, we'll be doin' it here where we are the law and not up there under the nose of Captain Woodes Rogers," he said. "Two hundred and ten men and the Belle of Erin, as staunch a vessel as ever flew the black flag, will be the first to change her registry. She'll take forty men, and there's Captain Cunningham's vessel, good for a hundred. Neither of us, if Captain Will will forgive me for speaking for him, would give our vessels up to you and I'll wager there's others of that same mind."

Indeed, as it turned out, no less than four vessels elected to continue under the Black Peter and the Sparrowhawk was one of them; Captain Edward England, sticking true to his vow to follow his master, gave up his command. The four vessels continuing on the account were to transfer to the admiral's fleet their men who favoured the King and take aboard the others who cared nothing for George and the Whigs.

Many of those who refused to accept the pardon believed the pirate's life was the only life for them, but many others could not have taken the required oath if they would. These were men who had been sold into servitude and had escaped; convicts, many of whom were branded on their foreheads; political refugees, and men wanted in Britain for capital crimes.

Buttons, though still determined to have done with pirating, felt more sympathy with the rebels than with the men who were leaving the account and felt sorely tempted to stand by them first. Jones had lost any influence over her; her only feeling was that if he wished to come with her, she would prefer it that way, but that if he chose to remain on the Sparrowhawk, that was his own affair; if he wished to poke his head into a noose, it was his own head, and be damned to it. Jones himself believed the whole project of the King's Pardon was a device to get the buccaneers to give themselves up for punishment.

"'Tis your head that will fit a noose," he said. "Set a thief to catch a thief and any of the older brethren, few they be, will tell you that Woodes Rogers, though never a Brother of the Coast, was on the account more than once. Stick by your rightful man, lass, and you'll stretch no hemp."

Carelessly Buttons mouthed the words of her favourite slogan:

"I'll cheat the gallows yet. That's why I am taking this opportunity." Then she became as tender as she could. "To-night's our last night together, man, an' I been a true wife to you, you know that. I've been buffeted about more than you have and I want to settle somewhere I can call home. Come with me, lad, let me show you the way." There was a note of pleading in her voice. Jones did not answer her and she went on, "Maybe bairns will come to us, Jones, an' it'll be a happy cot wi' all of us. Soft, too, and warm the nights. Hey, now, lad, tell me you've reconsidered."

"Have done. I've had my say and I stick by my word."

The tenderness, the woman in her, disappeared; once again she was the harsh man fighting for herself alone.

"I've done, mullet-head. I'll set my gear ashore this very night an' be well shut of you."

Forthwith she went to work to pack her gear into her chest. Her little leathern pouch had about a hundred guineas in it and this she stowed under her shirt. In the secret compartment of the chest she had some plate, both gold and silver, and she counted this over to see that it was right. Boots, greatcoat and all were gone over, blankets folded and made fast. Then she pulled all the stuff out on deck and called for another man to give her a hand. The two lowered the gear into a cockboat and then Buttons went back to the cabin and donned her arms: two pistols in her sash, cutlass in her baldric, stiletto and sheath knife at one side of her belt and at the other her axe. At that moment she hated herself for her feminine weakness of a short time ago, so, without looking at her husband or offering him God-speed, she left him and the Sparrowhawk. Her companion rowed her ashore and helped her stow her stuff above the tideline, safe in the bushes. Buttons took him to a tavern and bought him many tots of rum. Then she turned her back on the roistering town and returned to the shore.

To sleep in a tavern would have involved certain explanations, she knew; a sailor ashore did not sleep alone unless he was entirely drunk; besides, there were her possessions to protect. Wrapping her greatcoat and blanket about her, the girl lay down beside them and managed to snatch a well-needed rest. The absence of Jones, and it is no reflection on his manhood, went unnoticed and she awoke refreshed and ready for whatever the day demanded. She was yet far from New Providence and had to make some arrangements for passage. If Jones kept his mouth shut and set up no hue and cry for "his woman" she was safe. Her secret was his and hers alone.

The sun was high in the skies when she awoke and after a catlike yawn and stretch went in search of food. She found that in Mariaguana tavern doors were left unlocked at night; indeed, the occupants were in no fit condition at closing time to fasten latches. In the first one she came to many of the patrons still slept on tables or on the floor where they had fallen. Food and unfinished drinks remained on the tables and Buttons found fruit and bread enough to suit her needs.

Only on the decks of the vessels was there any sign of life, and the girl sat for over an hour on the little jetty waiting for the town to waken from its obscene and drunken slumber. She decided she would try to learn on which ship Captain England was taking passage and try to secure a berth with him.

It was after eight bells when the fleet sprang into activity. Smallboats and longboats began leaving the anchored vessels, bringing men and their personal gear ashore, dividing them, at first, into two camps, the one for rehabilitation and the other for—the freedom of the seas. Later on there would be another group, made up of cynics and daredevils who put no faith in Woodes Rogers' mission and who were, if necessary, ready to fight it out with him. These last numbered upwards of a hundred of the rebels and Buttons learned that their leader was none other than her husband, Jones. She giggled to herself at the thought of the boatswain leading anyone.

Captain England alone, of all the masters of the vessels, had lost his command. The Sparrowhawk was turned over to those men who were set and ready to defy the King's representative, and when its former master was taken aboard the Rising Eagle Buttons was happy to be given passage on the same vessel. By nightfall the transfer was complete. The three factions agreed to quit Mariaguana on the morrow. One last night was to be given over to carousing and wenching. Buttons, knowing such celebrations only too well, decided to remain on the vessel.

From Mariaguana the ships stuck close to the islands of the Lesser Antilles. They now proudly flaunted the Royal Ensign and beneath it the white banner with the red cross of St. George. Purification had already set in.

On the Rising Eagle only the meagrest duties were performed. The crew stood about in groups discussing the future, and men who had come from farms, who knew anything at all about the agricultural arts, found themselves regarded as fountain-heads of wisdom; they were kept busy answering questions. How were cows milked? And on what were chickens fed? Buttons listened to everything, absorbing all the information she could that might pertain to her new life and not knowing that much of it was false. Occasionally she thought of Jones. Would he come to her when they reached New Providence? she wondered. And would she, at last, adopt the clothes of her sex or continue to dress as she had always done? At times she wanted him more than she was willing to admit, at others she had difficulty bringing him to her consciousness. Her final decision was that if he did come back, she would dress as a woman, bear him children and keep his house; the idea appealed to her, but she was determined she would not lift a hand to bring him to her side.

The Rising Eagle on its last piratical cruise called only at Watling's Island where she dropped three Frenchmen and a like number of Spaniards. Then she crept among the cays to the Island of New Providence.

VI

From the roadstead the town of New Providence, if town it could be called, looked like all the other settlements in the Caribbees. There was a fort, called Nassau, and a few stone buildings remaining from the Spanish occupation which were now used as government buildings. The rest of Bay Street was composed of clapboard houses and stores and thatched mud huts. From the landing jetty to the fort, a distance of less than half a mile, the street along the waterfront was devoted almost entirely to business enterprises. Here every industry from the oldest profession to the happiest thrived side by side. Grogshops and taverns dotted the way, scattered among ship chandlers and dealers in stolen goods, shipwrights and ammunition sellers from whom you could buy anything from a pint of powder to the complete armament of an eighty-four besides shot, both ball and grape in any quantity, and drapers who sold long bolts of Lyons silks, Scottish woollens and Irish linens for any reasonable price. All the goods had been taken from honest bottoms by pirates and thrown upon this market.

A Thieves' Bazaar.

No honest merchant would ship to this port; indeed, a merchant's instructions to his captain were usually to avoid the Bahamas at all costs, to give them a wide berth and to do all his trading along the mainland coast. But for a captain to obey his patron was not always enough to keep his cargo from the Bay Street shops. The buccaneers roamed far and wide, and many a captain who had lost a cargo and then had been forced to put into New Providence for water saw portions of his goods already on display in Bay Street.

Your pirate was, in the main, a vain chap, loving fine clothes almost as much as he did rum and women. His first gesture when arriving at New Providence, usually in rags too filthy to stand another washing, was to repair to the shops and pick a new wardrobe from their varied stock. The quality depended upon his purse and his gullibility; since the shopkeepers were for the most part Spanish and Portuguese Jews, it was a lucky pirate who got full value for his money. Satisfied that he was the Beau Brummel of the Bahamas, he would strut about, from tavern to brothel, asking for kudos for his fine appearance and ending by getting as drunk as possible. An occasional sensible fellow would cache some of his wealth, reserving but enough for a night's entertainment, before giving himself over entirely to the pleasures of the flesh, but even then what few coins he had left in his pocket and such garments as could be removed from his drunken carcass were stolen by the wenches.

There was no government to speak of in the Bahamas. The place was a possession of the Lords Proprietors of Carolina, and New Providence was compelled to accept an administration man, a small-salaried official who usually managed to get rich in a few months and then return to England to live. There was a succession of these petty officials and they knew better than to try to impose the laws of the King on the people. There were stronger men than they in the community, men who could have them removed at will, men who demanded and took part of the income of all, pirates and merchant fences alike. And did the wench last night make off with some of her patron's equipment or clothing? Then she must share her takings with the men higher up. Captain Christopher Winter was one of these.

That worthy, at Mariaguana, had been stopped from taking a levy on the possessions of his own mates, but while still there he had been mistakenly informed that Woodes Rogers had already arrived. As one of the strong men of New Providence, he expected to hold the new governor as he had held the deputy commissioners. Now, as he raked the town with his glass, he could see that there was much gaiety, flags were flying, the one street was crowded with people; the harbour was filled with ships of all types, ten among which at least might easily have been mistaken for men o' war. There was great activity within the fort and much bustling about the government buildings. Before delivering himself and his men to the new governor Winter meant to have a word with that functionary and learn if his rights were to be respected; ordering his men to remain on board his vessel until he returned, he had himself rowed ashore, only to learn that Woodes Rogers was already a week overdue.

Manifestly, the Rising Eagle was ahead of time. To the pirate admiral there seemed but one thing to do, to turn back to sea and intercept the coming governor and confer with him on board the royal vessel; then he would know how to proceed. He discussed the situation with the other strong men of the settlement; to a man they agreed it was the only plan by which they might learn their status under the new regime; so it was decided they should accompany Winter. Chests were hastily packed and ordered taken to the jetty while Winter and his cronies sat over tots of rum in The Ball and Chain, a tavern frequented by officers. Outside there was a great huzzaing; a crowd milling in both directions, old friends greeting, women screaming compliments to old customers.

"A pox on them for their noise!" yelled Winter. "Let us go aboard and await our boxes. What say?"

Forthwith the five men rose in all their importance and Jim Fife threw down a coin to settle their score.

"Gangway! Gangway for the captains!" cried Captain Ben Hornigold as they emerged into the street; he had become a power in the Island since he had taken a French Guineaman worth three hundred thousand guineas and had cheated his crew of much of their share. "Gangway for your masters!"

"Gangway yourself!" cried a voice that Captain Winter recognized as belonging to a member of his crew. "We have no masters."

"What are you doing ashore, man?" he shouted. "My orders confined you to your ship."

"Aye, captain. But we come to take the King's Pardon and we're not asking yours. Zonder's your vessel and not a man jack, unless he be a fool, remains aboard. Too, master, we've taken what's ours, leaving you the vessel."

"Beshrewe me, I'll have the law on you!"

"Aye, that you will, but the terms of the King's Pardon are already known and all our ventures before signing are forgiven. Now we are ready to sign, Captain Winter. Are you? I have three guineas I got for your chased cutlass, the blade that was your pride!"

Winter went purple with rage, a rage so great that it rendered him inarticulate; Hornigold, about to draw his cutlass and cut down his friend's tormentor, abruptly changed his mind and led the captain back into the inn.

As each new vessel arrived in the roadstead, emitting gangs of hairy and dishevelled pirates, the din became greater. Ships were robbed of flags and pennons, regardless of what nation they represented, and these were strung from house to pole and to every staff that would support them. A keen observer, looking the flags over and attributing them to the nations to which they belonged, would have seen that one flag was missing. And in its absence he would have been struck by a fact that not even a fool could avoid.

The missing flag was the Black Peter.

For every ship in the roadstead from sloop to barquentine, and they numbered already more than fifty, there had been at least one Black Peter. Somewhere, secreted against the future, were upwards of fifty ensigns belonging to the Black Brotherhood.

If the same observer had become inquisitive and asked what had happened to the missing ensigns, he would have been answered by a laying of a finger against a nose and a slowly dropped eyelid. Perhaps certain pirates had gone in for collecting souvenirs. This, at least, was the charitable view to take.

Never had the merchants, both male and female, of New Providence known such business. The men at least were anxious to dispose of their stock in trade before the arrival of the law in the person of the new governor, and many a shop was closed at midday for lack of goods to sell, only to reopen on the morrow with the booty taken from a new arrival; many a longboat came to the jetty with barrels of rum which were sold to a fence who paid the market price and later disposed of it to a grogshop proprietor who, in turn, sold the liquor at a profit to the very men who had first stolen it.

The swarming pirates were spending money as if they had inexhaustible resources, apparently oblivious of the fact that upon accepting the King's Pardon they would lose their chief means of livelihood. But the morrow was to bring hunger and thirst. Gaunt men would wander over these fruitful islands eating cocoanut sprouts and any growing thing that seemed to promise nourishment; others would go about trying to trap the wild hogs to vary a diet made up chiefly of sea-food, and many would go mad and forget their vows and seek once again to go on the account. Returning, as one commentator put it, as does a dog to his vomit.

Buttons, for the very good reason that she cared nothing for rum and by her biologic make-up could not go wenching, was the more fortunate. She made two or three turns up and down the lone street, looking into the shops and taverns but sticking to her favourite drink of bombo and keeping her coins in her pocket. Every other hut and building on Bay Street was a grog-shop and they supported many curious devices. Here was The Bloody Hand, hard by The Rogue's Haven, both too small to accommodate their patrons; a step or so beyond The Sovereign's Bollacks was The Black Peter, and there were many more which dispensed with the traditional sign, letting their open doors announce to passers-by the business done within. When she tired and had seen all there was to be seen, Buttons began to think about the future.

Here were many men spending great sums of money, here the merchants were prospering as never before; here was opportunity. But of what sort for her? The merchants who dealt in stolen goods would be put out of business by the coming of the law in the person of the new governor; the women would go on for ever, but she was not that kind; the taverns might survive but only the best of them, for when the pirates' money was all gone, when it had all gotten back into the hands of the merchants, who then would buy their rum?

Buttons paused finally before The Black Peter, a building half of stone and half of wood, and then upon a sudden resolution went in. Rough tables, their legs sunk in the hard earth, were surrounded by long tables and light entered through masonic holes in the stout walls and through the two doors. A small bar was presided over by a former buccaneer of vicious mien but famous reputation who had made his place the favourite of all classes. The drinks were drawn by the owner but the tables were served by wenches who could always take a moment off for extra-commercial activities; too often business suffered because of absences and Buttons saw an opportunity for a man, a man such as herself, who would be always on the job. The landlord recognized her as the customer who always ordered bombo, which to his mind was no drink for any man.

"What now, Bombo," he called to her. "Have you decided to take a man's tipple? A tot o' good Medford rum, hey, now? It'll put blood in your young veins and give direction to your e'e, though I note that most of my maids are variously employed. Ha! Ha! Ha! You should have come earlier, Bombo, my lad."

"It's just that I would talk with thee, marster. Look'ee here. Twelve wenches you have on hand to wait on your customers and by my hide all but three are out of bounds. And those three are unfit for decent employment or else my eyes lie to me."

"Hi, it's the way of woman in all times and places, Bombo. An' would you have them different?"

"Nay, marster, not at all. All's fun and a bit o' profit to them and I say, let them have it. But look'ee there, azont the table abaft the window. Three thirsty men and nary a drink before them. Shall I take their wants?"

"Aye, do, Bombo."

In a minute she was back and said:

"Three stout rums, no water. There's men that are men, eh, marster? Three shillings I take it that might have gone to The Sovereign's Bollacks or to The Bloody Hand, had I not seen them agape."

"Aye, and you shall have a bombo at my expense."

"Nay, marster, thank'ee. You've a mind that I'm a sober lad. That is more than you can say for your wenches. Why not give me a place? When your customers demand more of your wenches than you sell, I'll still be here, to tend to the wants o' those less fortunate. What say, now?"

"Aye, it's a thought. Pray tell me why you, a fair lad of good bottom, yet stick to lime and forswear yon dames."

"'Tis no fault of mine, marster, but I've no great taste for either, which would be to your profit."

"Take a crown a day, your found and say that you're employed."

"Thank'ee, marster."

So Buttons went to work in The Black Peter as a bar-boy, the only one on all the Island, and many came just to see a lad who would steal a job from an honest, hard-working wench. They called her Bombo, as did the landlord, and, after the first derisive laughter, it was decided by many that her services were an innovation of real value. One could always be sure of getting a drink at The Black Peter and the custom of leaving a gratuity for the waitresses was extended to the prompt lad who never drank anything but bombo and who would not desert one customer for a more promising one. Buttons was a success from the day when Captain Jack Rackham, the famous Calico Jack, dandy and man about the seas, entered to the acclaim of the assembled pirates. Jack sat down grandly, his brightly coloured calico breeks but freshly laundered. He summoned a wench to take his order but, none being available, Buttons came to wait upon him.

"A lad, heh! What manner of man are you to take a wench's job? Hey? Answer me that!"

"You'd wait long and thirsty, marster, were you to await the comin' o' one of the wenches."

"So? When Calico Jack calls to a wench, she'll come or, by the Grand Chaco, Calico Jack'll know the reason. Send a wench to take my wants an' be damn certain she's a comely one. Hustle, lad!"

Buttons hustled, but Calico Jack was forced to face the fact that the women were otherwise engaged and so well engaged that they'd rather not forgo what they were doing even for the pleasure of serving him. Buttons explained carefully and Calico Jack, making the best of it, ordered a rum, straight, and a hearty one at that.

The man who called himself Buttons Read did not care much for the befrilled Calico Jack, but the latent woman that bore the same name and wore the same clothes thrilled at the very sight of him. She hurried to fetch his order and found him standing over his table, bringing his wide-cut breeks into their best advantage. After laying his drinks on the table Buttons had to pass by him on her way to another customer and Jack, in a spirit of fun, goosed her as she went by: if there was one thing the lad could not stand, it was being goosed. She jumped about eighteen inches and then she stifled Calico Jack's roar of laughter with a blow to the jaw that sent him sprawling over a nearby table. Furiously he regained his feet and drew his golden-handled cutlass, about to cut down the lad, when he found it torn from his hands and thrown into the corner and before him was a red-faced boy in the position of defence.

Thinking quickly, Jack spoke more to the customers than to Buttons.

"Deft, and a fine trick. My blade, lad! It slipped from my fingers."

Buttons hurried to retrieve the thrown blade and returned it handle first, saying evenly:

"I like not to be goosed, marster. Forgive me."

The quick-witted pirate noticed two things, the fact that in the general activity of the tavern the attack had gone almost unnoticed and the resolute, unafraid gleam in the lad's eyes.

"Too bad piracy's done for, my lad, or I'd have you as my bully mate on any vessel. You'll have to refresh my spilled drink."

"Aye, marster, in a trice."

Buttons hurried after the new drink. She was affrighted at her temerity in striking so august a personage, but Calico Jack now had a wholesome respect for the lad's courage. After his third glass of harsh rum, he called the bar-boy to his table.

"I've a mind to return to the account, lad, and I think that this Woodes Rogers be a sham, an illusion to frighten less hardy men than you and I. Would you have the occasion to return to deep water, to taking the filthy Spaniard and the dirty Frenchman?"

"Nay, marster, I'm through wi' that sort of life. At the best I was but an indifferent pirate and I am well content here."

"By Saint George for England, I'll do it! Here at New Providence to-day are the pick o' the lads o' courage of all the seas. I'll do it, lad."

Buttons had no opportunity again to declare herself against the venture, for Calico Jack leaped to his feet. Throwing a gold coin on the table to settle his score, he was out of the tavern in a trice. Then a shout from the street announced still another arrival and Buttons, running to the door, peered out across the water. She had seen that ship before and she would see it again, though she was certain that never again would she tread its decks. The Sparrowhawk slid gracefully to her anchorage and a single smallboat left her side. Buttons had no glass so she could not recognize those at the oars; she hoped that one of them might be her husband, or did she? Had Jones come to get her? To take her back or, failing, to denounce her as an impostor? Buttons liked neither prospect and she decided that if he had come after her she would dissemble, agree to accompany him and then, at the last moment, disappear; if he had come, repenting his former misconduct and ready to accept the King's Pardon, well and good.

She cared little for her single life while so many about her were enjoying the fruits of conjugal happiness, illicit or otherwise. She had sought definite information concerning the Crown Grants of Land that she had heard about, but she had gotten nothing but wild rumours and a meed of misinformation. Generally it was assumed that there would be twenty acres for a single man and twice that amount for a married pair, and the unfrocked priests and dominies were doing a startling business marrying repentant pirates to industrious trollops. Most of the wenches already had a dozen or more legal husbands and many of the men were married anew each night; no one remembered last night's ceremonies, least of all the officiating clergyman, for he was as drunk as the principals.

Each new arrival in the harbour was thought to be the new governor. Lookouts had been posted along the cays to send signals when he should be sighted and reports were received at frequent intervals, to the accompaniment of great shouts of joy and welcome; then half an hour later it would be learned a mistake had been made. All that the denizens knew was that the governor was coming, in a royal vessel they presumed; whether he would have a fleet under him with soldiers and marines to enforce the law, none could say, but it seemed unlikely the Government would send a man out single-handed to cope with such a problem as New Providence presented. Already there were over a thousand pirates and buccaneers assembled in the little town. They slept as a rule where they fell and at once became prey for the harpies of the shore; what the women of the town did not get, these foul beings took for their own. Many a pirate, knowing what his fate would be when he got drunk, would sneak out at night and bury his small hoard before giving himself up to drinking and carousing, only to forget in liquor where he had hidden his wealth. The beach beyond the fort was peopled by industrious diggers searching for this buried treasure.

The boat from the Sparrowhawk had Boatswain Jones at the tiller; he had been detailed to come ashore for news, an indication that on board all was not serene. The men beached their boat and joined the throng. Buttons, seeing Jones pass into the first dram-shop, knew that he would eventually arrive at The

Black Peter, she hoped still sober and in a good mood, for she didn't want to have to manhandle him.

"Eh, Buttons, lad," a voice called to her. "I heard you were here and I looked you up." It was Jones, amiable and pleasant as he could be.

"Hi, Jonesy. I thought you were still on the account."

"Aye, that I am and all the good fellows in the crew. A few chicken-hearted fellows decided they would be put ashore and we were to do it at Eleutheria, which we did, and learning that 'Is Majesty's Spit had not yet arrived, we came in to see. Do you still mind to stay ashore?"

"I do. I've work here as bar-boy, at a crown a day and my found. 'Tis a good berth and say the word, lad, and I'll have you fixed up in another. 'Tis an idea o' my own that each house should have a lad to do for the customers when the girls are busy."

She laughed a bit and Jones joined her.

"Whist, now, or you'll have me undone," she laughed again and then looked him over appraisingly. "You're a fine man, my Jones, and the nights here be long and lonely. You'll come wi' me?"

"For the nonce. I must be aboard by four bells i' the second watch."

Buttons sat him at a table and served him a drink of straight rum; then, when the opportunity offered, she took him up to her room. Later, when they were returning to the taproom, he whispered to her:

"You're a bonny lass, Buttons, an' I'll be needin' you as ye need me, but I've no taste for life ashore. Methinks piracy is finished, but I must have the seas beneath me. We'll part friends and I'll keep your secret to the death. Gi' us a parting kiss."

In the taproom the two had another drink together; then Jones went out into the throng, and as she watched his shoulders taking their way through the crowd, Buttons wondered if she would ever see him again.

"A good man he is, and were he to stay I might have fallen in love wi' him," she said to herself.

The crowds on Bay Street became madder and madder as the time passed. Many who had come ashore with small fortunes were already flat broke and preying upon those who still had money. There were fights and brawls every few minutes; at the least provocation fists would come up and swords be crossed. The women became, if possible, greedier and more demanding, prices went to unheard-of heights and only the blackamoors of the Island did any useful work. But even these poor suffered, for their little gardens were raided by hungry pirates, the pigs and cattle were stolen and even their persons robbed of the money they had gotten for their produce.

Realizing that it would be only a few days before anarchy would prevail, certain more responsible citizens tried to organize a temporary government; everyone wanted to be in on it, police were appointed only to be cut down by some former enemy, and within twenty-four hours the merchants were storing their goods and wealth within the fort, a fort manned by the very men they were seeking protection from. New ships arrived daily, dismissing their crews to accept the King's Pardon; of these only the stronger were able to retain any part of their wealth; the others were fallen on and pummelled and robbed even of their shoes.

And then complete pandemonium broke out. At the jetty stood a small post, and on the second morning after Jones' departure to his ship there appeared thereon a small announcement, held in place by a silver-handled poniard. Those who could read, read and pondered, and those who could not read had it read and re-read to them until they knew the wording by heart. It said, simply:

To CERTAIN MEN OF NEW PROVIDENCE

NOTICE that the undersigned is preparing to refit his twenty-four-gun vessel, the sturdy Rancour, for certain adventures that need not be detailed. To the men addressed notice is given to come at once to The Black Peter and to be prepared to sign the articles of agreement.

John Rackham, capt.

Buttons read and shrugged her shoulders. Like every other reader of the announcement, she hitched her trousers and hurried at once to The Black Peter.

VII

"Tankards and rum for all," called Calico Jack Rackham to the host of The Black Peter, "and I'll have the lad there to serve my company. The score, whatever it be, will be mine."

"Aye, Captain Rackham, as you wish." The landlord was worthy of a far better clientele. "Buttons, lad, give Master Rackham your full attention."

Several tankards and four flagons of rum were distributed where they would be handy to the captain's guests, who lost no time in slaking their thirsts.

"Drink, cheild," said the captain to one, "drink heartily, but know I want no part of a craven such as you be."

The man addressed tossed off his drink and sulked out of the tavern. When the taproom could hold no more, Calico Jack stood up and, rattling his accoutrements to gain silence and attention, announced:

"Gentlemen, for such you be, men of heart and men of great courage, your attention. Zonder lies the Rancour, as many of you know. With twenty-four

76

carronades she stands ready to meet friend or foe and all she lacks is a gallant crew. In New Providence to-day there are a thousand freebooters of all kinds; some of ye be cowards and cravens; one hundred and fifty I would say are men of undoubted courage, fearless and brave and willing to risk their necks against any who would seek to hinder them in their rightful pursuits. Those men are the ones I want. Those men, numbering one hundred and fifty, are alone asked to step up and give me their hands in fellowship and to sign the articles of the Rancour and to go with me upon certain adventures. The first articles are here in front of me and I will read them to you.

"'Certain adventurers of New Providence do herewith place their names or their legal marks beneath these presents acknowledging their acceptance of the leadership of Captain John Rackham for service aboard the bark Rancour for an adventurous cruise among the Islands of the Caribbean. They hereby promise to obey all his commands and the commands of those he chooses to place above them. They agree that the said Captain John Rackham shall have a third of all purchases and that his elected lieutenants shall each have three shares, and that all other officers shall, according to their station, have two and one and one-half shares respectively, and that all gunners, boarding men, musketeers and sail men shall have one share each.

"'That further articles of agreement will be signed once we are beyond the jurisdiction of King George. Amen.'"

As Rackham stopped speaking, there was a yipping, a blasting cheer from the men who, but a few hours before, had been ready to accept the King's Pardon. Then there was a rush among them to get to the table and sign their names.

"Silence! Stop!" cried Calico Jack. "You have forgotten my interdiction. The Rancour can accommodate but one hundred and fifty and that does not mean the first one hundred and fifty, but the one hundred and fifty men who are not afraid of Spaniard or Frenchman, Dutchman or——" the word came very softly from his lips—"Englishman." Then his voice rose again, hoarse yet resonant. "No others need sign. The men I want know I want them and what I want them for. The others know, too, that I do not want them." He laughed heartily. "Drink, my men, you all know me for a good fellow. But do not waste my time erasing your names from this paper."

He stepped aside and pushed the document forward where it could be seen and read by all. A voice from the outer rim called:

"Make way, you macaroons and scalawags! Make way for Will Fly who fights wi' his fists as well as wi' his cutlass."

The man began pushing his way through the crowd. He had once been champion boxer of the world and now he was one of the lowliest picaroons. As he pushed and shoved toward the table, he caught Calico Jack's eyes and what he read there may be surmised; he paused a moment and then let out a great half-drunken shout:

"Aye, master, 'tis I, Will Fly, but I want none of your articles. 'Tis a drink o' your neat rum I'm after."

The silent rejection of William Fly, a man whose fists everyone feared, had its effect; many others who were crowding up to sign found they had business elsewhere suddenly. At closing time almost the entire population of the town had read the document or had it read to them; up and down Bay Street, in tavern, grogshop and bordello, it was the only topic of conversation. Only sixty-eight names had been signed to the paper containing the preliminary articles, but every one of the sixty-eight was acceptable to the master of the Rancour; it had not been necessary to cross out a single one. Calico Jack called to Buttons and asked for his score. From a capacious pocket he took a leathern purse and tossed it to the boy, saying:

"Take what you will, lad."

Then, going to the table on which lay the precious document, he took another poniard, this time a gold-mounted one with beautiful Spanish chasing, and sealed the paper to the board.

When Buttons returned the pouch to its owner, it was considerably lightened, but Calico Jack paid no heed to it.

"That bit o' paper, lad, will not be complete till it bears your name."

And without waiting for a yea or nay he turned and went to his quarters.

For three days the paper lay on the table and each day more came and read and a few signed. On the fourth day a new sign appeared on the post at the jetty. Again it was headed:

To CERTAIN MEN OF NEW PROVIDENCE NOTICE:
The Rancour will sail on to-night's tide. Be on board with your gear before sundown.

Captain John Rackham, master.

Those who read did one of two things: they went to their lodgings and began to clear their gear or they ran to The Black Peter to count the names already signed. Buttons could have told them that since six bells in the morning the number had stood at one hundred and forty-eight.

At six bells in the afternoon Calico Jack, followed by six blackamoors carrying his chest and gear, stopped at The Black Peter and followed the example of the others; the list still stood at a hundred and forty-eight.

"A spike of rum, lad." When it was brought him, he said, "One hundred and forty-eight only and I had counted a hundred and fifty."

He tossed off the rum and asked for a quill and ink.

"A coin's toss to see who shall be first, Buttons, you er me. Heh heh! I'd forgotten I was to be one o' my own crew and there's still one name lacking, yours." Quickly he signed his own name and tossed the quill to Buttons. "Sign quickly, lad. There's no time for delay."

The quill lay where it had fallen.

"Nay, marster. I like thee full well, I do, but I've forsworn the account. I would stay ashore."

"Hey!" barked Calico Jack. "Who has said anything about going on the account? Not I. Nor my men. 'Tis an adventure and none the more or none the less. Sign and let's be off."

But Buttons folded her arms across her chest and shook her head.

"'Tis your last chance, lad," said Jack, placing his hand on the poniard but Buttons did not reply. Jack pulled the point from the paper and placed both in his pocket and, without so much as a farewell, he turned and left The Black Peter. Buttons turned back to her duties with a sigh; presently, unable to endure the suspense, she ran down to the jetty to cheer the last buccaneering expedition to leave New Providence. As she saw the happiness of the pirates who were returning like dogs to their vomit, she was almost sorry for her decision, almost wished she had accepted the final offer of Calico Jack.

Your pirate is as curious and inquisitive as a cat and many buccaneers who were unwilling to come to New Providence to accept the Royal Pardon came as close as they dared to witness what was going on. From their positions on the decks of their vessels, they watched longingly the gaiety and carnival of the shore. Their ignorance of how Woodes Rogers would proceed was what held them back. Would he come with a great fleet, surround the islands with ships of the line and men-of-war and hold all captive until they had accepted the Pardon or were at their foredoomed task of stretching hemp? None could tell, but it was the general opinion that every pirate on shore at the time of his arrival would be held strictly to account, that no ship might leave the roadstead until her papers were in perfect shape, and that those papers could be issued only by the Governor.

So, longingly, the pirates studied through their glasses the activities ashore and then sped to safety, only to return in a few days. Buttons had seen the Sparrowhawk a half a dozen times and had seen her disappear as often. But Calico Jack Rackham in the Rancour did not return the next day or any other day. He was sailing south, to Tortuga and to Cuba. Jack knew much more than he was given credit for.

The steady arrival of new vessels, throwing their crews ashore after they had found their anchorage, was all that saved New Providence from a revolt. Bay Street was a morass of muddy clay from the constant tramping of men; raiding parties were organized and, when a longboat arrived bringing rum to be sold, these gangs would meet the boats and take the casks to their shore rendezvous for themselves. Some they would sell or trade for food and provisions, but for the most part the stolen spirits warmed their own gullets. Many lived entirely on the shore or dunes, using pieces of sailcloth or boughs or trees and fronds of palms for shelter. Many of the wenches, losing their heads over some bonny fellow, accepted the conditions of their life and shared their lots.

The service at The Black Peter was vastly superior to that of all the other taverns and it now took control of the best trade, mostly captains, masters and officers. These worthies, wise in their use of rum and in their expenditure of money, awaited the coming of the law. Many were rich beyond the dreams of Croesus, others had tired of the dangers and uncertainties of piracy, all sought security from their enemies. They had made their piles and were now willing to sit on them and enjoy the view. Among them was Bart Roberts, a rare teller of stories, whom Buttons heard telling a yarn to the uproarious delight of his listeners.

"Up and down the seas he roved, a good privateer, with his papers sealed in his strong box. Don and Frenchman, it mattered not; Dutchman and Englisher were all the same. He'd sail up to them flying their own colours and when he got his grapples out, he'd push up the Black Peter.

"'How now!' would cry the captain of the captured vessel. 'By my eyes, you're a filthy pirate and had I known it, I'd laid you by the heels.'

"'Nay,' says the fellow. 'I'm a privateer and I make war by my King's orders and consent.'

"Then he would conduct the captured master to his quarters and bring out his document, its lettering in wide and beautiful flourishes and covered with big and little seals in gold and other colours. The unlucky men would try to read it, but 'twas in Danish and it looked all regular and honest and, though they grumbled that they knew not the Danes were at war with their King, they had to submit. The man kept on until one day he took a ship on which there was a Dane who could read the language."

Bart Roberts stopped to have his own laugh and to put his listeners on edge.

"The unlucky captain called to his Dane to read for him the words on the document and the Dane read, he did, he read that this precious bit of paper entitled the owner to hunt wild pigs and wild goats on the Island of Christianstad and nothing more."

There was a great burst of hoarse laughter and a pounding on the table for more rum. This was the kind of humour beloved of all pirates and it even drew a laugh from the sad-faced Stede Bonnet, or Major Stede Bonnet as he was known.

Years before the major had made his fortune in the army and had retired to live his declining years in comfort in the Barbadoes. He had been married for years, but the exigencies of a soldier's life had given him but little time at home and to his wife and children he had become scarcely more than a casual visitor, welcome because of his support. Upon his retirement he found that his family cared little for his company; in fact, his wife turned out to be a shrew and he only a henpecked man. He stood it as long as he could and then decided to go a-pyratin'. Rank amateur though he was, he purchased a vessel, recruited a gang of cut-throats and went on the account. His first meeting was with none other than Teach, known as Blackbeard, who laughed long and loudly at the major's attempt to be a buccaneer. Teach invited Bonnet aboard his own ship the Revenge and while he was entertaining his visitor sent a lieutenant to take command of Bonnet's vessel and sail it off. Later the major regained command of his own ship when Teach got into trouble and, sailing it immediately into Charleston, confessed to piracy and received a pardon.

But the thought of returning to his family was too much for him. Changing his name to Captain Thomas, he secured another ship, this time taken in true piratical fashion, and returned to the account; his contribution to the history of buccaneering is that he alone, of all pirates, actually made his victims walk the plank.

Bonnet was now in New Providence only to dismiss such members of his crew as wished to take the Pardon. In the morning he would sail with the recalcitrants because between the dangers of the sea and the terror of his wife's tongue he had no choice; he would sail and, though he could not guess it, he would be taken a few weeks later off Charleston and a month or so afterward be hanged there at White Point.

"And the King's Pardon, what of it?" Captain Charles Bellamy was saying. "Who gave the King the right to pardon such as us? By our very lives we have shown His Majesty that we have forsworn all allegiance to his crown; therefore and manifestly, he cannot pardon that which is not his." He looked about truculently. "I shall accept his pardon, but I shall reserve the right to abide by it or no."

Bellamy was a famous haranguer and disputant. When he was gone Captain Johnson would tell of his greatest speech, made to a captain whose ship had just been taken by Bellamy's crew.

"I am sorry," he cried, "that you cannot have your sloop again, for I scorn to do anyone a mischief when it's not to my advantage, but you are a sneaking puppy, and so are all those who will submit to be governed by the laws rich men have made for their own security because the cowardly whelps have not the courage otherwise to defend what they get by their knavery. Damn them altogether for a pack of crafty rascals, and you, who serve them, for a parcel of hen-hearted numbskulls! They villify us, the scoundrels do, when there is the only difference that they rob the poor under the protection of the law, forsooth, and we plunder the rich under the protection of our own courage. Had you not better make one of us than sneak after these villains for employment?"

While the captains discoursed in merriment and peace within The Black Peter those outside were in a different mood. Stede Bonnet might be the laughingstock of the pirates, but when it was known he was refusing the King's Pardon he was besieged by recently penitent pirates for berths on his ship; better by far to die a pirate than to starve to death in righteousness. Brawls, burglaries and killings made the richer of the people pray for the speedy arrival of the new governor.

Then came the news he had been sighted and this time there was no correcting of the report within the next half-hour. From Grand Abaco came the first report; hours later his two vessels were sighted off the Hole in the Wall. Another full day and they were seen passing Barry Island and on the next would appear to view off New Providence. The spirits of the people picked up at once; perhaps the delay had been for the best since it had rid the town of many trouble-makers and made the balance amenable to the King's law. But the two ships were coming too slowly and many more riots and deaths occurred before they appeared two days later off the bight. As the sun arose the first lookout cried the news, and men left their women and their beds and in shirt-tails came to see with their own eyes, and shouted back to the women who came too in what they had on and what they had not on.

There, commanding the western entrance of the roadstead, stood the King's two vessels, placed at right angles to each other so that they might broadside either the town or the vessels riding at anchor should either show fight. A longboat was pulling out from the larger vessel, a barquentine, and three splendidly dressed macaronis stood in the shrouds. As the boat neared the landing jetty, a boatswain cried out:

"Make way for the King's men."

But it was as if each man thought some other was being addressed and no one budged. One of the officers called:

"Ready, take aim!" Six muskets were pointed at the crowd. "Now, you ruffians, fall back and make way for His Majesty's representatives."

"Holy Murther," yelled an Irishman. "The b'ys have come to shoot us instead o' bringing us the r'yal pardon."

Laughing at the sally, some fell back and made way for the officers to step on to the jetty.

"Make way, I say, make way!" one called repeatedly.

But already the crowd had taken up the shout and were running down Bay Street screaming to the almost empty houses that the Pardon had come and all were free men again.

"Who is in command here?" called the macaroni. "Bring him before us!"

The Irishman was neither silenced nor frightened.

"Sure, your lordship, here until you set foot each man was king in his own right. Now that your lordships are here we all abdicate."

There was another shout of yippy laughter and the crowd fell back so that a lane was opened for the officers.

"What way His Majesty's Fort Nassau?" asked an officer.

"Forninst ye. Down the lane until you bump your Royal beak," a harpy called.

"But one cannot walk through this mud. His lordship would not condone it. It must be cleared up."

"How now, my lords, which of ye be the Lord Governor?"

"His Lordship remains aboard until this afternoon. Before he comes this sty must be cleaned up. To the brooms, and quickly, my lads."

"Aye, bring ye brooms to the Bahamas, that's never known a broom and none the worse for it?"

Buttons was thrilled by the finery of the officers, but not over-awed; stepping up briskly, she saluted.

"Sirs, what you seek may be had at The Black Peter, which is there azont the stone building. The chief men of the town are awaiting you." Buttons had an eye for business. "May I guide your lordships?"

"Pray do, lad, and as quickly as possible."

Buttons leaped from dry spot to hummock and was followed by the three officers who were in turn followed by the squad of infantrymen. At The Black Peter she stood aside and bowed them in; two men were placed at guard in front of the door, two were sent with a corporal to make a reconnaissance of the old fort and the others were returned to the jetty to protect the boat.

Inside The Black Peter the officers found none who were willing to accept even temporarily responsibility for the settlement; there must be, they insisted, someone to turn over to the King's Governor the town and its people.

"Where is the Deputy-Governor, the representative of the Lords Proprietors?"

"Oh, 'e," volunteered a former captain. "When 'e 'eard you were coming, 'e went to Lunnon to raise the old 'ob. I wouldn't be surprised 'ad you passed 'im in your coming. 'E's been gone these six weeks."

Ultimately it was decided that at four bells in the afternoon Governor Woodes Rogers would come ashore and take possession of the town, the island and all its people in the name of King George. Details were organized to go into the fields and bring into town great masses of boughs and fronds to provide a dry footing for the Governor. More flags were brought out and what merchants were left closed their shops, only the women and the grog sellers continuing business.

VIII

When it was seen that there were to be no immediate reprisals an old, toothless fellow, a Captain Sawney, known locally as Governor, consented to be placed in charge of all details. He had, years before, been a member of the Mission pirate republic at Madagascar and had held some office under that idealist. He was looked upon as a law-maker and it was he who gave the orders that Bay Street must be covered so that the good Governor might not muddy his shoes and who roughly trained a couple of squads of former soldiers to present arms, stand at attention and offer a salute; they were to act as a welcoming guard and help in any ceremonies to be determined upon by the young macaronis.

Buttons went from The Black Peter to the jetty fifty times that day and then decided to take a leave of absence to welcome the new Governor; she still had her job but at reduced pay, for business had fallen off to such an extent that only six of the original twelve wenches who served the tables were still employed. Bringing out her finest shirt and breeks, no less gay than those of Calico Jack, she dressed in her best. A sash with pistols, a baldric to carry her cutlass, a wide sweeping plume in her hat, and she was as gay a macaroni as one might find off Rotten Row.

At two o'clock a bugler and a drummer announced that the new Governor had left the Royal Frigate and was coming ashore, preceded by several longboatloads of marines. The small boat fleet made for the landing jetty in fine order, and the first squads clambered up and fell into line. There were fifty of the marines and line officers and another dozen aides-de-camp to the Governor. By the time the diminutive figure of Woodes Rogers appeared on the jetty, the former pirates had made a lane the full length of Bay Street. Eleven hundred rogues in their rags and finery, ill-assorted and disreputable, formed a gauntlet only a brave man would care to run.

Buttons observed the activities at the jetty and then decided to get closer to the Spanish building which had been designated as the future Government House where the real ceremonies were to take place; here old Captain Sawney was to act with the new Governor whose ceremonial plans demanded that something be taken over. As the girl hurried down the frond-laid path she passed many a familiar face. Here were Tom Cocklyn, known as Bloody Tom, and Pierre le Grand or, as he preferred to be known, Peter the Great; Captain England was there, puzzled and not knowing whether he had done right or not. Beside Ben Hornigold stood Edward Teach, called Blackbeard, and, but a few paces beyond Captain Winter, Buttons saw John Martell, him of The King's Fancy.

"I heared, John Martell, that you were languishing in a Spanish Town gaol," she laughed. "Did the walls fall down?"

"Nay, Buttons, lad. But I found in the Deputy-Governor a rare friend, and when I told him I wanted to accept the King's Pardon, he gave me leave to come to New Providence."

Buttons went on, nodding to acquaintances as she met them, Captain Roundswivel, Bart Roberts, Sample and Vane.

"A fine bunch of snivelling cut-throats," she averred to Captain La Bousse beside whom she took her place.

She faced the sea and saw that the Sparrowhawk had returned to watch the proceedings from afar. All her sails were set and it was only with difficulty the helmsman kept the vessel from scudding before the wind.

From the jetty came the sound of drums and bugles and the little music corps started the procession to the cheers of eleven hundred gullets. Every man jack in line pulled out his cutlass and held it aloft, making an arch through which the law in all its dignity must pass.

"My lord guv'nor walks a pretty step," said La Bousse.

"Aye, that he does," Buttons agreed.

"I mind the time," went on Oliver La Bousse, "when the man himself was on the account. Aye, I was in his crew, lad, a boy like you be. It was a merry company for such a hard master, for hard he was and stern and unyielding, but withal a gallant captain. He was a privateer, with his papers in reg'lar order, and he took the French and the Dons all according to law but, mark ye, he was not adverse to picking up a fine Dutchman and even another Englishman if there was a profit in it."

"A fine-looking fellow, though a bit small for such a great post," Buttons interjected.

"Small, but a demon in action, I can tell you. And not above a good laugh either. I mind the time we were off the coast of Brazil and our vessel was fired upon by the shore batteries. Now that was a signal for war with the Portuguese and the master landed his men under the fire of the batteries and took the town, a small affair and hardly worth the powder to protect it. It seemed that several attempts had been made to take the place and the people had become pretty nervous and fired on every vessel that flew not the Portuguese ensign.

"All this was explained to Master Rogers and, seeing he'd lost no men, he took it as a grand joke. The town was to have a religious ceremony and they came and asked the master to supply some music; one of our shots had pierced their music-box and they lacked the means to celebrate. Master Rogers was pretty quick to say his men would be happy to supply the music, forgetting that not one of them understood any of the Papist gibberish. So the procession was formed and off they go, the good fathers singing their hymns and followed by a bunch of drunken British tarry-breeks, playing 'Way hay, up she rises.'

"At the end of the procession came the Portuguese Governor and our gallant master arm in arm, drunk as lords, carrying lighted candles, one singing in his own tongue, and his mate in another. Aye, lad, it was a curious sight.

"After that a great party was held and I won't tell you how kind the Portuguese girls were to us, generous too, and if ever you come by one of those wenches, tarry a bit, lad, be in no haste to leave her. Well, we invited the Governor and his staff and all the priests and monks to a party on board the Duke and it was three days before one of them was sober enough to go ashore. Aye, we had to lower them by ropes into the longboat to be shut of them. Ha! ha! ha!"

Now the musicians had come abreast of Buttons and her companion and the two brought out their cutlasses and held them aloft. Following the musicians came the marines, fifty strong, and behind them, at a decently impressive interval, the new Governor and his staff. In their tall perukes and periwigs, silk stockings and satin small clothes they made a show worthy of London and one that was not wasted on the yet-to-be reformed pirates. Never had the Islands seen such a sight; this was the law in all its dignity and impressiveness, this, indeed, was the legal authority under which the Islands from now on would be ruled. The infantry went by in their red coats, buff breeches and long black leggings with silver buttons and then one could behold the grim visage of Woodes Rogers as he advanced to the Government House.

His face showed he had strength, for each pirate as he passed him brought out his pistol, or pistols if he had them, and fired them above the small Governor's head. Another man might have balked and ordered the ruffians disarmed, but not Woodes Rogers. A shot might find his back but the law would go on.

On he came, looking hardly to the right or left, until he was abreast of Buttons and La Bousse. Here he paused and Buttons wondered if it was from fear; he had but another fifty paces to go. But he had recognized La Bousse and was hailing him as an old friend.

"Ah, Oliver, my man. It's a fine thing to see you here. But tell me how you, a Frenchman, expect to receive His Majesty's Pardon? It applies only to loyal subjects."

"Hola, my lord gov'nor, but I've ceased to think of myself as anything but British and, like all your countrymen, I'm willin' to try anything if there but be a profit in it."

It was a nervous laugh that came from Woodes Rogers' throat. He glanced towards Buttons and his eyes brightened.

"Your name?" he asked quietly.

"Buttons, your worship, an' His Majesty's loyal servant."

"Aye, Buttons, eh! And before that?"

"Read, worship, Simon Read, of old Bristol Town."

"Aye to all that." The Governor was impatient.

"And before that?"

"I'd no name, worship, I'd not been born."

The Governor's hand came out and pinched her cheek.

"By my faith, I'd say you were a wench before you were named Simon. But I've no time for that now."

He resumed his march to the official residence while a young girl dressed in man's clothing, one who had never worn anything else, felt a chill hand grip her heart. Was this the law? Omniscient? She was now eighteen and no one had, in all the years before, questioned her sex. She wanted to run, to hide, to be away from this strange thing that was called the law and was vested in the person of Captain Woodes Rogers, Governor General of His Majesty's Colony. But her cutlass was still held in a firm hand and, when the Governor had passed and was followed by roughly formed battalions of pirates, La Bousse turned and said:

"What did he ask you, lad?"

"Nothing! He merely wondered that one so young as I should be on the account," she lied.

A lie would save her skin for the moment but Woodes Rogers might remember the lad he thought a wench and send for her and then no amount of dissembling would help her. She would be undone.

As the last of the procession passed her she joined with them and went to the steps of the official residence to listen to the proceedings.

The drummers and buglers led off with a flourish and rifles and then My Lord the Governor took the centre of the stage. He called attention to the condition of the settlement and told the assembled people that Lord Sutherland, thinking only of the welfare of His Majesty's subjects, had appointed him to clean up the place and make it a proper and law-abiding community. Then he read the King's Pardon to all offenders, reserving to himself the right to pardon traitors and murderers, for what pirate had not committed the violent act some time in his career? All those who wished to accept the pardon must come to the Government House in person and put their names down in the great book that had been provided for the purpose.

As Woodes Rogers finished speaking, almost as a period to his last remarks, there came the boom of a cannon, a single shot fired from the harbour; those near-by said the shot travelled just above the low roof of the Government House, in fact, just over the head of the new Governor. Every eye turned towards the harbour where a small puff of smoke could be seen wafting its way from one of the larboard guns of the Sparrowhawk and where that vessel, no longer held against the wind, was scudding before the breeze toward the western end of the channel. In her mind's eye Buttons saw her husband standing behind the offending cannon and offering, not a salute of respect, but a gesture of contempt for the new law—and she wished mightily she was beside him.

Mary Read, known as Buttons, was finding she cared as little for law and order as she did for piracy.

IX

My Lord Governor heard the shot fired above his head, but neither by word nor action did he acknowledge the fact. Those closest to him said he merely glanced in the direction of the roadstead, at the Sparrowhawk now under full sail, and went on with his task. Arrangements were completed for the signing of the Pardon and for the swearing of allegiance to His Majesty, King George.

But the Governor's work had just begun.

There was a division among the pirates, a division that would continue to harass the government for many years to come, the conflict between those who had and those who had not. In the days just before the Governor's arrival, in that time of bestiality and carousing and celebrating, many who had arrived comparatively wealthy had found themselves reduced to pennilessness; the merchants had the money and that was the end of it. As the King's promise had it, each man who accepted the Pardon and swore the oath was entitled to twenty or forty acres of Crown Lands, but of what use were his acres if he had not the money to stock them, to buy the necessary implements to cultivate them and to build his home? No provisions had been made for financing the new farmers. Many signed and took their land and then went out to look at it; they looked long and when they were through looking, they began to think.

In the Caribbees the news that Great Britain had, at last, put down all traces of piracy, had with a single conclusive gesture wiped the crime from the high seas, had a salutary effect. In the far-flung ports of Europe and South America, even unto Africa and Asia, the news was received with general rejoicing among the merchant shippers. New vessels left the ways, new cargoes were shipped to colonial possessions. Best of all, the golden wealth that Spain had hoarded in Mexico and Darien was placed in capacious bottoms and sent under practically no guard at all to her home ports. Was not the sea free of English freebooters and pirates? Had not the Crown Secretary assured all the ambassadors that they no longer had to pay for expensive convoys and for heavy insurance premiums?

The shipper might accept the word of the Crown Secretary, but Woodes Rogers knew by personal knowledge that no fewer than five pirate ships were still afloat. There were Teach and Stede Bonnet, both who had taken the Pardon and then repented, there was Captain Jack Rackham; too, there were the Sparrowhawk under Will Cunningham and Captain Dennis McCarthy in his little sloop. Where were they? Where made they their rendezvous? It was too early to say; it would take a bit of time for them to come together and lay a base from which to operate.

A pirate without a base was not very dangerous; he could make his purchases over a wide area, but unless he could dispose of his booty, they were only a liability. Certain ports were known to be still open to the buccaneers and these ports were guarded by English frigates. No chance unless—well, there was one way out, and that was the way the remaining pirates took.

In the roadstead before New Providence stood upwards of sixty vessels, some armed to the teeth, others with but fore and aft falconets. All, or at least most, bore names that once had struck terror to the hair and hearts. The larger, especially the speedier ones, might be commandeered and placed in the King's service. Manned by former freebooters, in accordance with the Crown Secretary's favourite philosophy of setting a crook to catch a crook, they would prove effective. A call was sent out for volunteers, but only a few answered.

Recruiting posts were set up along Bay Street and a bonus was offered for enlistments for a single year, all, Woodes Rogers thought, that would be required to lay the last of the rapscallions by the heels. But what were five guineas to men who had dealt in thousands? Five guineas, hardly the price of a single night's fun! The bonus was increased to ten, to twenty and twenty-five before enough men were enlisted to send out a snow. A snow to catch the Sparrowhawk! A snow to lay Calico Jack, or Teach, or even henpecked Stede Bonnet by the heels! No wonder there was laughter on Bay Street. And out on the dunes there was more laughter where men were tired of being penniless and eating shellfish and other sea food. They wanted money and in their experience there was but a single way to get it.

The Governor recognized the gravity of the situation outside the town. He was of two minds how to deal with it, but decided first to try peaceful means. Calling Captain James Fife, a truly contrite pirate, to the Government House, he pointed out to him that his former men were ringleaders of the revolting factions.

"Go, captain," said the little Governor, "and make these old associates of yours see eye to eye with you. Tell them to return to the settlement and tell them that if they are hungry and without houses they can enlist in the King's forces and thereby become self-respecting subjects of His Majesty."

Captain Fife knew his men and was reluctant to visit them. When he asked for time to think the matter over, to ponder on how he was to approach these men he knew for blackguards, the Governor led him to the steps and pointed out to the snow, now in the service of King George, sailing to do battle with the runagates. Another ship, a larger one, would sail the next day and all that was needed to turn the entire fleet into a Bahaman navy was the enlistment of the men out on the dunes.

The Governor was right. Despite the laughter, there was considerable enthusiasm in the town for the little snow departing on its desperate mission and many who remained ashore wished they had gone along to see the fun. What New Providence needed was excitement, after all. The snow's departure brought many to the King's service and, on the following day, a barquentine with a crew of eighty, a brig with fifty and the two Royal Frigates left with colours flying.

Feeling that he was at last part of an honourable government, Captain Fife agreed to go as missionary to the men on the dunes. It took him three days to prepare for his hour's journey, to rehearse his message to the rebels and get his answers to all possible objections by heart, though he needed, as it was seen when the results were known, no time at all. He set forth on foot, without music or fanfare, and walked straight as a crow flies or a ship sails into the camp of his former friends. And they, liking him none too well and caring nothing for his carefully rehearsed speech, set upon him and beat him to the sand.

90

That same night afar to the south was heard the heavy cannonading of a sea battle, sounds indicating that war had been declared between two or more nations and that the issue was being decided somewhere in the Bahamas. For two hours the cannonading continued and then subsided as quickly as it had begun. And the silence hung heavy on Bahaman ears while the people awaited the news.

On the seventh day of the reign of Governor Woodes Rogers two things occurred. Shortly after dawn came the news that the body of Captain James Fife had been found on the dunes, horribly mutilated and recognizable only by its clothing; he had been set upon by persons unknown and beaten to death and his body torn to pieces. Before the news of the crime had penetrated through all of New Providence, the brave fleet of the Bahaman Navy limped into the roadstead. They brought with them a battered little sloop, the Belle of Erin, and came to their anchorage. Then a longboat put out from the larger frigate and the whole town hurried to the landing jetty to see with their own eyes what had happened.

As the longboat neared the shore there were seen, sitting in irons, Captain Dennis McCarthy and his mate. Another boat followed with seven others, all that remained of the desperate crew of the Belle of Erin. Honesty forced the captain of the frigate to admit later that the Irishman had held them off for two hours and that it was only when McCarthy and his mate alone were able to hold their cutlasses in their hands that the little sloop had been boarded and taken. A detail of soldiers hurried from the fort and formed a hollowed square and the prisoners were marched or carried to the prison within the walls of Fort Nassau.

Now the good Governor was greatly wrought up by the news of what had happened to his emissary on the dunes and, failing to find an immediate object for his wrath, he took it out on the little crew of the Belle of Erin. While the captured pirates were still on their way to prison he came out on the steps of the Government House and ordered them to an immediate trial; even before the judge had mounted the bench carpenters were at work building gallows across from the Government House. There were nine pirates captured and there were nine gibbets; no one about to go on trial would be found not guilty.

Nor were any of the former pirates admitted to the trial. At eleven a crier came to the gate of the fort and, after a riffle on the drums, announced that nine unregenerate pirates had been adjudged guilty of piracy on the high seas and other crimes and sentenced to be hanged by the neck until they were dead, "and may God help their souls."

Promptly at noon the condemned men were led through the streets with nooses about their necks behind a drummer who beat a funeral drum. With the lone exception of Captain McCarthy the rogues presented a lugubrious appearance, a hang-dog mien that would have been funny had it not been so tragic. McCarthy laughed and gibed at the onlookers, calling first to one and then to another, asking them how his new kerchief fit and did they not think it should be of another colour. To some he prophesied a demise in the same manner as his own. When the condemned men had been paraded up and down Bay Street as a warning to any other pirate who might have an ambition to return to the account, they were lined up before the Governor's House. That worthy came out and made a short, vivid speech, not to the prisoners, but to the audience. These were the first to suffer the viceregal wrath; the next would be the murderers of the King's emissary, Captain James Fife.

"How now, your worship!" Dennis McCarthy cried. "Am I being hanged for not accepting the Pardon or for the murder of Captain James Fife? I did neither, nor was I taken in the act o' piracy. I was sailin' about my own concerns when I was attacked by these rogues. May I ask for what I am to be hanged?"

"Silence! You are a bloody pirate, unregenerate and criminal, and as such you deserve no better then you're getting. Sergeant, take these condemned men and let them stand beneath the gibbets until such time as they have made their peace with God. Then hang them as the King's Court has decided."

How the sergeant was to determine when the pirates had attained the proper spiritual condition was not said. He went about his task methodically, assigning the first gibbet to Captain McCarthy, the second to his mate, and the rest to the others as they came. For forty-five minutes the condemned men stood until one fainted; it was then assumed he had made his peace with his Maker and he was revived with cold water and forthwith hanged.

"Must I faint before my hemp is stretched?" McCarthy asked.

Two others burst into tears as they saw their mate hanging, feet clear of the earth, and the sergeant, feeling that this was a satisfactory sign of contrition, ordered the hangman to proceed. Another was seized by fear and acted like one taken with the palsy; he was hanged at once. But nothing could suppress the humour of the pirate captain.

"Sergeant," he croaked, "ye'd better bring some lanterns for the coming av the night. The only sign of repentance ye'll be gettin' from me is a yawn or that I've fallen asleep."

At three in the afternoon the eighth man was hanged and Captain McCarthy still stood gibing at the sergeant and the onlookers. He recited the heroic deeds of those hanging on his left, pointing out that they had died as courageous men and that the best part of being hanged was knowing that he would meet them all, fine fellows, in heaven or hell.

At half-past three it looked as if the captain's prediction that the sergeant would have to take a yawn as sign of his repentance was coming true. He had tired, and he was willing to admit it, of addressing a blathering bunch of yellow-bellied scoundrels who had no more courage than a Spaniard and he was sure that he himself would have to give the signal for the tightening of the rope.

"And I'll not be doing that. If ye cannot make up your own minds, to hell wi' all o' ye."

But the captain was breaking under the strain and there were shouts from the audience who were tiring more quickly than the condemned man. The sergeant visited the officer of the day and then returned and stood before McCarthy.

"At eight bells you will hang."

"Eight bells, is it? Foine!"

And then came the patient wait as minute followed minute; though they seemed hours to those who watched, those minutes must have raced precipitately over the courageous man's head.

Then from the warships in the harbour there began the tolling of the hour of four. When the last bell sounded, the rope would tighten and the soul of Captain Dennis McCarthy would join the souls of his fellows in heaven or hell, as the case might be.

But McCarthy had not had his last gibe, he was not yet finished. He had reserved his best quip for the last. As the hangman placed his hands on the rope, he cried:

"Some friends of mine have often said I would die in my shoes but I'd rather be making them liars."

He kicked off his shoes just as the hangman pulled his feet from the ground.

X

Buttons Read had watched the executions, had seen each man's feet leave the ground, but with no special qualms. She had quit piracy not through fear of the final humiliation of hanging, but because she had found the life unexciting and almost inactive. There had been more fun tending tables in a dramshop, but since so many pirates had taken the Pardon working in The Black Peter was also becoming an affair of dull routine. Business was at a low ebb and Governor Woodes Rogers was trying to regulate the hours of the taverns and the conduct of those who drank within.

The new Governor's reforms were proceeding slowly and cautiously. He wanted to know his strength before he put his full weight behind his authority. He had behind him only two frigates and fifty loyal troopers on whom he could rely and out on the dunes he had enemies estimated to number two hundred. There was constant contact between the people of the town and the beach-combers for the women circulated freely, coming into town to earn an honest crown and taking food to their lovers in the camp. The rebels had no arms for they had pawned or sold everything they owned of value. It was even the case that when differences of opinion brought them to violence they were forced to fight in most unpiratical fashion with their fists. Between what their women could make in town and the wild fruits and vegetables they could find and the fish they could take from the beaches, they managed to live, but many had little more than breech-clouts to cover their nakedness and all were bearded and long-haired and unkempt, while most were desperate.

Buttons eagerly scanned the horizon each time the fleet left port in search of the runagates Rackham, Teach, Cunningham and Bonnet. She prayed, if praying it could be called, that Boatswain Jones would be spared, for she knew that if he were captured and the Governor learned it was he who had fired the shot that had punctuated the inauguration ceremonies, he would hang higher than any other.

Then came the news that Teach had been taken. He, the most ferocious of all pirates, noted for his cruelty, had been chased up a little creek by a young, beardless lieutenant in the King's Navy. Lieutenant Maynard was the young hero's name; on the twenty-first of November, 1718, he had run Blackbeard's ship into shallow water, grounding it, and in his own vessel that drew less water had managed to come up under the pirate's bow. The daredevil had gone too far, it seemed at first, for Teach and his men boarded the H.M.S. Ranger and the fight was conducted on the pursuer's deck; it lasted for two hours and when Teach fell dead with over twenty wounds in his body it was found that the young lieutenant had escaped with only a few scratches on his sword hand.

The pirate's head was removed from his body, hung to the bolt-spit end on the Ranger and taken to Charleston, South Carolina, as evidence of the law's victory.

The news of Teach's death came as a blow to the rebels of the Bahamas. Teach taken! Blackbeard dead! The heart went out of many and some two score came into New Providence and signed, somewhat belatedly, the Royal Pardon and the oath of allegiance. Almost on top of the news of Teach's death came news that Stede Bonnet had been taken alive with all his crew and, at a quick trial, had been found guilty and sentenced to be hanged. With him went to the gallows his entire crew and the final wording of the sentence struck terror into the heart of every unregenerate rebel.

"You are to be hanged by the neck until you are dead and then your body is to be cut down and buried between the high and low water marks in the swamps." Aye, their graves were not to be at sea nor in dry soil, but in the unreclaimed and worthless lands, inhabited only by reptiles.

Many other rebels came in and accepted the Pardon and then, because they were still penniless, enlisted on the side of law and order in the King's forces. Some were assigned to the garrison within the fort, others to ships formerly on the account. Buttons Read watched all that was going on with a most interested eye. The Black Peter was now almost bereft of wenches, only two remaining to combine housekeeping with their regular employment, and business was very low. Then came the final humiliation. The landlord insisted that if the lad wanted to keep his job he must go into the scullery when he was needed and help with the work. With almost two hundred guineas in her chest, Buttons quit the place for all time.

One of the improvements instigated by Woodes Rogers was the founding of a bank. Its charter was already on its way from London and, knowing the character of the depositors and fearing them almost as much as the rebels on the beach, he had set a platoon of loyal marines to guard the deposits. Buttons, knowing nothing of banks and bankers, was unwilling to trust her wealth to it. She went to Captain Sawney and told him her predicament. The captain was too old to fight for his own, he told her, and he was letting the King's troops guard his money and advised her to do the same. But, bred to lawlessness from babyhood, Buttons looked upon police and soldier as her natural enemies and it was not until after certain desperadoes from the dunes, demanding liquor and food, had made several forays upon the town, each more successful than the last, that she could bring herself to place her wealth in the Royal Bank.

Bay Street was no longer the gay thoroughfare it had been on her arrival. Most of the shops were closed, the taverns were for the most part empty and the people stood about in groups with nothing to do but talk. News percolated in that so and so had taken a fine ship, that things were booming in Tortuga and on the Spanish Island, that place the Spaniards called Hispaniola. Not only had a fine ship been taken, but incoming vessels reported the seaways crowded with all manner of sail and great rejoicing in Spain over the safe arrival of many ships of the Gold Fleet. In New Providence there were many itchy palms and behind many huts and houses men might be seen practising with the broadsword and cutlass. Thrust and parry. Guard and touché. Too many were practising and it came to the ears of the Governor. He decreed that only those in the service of His Majesty might bear arms.

Very few gave up their arms. Buttons buried hers at a point between two palms on a prolongation of a line that extended from the jetty post to a lonely rock a mile beyond the settlement. Two pistols and a cutlass were wrapped in heavily oiled silk and consigned to the soil for safe keeping. She had no use for them at the moment, but who could tell? Who knew whether or not the rebels on the beach might not decide to take the town and destroy all loyal subjects of His Majesty?

Rumours about treasure ships and the resumption of trade, all varying in their reports of the amount of wealth transported, might have been only rumours, but the news about Teach and Bonnet was genuine; it was read from the steps of the Governor's House.

The taking off of these two pirates, one noted for his terrorist methods, the other a mild-mannered man who sought only relief from his wife's tongue, but whose death was magnified in importance by the great number of men hanged with him, made a great stir. It was, the law pointed out, the turning of the tide, a certain sign that piracy was dead, and it was used as a means to stimulate recruiting. The desperate Will Cunningham and the brave Jack Rackham were still afloat and raiding at will. At least, so rumours had it; these rumours included other names unknown to Buttons but, quite evidently, familiar to others of New Providence.

Among the ships sailing bravely forth from New Providence to do battle with the forces of the right was H.M.S. Morning Star, formerly the pirate ship of Captain William Lewis who had been murdered in his sleep by his mutinous crew. She was manned by fifty men, or rather, by forty-nine men and one Mary Read, known as Buttons and still posing as a young man of the sea.

Boredom had driven Buttons back to the sea. She had dug up her pistols and cutlass, signed the King's Articles and taken service under Captain John Massey in the hope of a bit of excitement and perhaps the slight expectation of meeting up with a certain boatswain who was her lawful spouse.

John Massey had been a former boatswain in Captain Jack Rackham's crew and before that a soldier in Flanders under the Duke of Marlborough. This newly established master was a gay fellow and when he got his crew lined up he announced that a soldier made a better sailor than any man of the sea and designated Buttons as his first mate or chief officer because of her experience in France. The lad protested that he knew nothing of navigation but the appointment stood, the captain protesting that a few good soldiers were what he needed among his own men.

"Then you do not know the men of the sea," Buttons said. "I've seen greater courage on a deck than ever I saw in a battle on land. On deck there is no place to run and a man must fight or die. On the battlefields there are many holes where a coward may hide."

"We shall see," the captain returned.

For two weeks the Morning Star cruised about the Islands, the men looking into hidden harbours, sending reconnaissances up creeks and rivers, even hiding themselves in the hope that some marauder might come upon them. The captain went so far as to order his guns covered so that from the distance he might appear to be a merchantman or trader and lure some venturesome pirate into attacking him. But there were no pirates in their way. Then one night about dusk they heard to the east of them a heavy cannonading which ceased even as they listened. Crowding on all his canvas, Massey pushed his ship in the direction of the shots; through the dark tropical night they journeyed, every eye straining and every ear alert. Buttons couldn't help wondering how sincere the men were in their efforts to overhaul and capture the pirate, if pirate he was; she suspected that most of them were aboard the Morning Star only for the excitement and would rather see a good piratical job than lift a hand to stop it.

Dawn came and but half a league to the eastward was a sight that every ex-buccaneer on deck must have witnessed with a thrill. A pirate he was and about to make his purchase; it was evident he had taken his ship just before nightfall and, sure of his success, had waited until the coming of the next day to raid her.

"All hands to the guns. Musketeers, aloft. Make grapples ready!" the captain shouted. To Buttons, who was on the quarterdeck, he said, "Mr. Read, bring her up under the bow of the pirate. Then we'll have the bastard between us and, if there's any fight left in that merchantman, she's as good as ta'en."

"Mister" Read did as he was bid; at least, he passed the command on to the quartermaster at the wheel. Shortly the royal vessel drew near enough for the crew to see the results of last night's cannonading; the merchantman was sorely hit and in danger of sinking as soon as the other ship cast off. The Morning Star came under the leeward of the pirate and the captain shouted to the gunners to prepare to fire. The pirate flew no flag and Massey must show his colours or his papers before he could begin the attack. On the quarterdeck a sailor stood ready with a slight bundle of bunting which on command would be sent aloft and then released to the winds, telling those on the pirate vessel just what business the newcomer was on.

At this crucial moment Buttons acted outside the line of duty. She left her post and hurried to her cabin, returning immediately with another small bundle of bunting which she handed to the lad at the halyards; with the same gesture she took from him the one he had.

"Make it fast, lad, and when the master commands, send it aloft," she said quietly. Then she said to the man at the wheel, "Hard a leeward, man, and hold it!"

The Morning Star, a sensitive thing, answered immediately; she turned, as if on her heel, and came up alongside the pirate.

"Take aim, gunners. Aloft with your ensign. Hard down on your helm," cried the captain.

"Break out your ensign, Gunners fire!" again ordered the captain.

But there was no burst of flame from the starboard guns of the Morning Star. Buttons looked aloft and then led the crew in a great shout of laughter. The pirate, seeing how things were, joined in the laugh and Captain John Massey, looking aloft to focus his eyes upon what the rest of the crew was looking at, saw a flag he had seen before, the Black Peter of Piracy.

Again Buttons laughed her deep laugh and the crew joined her.

Why shouldn't they laugh? They were once again on the account. Once again they were happy as every man who has found his work is a happy man.

BOOK THREE - CALICO JACK AND HIS ANNE

I

Buttons' act in sending up the Black Peter was not as unpremeditated as it seemed. She was closer to the men in the forecastle and those between decks than she was to those on the quarterdeck, officer though she was, and she had guessed before the vessel left New Providence that the crew planned to rebel at the first opportunity; perhaps not the first but the best. John Massey, she knew, would have been no match for most of the known buccaneers and especially not for the man he had been planning to attack and his crew. For on the quarterdeck of the pirate ship Buttons had caught a glimpse of the captain's brightly coloured breeks.

She was no Howell Davis in any sense. John Massey had already been on the account, as had his entire crew. Buttons had simply given direction to a situation which she recognized. There were fifty men aboard the Morning Star; Calico Jack's vessel had left New Providence with a hundred and fifty or, well, a hundred and forty-nine. Suppose the Morning Star had attacked the pirate? The only possible outcome would have been that that gallant macaroni, Calico Jack Rackham, would have been master of both vessels by now.

The crew of the Morning Star and the Rancour threw out their grapples, not without some raw jests, and in a moment were fraternizing on the larger vessel's deck. The men of the Rancour complimented the men of the Morning Star on having seen the light and heard the strong clear call of piracy. To the men of the Morning Star it was a moment of homecoming. Buttons and her captain went at once to the cabin of Calico Jack to make their amends and ask to be allowed to sign his articles. Jack greeted them like lambs returning to the fold, bringing out flagons of wine and rum and ordering a general holiday for both crews. Just two days before he had taken a Yankee rum ship and stripped it of its cargo, turning the ship about on the condition the captain should not report who the pirate was.

Jack was glad to see Buttons, whom he remembered as a lad of great courage and pugnacity. While in New Providence a number of his men had fallen under the influence of the rejected pirate William Fly, once champion prize-fighter, and the gentle art had taken his crew by storm. In the month they had been cruising all issues had been decided; there was no question who was the best fighter on board, but now, with fifty new men, the contests could be continued. Calico Jack was all for matching Buttons against the ship's champion. He was pointed out to her—and Buttons, knowing nothing about boxing, decided then and there that she was his master and agreed to meet him at any time.

By six bells in the forenoon both crews were fairly drunk and the old home week celebration showed no signs of letting up. Buttons, like the other top men, rarely drank to excess, sticking to wines and the simpler beverages, such as bombo. In the conference held in Calico Jack's cabin it was decided that the officer personnel of the Rancour would take command of the Morning Star and the officers of that vessel would fill the vacant positions under Calico Jack. Captain Massey gave up his command to Jack's chief officer, accepting that worthy's place on the Rancour, and Buttons became second mate in command of the forward watch.

"A drink to seal the bargain, a strong drink for it's a fine bargain to all of us," cried Jack. "A loving cup it must be and all must drink of it or be set down as traitors. Oh, Anne, m'love, come forth and help us seal our bargain."

A soft, almost musical voice, came from behind a closed door and Buttons looked up as it opened on what she believed to be the most beautiful woman she had ever seen.

All hats came off as Calico Jack announced grandiloquently:

"Gentlemen, Anne Bonney, as bonny a lass as ever warmed a buccaroon's heart."

The woman, tall, blonde and fully developed, dropped a curtsey that proved she knew the ways of the world. She had rosy cheeks and when she spoke it was with a rich Irish brogue that betrayed her nationality.

"Gentlemen, welcome be you to the Rancour."

Jack quickly filled a large chalice of silver with rum and again bowing gallantly asked the girl to sweeten it for them. This she did, taking but a small sip and passing it back to him.

"To you, Massey, whom I shall call captain as long as you remain loyal."

Massey drank and the cup went from hand to hand until it returned to Calico Jack who drained it to the dregs.

"A true, piratical bond. Let none of us betray it."

Anne Bonney stared at Buttons until that young officer began to feel uncomfortable; there was a penetrating look in the very blue eyes that seemed to see right through her. Buttons sought conversation with Calico Jack.

"This brig you've grappled, master? What of her?"

The pirate slapped his thigh and let out a roar of laughter.

"By my bollys, I'd clear forgotten it. We took her just afore dark fell last night and at first we thought she'd sink. Our carpenter says she'll last till she gets to New Providence or wherever her master's bound."

"But what of her? What does she carry?" Buttons persisted.

"Nothing o' value. She's a prison ship, bound for the plantations and with a cargo from Newgate. There's forty poor wretches in that hold o' hers and, by Harry, I mean to send them a drink to celebrate this event."

To a negro beside him, he said:

"Have a small cask o' rum sent to the prison ship and see that the convicts get a full measure each afore the crew drinks."

"What else has she aboard?" asked Buttons, more to avoid Anne's penetrating gaze than to engage Jack's attention.

"Beshrewe me, I don't know. Her captain and her chief officer were killed by our shots and the crew battened themselves below decks. Let's have some stench bombs and rout the rats out. Hey, now, for some real fun. Bring stench bombs and grenades and we'll have these landlubbers on their crapulous deck in no time at all."

Calico Jack led the procession from the cabin. Buttons, because of her youth, was waiting in place at the end of the line when she found her exit cut off by Anne.

"You're a broth of a lad," the woman smiled. "A blessin' to any colleen's eye. What might your age be, now?"

"Seventeen, madame," said Buttons. "But I'm large for my age."

"Aye, I can see that," said Anne as she moved over to Buttons' side. "Aye, you're all of an inch the taller. A fine couple we'd make now, you and me." She linked her arm in that of Buttons and felt the arm as her hand passed. "An' a fine arm to go about a wench's waist."

Buttons, decidedly uncomfortable, suggested they follow the others to the deck of the prison ship.

"'Tis not very gallant o' ye," protested Anne. "'Tis no tribute at all to me charm and beauty."

"You're very lovely," said Buttons quietly. "And you be my master's spouse. I fear lest he discover us thus."

She sought to be free of Anne's arm.

"Nay, lad, 'tis seldom enough a lass the likes o' me sees such a comely youth. Tarry a bit, an' tell me o' your life. How long, now, have you been on the account?"

101

"Less than a year, madame; in fact, but a scant nine months. I was in the army afore."

"Ah, now. There must have been some grand battles. You must tell me o' them. What did you in them, now?"

"I was an artilleryman first and than a mounted trooper. I cared little enough for the life. Indeed, madame, until I saw the Black Peter this morning, I've had scant thrills in my life."

"I'll not grant that. What I want to know, my bonny lad, is what about the wenches you've had? Not many, I'll warrant, by the blush that mantles your soft cheek. But some, yes? Tell me o' them. An' don't harry me wi' lies."

Buttons stammered, trying to say her carnal life had been that of soldiers and sailors, that there was no one woman in it.

"Go on wi' ye! Cadgilly now. We be alone an' I'll not let you go. Somewhere in the Islands there's a wench, I trow, who's eating her heart out—"

"Nay, woman, I tell you there's none. I'm a lone lad and I care not much for wenching. Indeed, I've had none o' it and I want none."

Buttons let her indignation put its mantle about her as a protection. Then she firmly released Anne's arm from about her and made for the door but Anne was too quick for her. In desperation Buttons cried:

"If my master should find us here, 'twould not go well with either o' us. Nay, woman, I'll not tarry. 'Twould be the death o' both o' us."

Anne gave a short mocking laugh.

"Did not Jack tell me how you laid him low, you a mere lad, back in some tavern in New Providence? Do you mind that Jack remembers and may be afeared o' ye? But whatever he thought, I could explain it to him. Come, gi' us a buss and the devil take them all."

Buttons stood adamant against the wall but Anne came and placed her lips against hers.

"No fire at all, at all," she laughed. "What sort of a lad to have wi' you? You're no good entirely."

But Anne Bonney seemed to enjoy bussing the terror-stricken Buttons. She repeated the gesture a dozen times before she seemed satisfied.

"Nay, Jack 'ud not mind if he should catch us, not if I told him the truth. I know my Jack too well. Hey, lass?"

Before Buttons entirely grasped her meaning, Anne went on:

"I could explain to my Jack that I have longed for the companionship of a woman o' my own age and here stands one before me. Did you think for a moment you had hoodwinked me? I knew you for a wench the minute I laid eyes on you." She laughed quietly. "Is it my Jack you're being coming for?"

"Nay, madame, I came not for Calico Jack. I came but for to be a buccaroon. 'Tis all I ask. Save that you do not betray me and discover my sex to my master. I've always been a lad and I've no mind to change."

Anne stood, arms akimbo, blocking Buttons' escape from the corner of the cabin. The Irishwoman looked long and steadily into the other girl's eyes.

"Nay, lass, I'll not betray you whilst you mind your duties, but if I ever see you making for Calico Jack I'll heave your heart on a spit. Misunderstand me not."

Buttons did a very unmanly thing in taking her master's wench into her arms and kissing her. Then the two sat at the cabin table and Buttons told her story, leaving out a few details.

Then Anne told hers.

"I'm no strumpet, lass," she began, but Buttons interrupted her to say quietly:

"Call me lad, not lass. Let not your unconscious tongue betray me."

"Oooee, aye! Forgive me, lad!"

The remark brought a slight constriction to Buttons' heart. Not since her last night in Bristol had she heard that cooing sound and then it had come from the lips of Moll Read. Now that she was an avowed pirate, she felt closer to her mother than before.

"Aye," she said to herself, "like mother like daughter."

Anne told Buttons that she was the natural daughter of a distinguished Irish barrister who had fallen to evil ways and had been born in Cork some twenty-one years before. Her father had loved her mother, a governess in his wife's home, and when Anne was born the lovers had taken the child and fled to Carolina. Here her father, as lawyer and merchant, had prospered so greatly that he had become a planter and owner of a great acreage with many slaves. Anne's mother had died when she was fifteen and she had taken her place as head of her father's house.

She was courted by most of the young bloods of Carolina but she liked them not and had an affair with a man of whom her father disapproved. He insisted she give up her lover; she refused and her father, through the great power he had built up, was able to have the man transported. To show her contempt, not only for her suitors but for her father, Anne married a sailor and brought him to her father's house. The enraged parent saw them both to the door and forbade their return. Anne donned man's clothes and was signed aboard her husband's ship, but almost before the marriage could be consummated Calico Jack had taken the vessel and Anne had fallen in love with him. There had been no marriage ceremony and, to Anne's mind, none was required; nor did she regret her ill-planned life.

Almost as soon as she finished her story the two women heard the shouts of the men on deck; the stench bombs had had their effect and the crew of the prison ship had come up. Jack lined them up before him and was mocking them.

"It is customary for a man in my position," he began, "when we take a ship, to offer the crew of our prizes an opportunity to join in wi' us. We offer this chance to brave men only and never to cravens such as you be. From the cut of your vessel I take it ye be King's men and that's the better for us. Stay, for our sake, in the sarvice of his bleedin' Majesty."

Then his voice hardened.

"Such as you deserve nothing better than death, but this be a great day for us, we have gained many brethren and I choose to let you live, to let you continue, and I think it best that the honour to join wi' us, denied to you for your coward-ice, be offered to the men in the hold of your vessel, those who lie helpless in irons."

Again his voice took on a harsher note.

"You who are leader amongst such a craven crew, go below. Release your prisoners and have them on deck. It's a whimsy o' mine, but it'll be honoured by the likes o' you. Step fast!" As the man stepped out and gave the word to four others, Calico Jack shouted, "Have off their irons. I like not to see my fellow-man in constraint. Speed your movements!"

The five men disappeared below decks and within a few minutes there came to sight the first of the prisoners, his eyes blinking against the unaccustomed light. He was a deplorable figure, a sneak thief, and more afraid of these gallant brothers than of the judges who had sentenced him. Here, he must have thought, were men who gloried in their crimes and feared no man, whatever his station. One by one the prisoners came on deck and they were much like the first. Long hours and days in Newgate had not improved their looks and they were indeed a hangdog crew. Thirty-five came on deck, among them three women, drabs, and no better than the males. The man who was the leader came up and saluted Calico Jack.

"Master," he began.

"Call me not master. I'm no master to cravens. Captain Rackham to you."

"Captain Rackham, sir, there be sick women below, unfit to come on deck. What shall be done about them?"

"Am I to be wet nurse to convicts? Let them stay where they be. But wait a minute. I'll have our leech down to see what can be done. Call the doctor! Where's that blackamoor? Hey, you there! Begin your distribution o' rum."

Anne Bonney stepped to the side of her lover.

"My captain," she said quietly. "May I go and see what help I may give these poor unfortunates?"

"Aye, lass, as you will. Take care not to lay your hands on them nor on anything they used, lest you get the pox. They are a filthy lot. And go not alone. The leech will be going aboard, and take the lad Buttons wi' you."

"Come, lad," said Anne to Buttons. "And bring a pannikin wi' you for their rum ration."

The two clambered over the rails of the two ships and Buttons led the way to the companionway from which she had seen the other prisoners emerge. She went first and then reached for Anne Bonney's hand and helped her down the ladder. Between decks it was almost pitch dark and if it had not been for the moans of the sick, they would have been unable to find them. A lone lantern lighted the entire deck and, lifting it from its mountings, Buttons led the way.

She found the sick convicts lying on straw pallets on the floor, their chains beside them. None were able to rise; two were delirious, and one who had been hit by one of Calico Jack's shots was already gasping out her last breath.

As the two women approached, there rose an instant pitiful cry for water and, going back to the companionway, Buttons called aloft for rum. The pannikin was passed down to her and she went from prisoner to prisoner, holding the rum to their lips while they sipped. While she was so engaged the leech arrived and, of one woman, remarked to Anne and Buttons that she was almost done. Buttons turned to hold the lantern to the woman's face and gave a gasp. It was her mother, Moll Read.

"More o' that rum! It'll quicken her pulse," she cried.

She poured a goodly swallow into the woman's mouth and was rewarded by seeing her open her eyes. A long quaver racked the woman's body and she tried to rise.

"Easy, Moll darlin', easy now," Buttons said. "Here, you leech, lend me a hand to get this woman on deck. And you, Mrs. Rackham, fetch a pallet wi' you. Now!"

Between them they got Moll Read to a shady nook beneath a cockboat on the upper deck. Buttons got water and a cloth and washed her mother's face and hands; then she hurried to the galley for broth and bread. Moll Read responded to the treatment or to the rum; for over an hour she talked and then lapsed into a fitful slumber. Buttons stayed beside her and the doctor felt her pulse from time to time.

Moll Read, Buttons learned, had at last been caught in the act of crimping a sailor; she had grown careless and was easily taken. The judge found evidence that she was an old offender and ordered her transported to the colonies to be sold into servitude. In the hold of the filthy prison ship she caught a cold, and since she was without medical care, it had developed into a serious illness.

She was happy to learn that her daughter was a fully accredited pirate and an officer in the service of the great Jack Rackham.

"Aye, lass," she whispered. "Blood'll tell. Your father, now, was a brave mon, fearing none and dying like a hero, I heared tell."

"My father? Was he known?"

"Aye, to me, lass, only to me. When you left Bristol, 'twas in his vessel. Captain Skinner he was and he died at the hands of his own crew."

"I know! I saw him killed! My father, and I made no attempt to help him."

Buttons saw again the master of the Cadogan, lashed to the capstan and being beaten and torn with broken bottles by the men he had marooned.

"Did Master Skinner know I was—his daughter?"

"Nay, lass, he did not that. To him as to all but you and me you were Sime Read's son."

Moll Read lasted through the night, but with the coming of the new day she passed on to whatever reward she was entitled to, leaving a puzzled daughter who could not tell whether or not in her last moments her mother had been speaking the truth.

After Moll's body had been given to the sea, the carpenters of the Rancour and the Morning Star made some hasty repairs to the prison ship and she was sent on her way. Before releasing the vessel Calico Jack destroyed the papers of all the convicts and threw the irons which had bound them overboard.

"If there be men among ye," he said to them, "ye'll take this ship to some other port than a British colony. Though we be fellow criminals i' the eyes o' the law, I could not use ye. Thieves ye be and a single thief in a gallant crew such as mine would create havoc. Off wi' ye!"

When Mary Read transferred her chest to the Rancour, she found herself in a most unusual situation, one of three women on a pirate ship. With Anne Bonney was a Mrs. Anne Fulworth, a middle-aged Englishwoman whom Calico Jack had brought along to serve his mistress partly as duenna and partly as maid. In Anne Buttons found, for the first time in her life, a companion of her own sex, sympathetic if a bit headstrong and self-willed. Anne delighted in watching this woman disguised as a man making her way in a world of men and making a success of it. She saw Buttons place a blow on a sailor's chin that sent the man spinning across the deck; she saw this woman, girl if you will, undertake tasks that were beyond the powers of many men and at times Anne would break out a-giggling at some thought of her own.

The two ships rode in the quiet sea, still grappled together, and the crews were constantly visiting back and forth, much to Buttons' disgust. She admired Jack Rackham but considered him a little short on discipline. That foredeck, for instance, was filthy but 'twas not her task to attend to it; that was in the province of the first officer. Buttons' only duties were to take the quarter-deck mornings and evenings. Her new master, she soon found, was an all-round good fellow who saw piracy as a great lark as well as a profitable enterprise. While the two ships stood together nothing would suit him but that the two crews should determine which was the superior in boxing.

The bouts were held in the waist of the ship, in full view of the quarterdeck; there was plenty of room on the rails and in the rigging for the spectators and the boatswain acted as referee.

The bugler called the men on deck and Jack announced the addition of a new champion, "this lad here, who's your second mate, an' who deals death with either hand."

Buttons joined in the laugh that followed and agreed to meet the winner of the semi-finals. She was shortly to wish she had not been so precipitate.

When the bouts had been first arranged, it was the custom for a man to enter the imaginary ring and, looking about him into the faces of his fellows, pick out his adversary. The challenged was in honour bound to come down and ex-change blows with the challenger. Did he refuse? Then he was dropped or pushed to centre by his fellows and made to fight. Many did not know how to use their fists and were unmercifully beaten by those who did. Shortly it had developed that certain bullies would pick on the weaker, refusing any sugges-tions that they meet a man more to their credit and the result had nearly been the ruination of boxing on the Rancour. When Buttons joined the ship a man might still step into the ring and make his own challenge but the spectators had now the right to veto the challenge and suggest or demand a worthier opponent; since this condition had been laid down the bouts had improved and Rackham had added weight classifications, light, middle and all-weights; if a man triumphed against one in his own class, it was not uncommon for his fellows to pit him against the heavier men. Buttons, though stout and well-developed, fell in the middle-weight class and might be called upon to meet both the heavier and lighter men.

Calico Jack, a showman as well as an enthusiast, blew his whistle and called the names of two of the crew to meet each other. Both, happily, were willing and leaped to the centre. They removed their arms and top clothing and sprang at each other.

Buttons had fought often but never had she boxed. All she knew of boxing was that one man put up his fists and tried to blow his opponent down; that, in the end, one asserted his mastery or failed. Now, though she watched closely, she could see only one difference from the fighting she knew; in fighting you fought as you were and in boxing you stripped to the waist—and she was not stripping to the waist for any man or any group of men.

The two men on the deck were pummelling each other to their heart's content; blood flowed from both noses, eyes were blackened and each man seemed determined to beat his opponent into a condition bordering on death. When one fell the other jumped on him with his feet or fell on top of him to knock the breath from his body. At last one man could no longer rise; his conqueror was acclaimed by loud huzzas and then retired, only a little less beaten than the fallen one.

Buttons turned to the captain and said:

"A good fight, master, but what purpose is served?"

"It's all good fun, lad, and it hardens the men," Jack Rackham said. "Too, it sharpens their wits and in an engagement, should they lose their weapons, they'd be a match for a well-armed man."

"Aye, master, but the fallen one. It will be many a day before he's fit for his duties. And the winner's worth but little more."

"By my bollys, you've no stomach for the game, lad. Is that it?"

Another bout was already in progress, and like the former boxers, the two men had removed their shirts.

"Call it that, master, if you will," said Buttons. "I do think that for a man to leave the quarterdeck to engage with one o' the crew would be bad for discipline. Suppose the officer should be beaten, blowed down. Where then would be his authority?"

"Come, lad, come. 'Tis a coward's fear. Either you'll box or you'll not. 'Tis for you to say."

Behind her Buttons heard a giggle, and she knew that Anne Bonney was enjoying the discussion.

"'Tis no coward's fear, master. I speak the full truth. Am I beaten only to lose my station? You say not. But wi' the men my orders would meet with mocks. 'Tis a great risk and I'm not willing to run it."

They were interrupted by the shouts of the crew; one of the boxers had been felled by a blow to the face and in falling his head had struck the deck a resounding thwack. He lay where he fell. Buttons hurried down the ladder to the deck, for the fallen man was of her watch. Calling for rum and water, she spilled the water over him and then forced some of the fiery liquor down his throat. As there was no response she shouted for the leech, and when that worthy came he declared the man was dead.

The word that he was dead infuriated Buttons and when she heard the victorious cackle of the killer, she turned upon him in rage.

"Craven," she shouted. "You've not the guts to fight one of your own heft. A smaller man's your meat!" and before the surprised man could retort she was upon him.

Her first blow caught him on the chin and spun him about but he quickly regained his footing and came to her with head down and arms flailing. Buttons ducked him and then placed her right under his heart. Her opponent's method was to crowd in until stopped, then to retreat and weave in again, head down. Buttons repeated over and over again the blow to the heart without the man learning to protect himself. Then she got in a fortunate blow to his face, an uppercut that threw his head back and set his powerful arms flailing above his head. She stepped in and caught his wind with her right and led up with her left to his chin, snapping his head first forward and then back and laying him gently at full length upon the deck. She toed his fallen body with her foot and without further ado returned to her station on the quarterdeck.

"Well done, lad," said Calico. "The man must 'ave weighed three stone more than you and he's fairly out."

"Take back, master, what you said about a coward's fear."

"Aye, cadgilly, Buttons. Sure you are no coward nor did I think it."

"'Tis well, master, but I've a mind to be done wi' this silly sport. Let the men box, as you call it, and I'll tend to my own station."

Friends of the fallen man, the man Buttons had downed, cried for more and Buttons' own watch cheered her with huzzas.

"Muster Read," called a loud voice, "you're a mon to sarve under."

And from the rear she felt the hand of Anne Bonney on her shoulder, a pat of approval, but she did not look around.

II

While the two ships stayed together, there were several conferences in the captain's cabin on the Rancour. Calico Jack wanted the men of the Morning Star to acknowledge his leadership and suzerainty; this they were willing to do but there was more discussion about the percentage of the loot the admiral was to take. Rackham began by demanding a third of every purchase but wound up by accepting a fifth, his other officers to receive two shares out of every hundred established. With this simple agreement and an established rendezvous which each vessel would visit once every three months, the two ships parted company.

There was, to Buttons' great satisfaction, a noticeable tightening of discipline after the departure of the Morning Star. The one hundred and fifty bullies originally signed by Jack had been augmented by a dozen recruits and depleted by half that many deaths. Each morning the men fell to with a great will and by noon the vessel sparkled in the tropic sun. Calico Jack was essentially a lazy man; often he chose to cruise about off the lanes of travel, loafing and enjoying the charms of his blonde mistress. He had a long hammock swung low on the lee side of the quarterdeck and covered with a canvas awning. Here the two would loll for hours, Jack smoking his long cigarros and sipping bombo, Anne singing to him in her throaty contralto. From this vantage he could watch the operation of his ship, the man at the wheel and the officer on watch.

Jack did not require his officers to be navigators but engaged men for that duty, demanding in his staff only courage and leadership. Both Massey and Buttons gave him these.

It was on Calico Jack's vessel that a talented man, one who could play a musical instrument or sing or do gymnastic feats, was always allotted an extra share of the prize money. Some who were excellent were given a full extra share and others anything from a tenth to half a share for their entertainment value. Jack loved the carnival, the picnic, anything that savoured of theatricalism. At his favourite rendezvous on the north coast of Cuba he would take most of his crew ashore and there make merry with the women of the town. There would be music and dancing in the fields and woods, great amounts of eating and drinking, a riotous time for all. Too, he paid close attention to his vessel's larder and when anything ran low he went in search of a ship whose cargo would replenish it. And he listened to the temper of his men.

On one occasion he said to Buttons:

"Flour and rum are low, lad. The men haven't been drunk in a fortnight and they're talking. Lay over towards Tortuga and the Spanish Island and we'll take a Yankee. Double your watch aloft and an extra bottle of rum to the first man to report a sail. That'll keep the men hot."

Jack found his Yankee skipper with both flour and rum aboard, a fighting master, a Salem man who had no intention of giving any part of his cargo to a damned pirate. But a man with only a single falconet mounted forward on his vessel may be of very great courage and still lose his ship. The Salem man did just that. Rackham was all for hanging him to his own yardarm and still the fellow only said:

"Hang away and be damn' to you for a pyrate," and folded his arms to await his fate.

Jack laughed at him.

"Know you me, man?" he asked.

"An honest man would know no pyrate and I be an honest man."

"Would you know Blackbeard were he to take your vessel?" persisted the buccaneer.

"I'd not. In thutty year at sea you're the fust pyrate to take me. Hang me so that you'll be the last."

"Nay, man, if you know me not, you shall go free. I want no man running about saying my name to the King's men."

The crew of the Rancour transhipped the merchant's cargo, rum and flour, dried meats and hams, bacons and some vegetables, such as potatoes and other roots. In the cabin's chest they found fifteen hundred pounds in gold and silver and they took that and sent the captain, crew and vessel about their business. They sailed away to the shouts of defiance of the fighting skipper. It was all fun to Calico Jack Rackham. Despite what he had said to the skipper, Buttons knew that Calico Jack was not so stupid as not to know that in reporting the piracy the vanquished skipper would certainly mention the pirate's outstanding characteristic, thereby revealing his identity. The brightly coloured breeks, which, Buttons learned, were made for him by Anne, were identity enough for any of the King's men.

After the purchase Jack gave liberty to the forward watch for twenty-four hours, letting each man celebrate to his heart's desire. When their time was up, the other watch took to their tankards and won forgetfulness. Then he went to his quarterdeck rail and piped all men aft.

"You've had your fun, my men, and now for work. We are to go to La Desirade and lay in wait for the Gold Fleet. While we are sailing in that direction we will resume our drills. I want each and all of you to be bright and sprightly, to do your task as well as possible, because I love you all and want to lose not a single man of you. Mind you, the fun's o'er and this is work for men of bowels."

Calico Jack returned to his hammock and his mistress, but while the men were below or aloft at their tasks he would quietly order the bugler to sound for an attack when they least expected it. Then he, too, would leap to his station and sing out his orders loud and strong.

"Larboard cannon load! Larboard cannon point! Topmen and musketeers aloft! Pistoleers to your stations. Lay hard on the helm! Larboard cannoneers fire! Reload. Stand by to board. Grapples out!"

By the time the whole drill was complete the entire crew would be on the larboard rail ready to board the imaginary prize.

"Good men all," Jack would shout in approval. "A little more speed the next time."

But the general purpose of the drill was fulfilled; each man, no matter what he was doing, would hurry to his station as soon as the bugle sounded and be ready for friend or foe, preferably the latter.

"Blight me," muttered a man called from his slumber, "if ever I heared the like. 'Tis a false alarm that macaroni on the quarterdeck gi'es us. Did he, I wonder, e'er hear tell of the lad who cried 'wolf'?"

"Bridle your tongue there you!" cried Buttons harshly.

"An' the same to you, sir," cried the man. "'Tis a fool's errand we are on. Callin' a man from 'is sleep." Muttering he went back to his bunk.

And Buttons knew there were other mutterings. On board the Rancour were several men who considered themselves better able to captain the vessel than Calico Jack; each watch had its own favourite "sea lawyer" whom it was eager to put forward as master of the vessel in case anything should happen to the present incumbent. But when she called this state of affairs to his attention, Rackham only laughed.

"I'd not have it different, lad. It keeps them on their toes. If each watch has a second leader ready to place on the quarterdeck, they'll back up their man with the only quality I require, courage. 'Tis said, and rightly, too, that any buccaroon is worth three ordinary men and you can do your own arithmetic when I tell you that any one of my men is worth two ordinary buccaroons.

"Think not I do not know the fellows who when in their cups come aft and shake their fists at my cabin door. As long as I lead them they'll swear by me and vent their wrath on the next prize we take."

"We're to attack the Gold Fleet, master, an' how do you know where you'll find them?"

"'Tis chance, most like, lad. But the word has gone out that the buccaroons have been wiped from the English seas and if I think aright, the Dons will be rushing treasure from every port and in every kind of vessel. There'll be so

112

many of them that we'd have to look sharp to avoid them. Our task will be to take the richest."

"And so we go to La Desirade. You think it a likely point?"

"So, lad, the most likely until we learn better. We are not so well liked at other islands and from there we can cruise about, darting out of our shelter for any likely looking sail and keeping to cover when danger shows. What would you?"

"'Twas only an honourable question, master. I did want to know your intentions."

"Well, you have them for what they're worth." Then, looking at Buttons narrowly, he continued: "Methinks you like Mistress Bonney full well, lad. An' I approve o' it. But mind your feet."

Buttons blushed to her hair and, saluting, turned to her cabin. She had sworn Anne Bonney to secrecy and hoped that Jack's mistress would be true to her word. More than ever, now that she was on the account in earnest, that she was rising through the ranks to command, she must keep her sex a secret from all. Once it became known that a certain mate, Buttons Read, was a woman, she would be laughed off the seas. No master would sign her on his vessel, no crew would take orders from her. Indeed, her very presence on any vessel would mean an end to all discipline.

In her cabin she found Anne and Mrs. Fulworth. Anne was sewing on a set of new breeks for the pirate, a gaudy pattern in printed green and red stripes, and the duenna was darning his socks. A lucky man, that Calico Jack, and one who knew women's full value. Buttons shot a signal to Anne to be rid of the other woman, but Anne signalled back it could not be done. Buttons saw something was amiss and, rather than take any chance speaking before Mrs. Fulworth, returned to her station.

It was Massey's watch; while Buttons was idling on the quarterdeck Anne came up from the cabin and invited her to sit with her in the master's hammock. Buttons wisely chose a cushion thrown on the deck and looked into the honest blue eyes of Anne Bonney.

"Mistress, have you told anyone that which you alone should know? Mrs. Fulworth?"

"Nay, lad, my lips are sealed, a woman's word to a woman. Have no fear. Why do you fear?"

"The master," said Buttons, "only this moment past advised me to mind my step, lest I go too far wi' you."

"I know. He's put Madame Fulworth on the cat, to watch me and thee. I have no fear. 'Twould be a rare laugh on Captain Calico to learn he were jealous o' another woman." She giggled loudly enough to attract the man on watch. "Aye, I have no fear for ye, Buttons. Did I not with my own eyes see you take that bully to account an' wi' your fists? There's no man on board but fears your displeasure an' that you may blow him down. An' that goes for my master, Captain Calico, too."

"Nay, mistress, 'twould be mutiny to strike the master. Hanging at the yardarm would be my reward and I've no mind to tread the air."

"I would say," said Anne, looking nowhere in particular, "that Captain Calico might care as little for those fists o' yours as his lowest man. Have no fear."

Buttons did have a fear and it was not lessened as she went down the ladder to the deck and saw Jack Rackham lounging against the rail where he had had a full view of the two while they were talking. A cruel light was in his eyes and Buttons resolved that she had had her last word with Mistress Anne. She wished now she had denied her sex the first day when Anne had guessed it, but now it was too late to think of that; a woman's tongue wags loosely and sometimes unwisely. Yet she could find no fault with Calico's mistress; the woman had good sense and a world of experience and Buttons had won her admiration. Often, good-humouredly, she had deplored Buttons' disguise, saying she herself would not be the best man alive.

"There's nothing happier, Buttons, than a well-loved woman an' I'm all o' that. I got me a brave and fearless man, an' a strong one a' that, an' I wouldna change wi' you or any man." She laughed happily.

"Nay, mistress, I could not change now for I know no other life than the one I live. To put skirtles on me now would be to make a mock o' my true sex. I'll ha' to go on in breeks until I die."

Buttons might decide to be seen no more in the company of Anne Bonney, but, after all, she was only a second officer and Anne was the captain's mistress and could go anywhere and did. She would come, with or without Mrs. Fulworth, to Buttons' cabin and sit with her sewing or knitting, not caring what Jack thought. She did not greatly fear her lover's wrath; she knew that if his jealousy were to get out of bounds she would not hesitate to sacrifice Buttons' secret for her own safety. Too, Anne believed, and rightly, that she had Jack wrapped about her little finger and she meant to keep him so.

At La Desirade the Rancour approached not the settlement Buttons knew so well but a small harbour to the south. Behind the harbour was a high hill and there Calico Jack posted his lookouts with powerful glasses to sweep the horizon. With Anne Bonney Jack spent much time ashore, leaving the vessel in the hands of Massey and of Buttons Read who was greatly relieved to have the pirate's mistress off the ship and in the company of its master. The lookouts made their reports not to the vessel but to the tavern where Jack Rackham sat enjoying himself, caring nothing for the mumbling of his crew; by the time a real treasure ship came along they would be in a mood of no compromise.

On the sixth day the call came and Calico Jack came out to the Rancour in his gig and he came alone; Anne Bonney had been left ashore, but not alone. Mrs. Fulworth had been sent ashore to keep her company and to chaperone the wench. For the first time in days Buttons breathed easier; if she had known more about the masculine impulse of jealousy she would have been afraid. Calico Jack's face wore a frown and more than once Buttons looked up from her task to find his hard black eyes fastened on her.

Had Anne Bonney betrayed her? she wondered finally.

But Jack had little time for lowering. The ship sighted by the lookouts was a good four miles to the starboard, and to overhaul her meant a long, hard chase. Jack's plan was to determine the vessel's course and then try to overtake her during the night; he succeeded in doing just that only to find that she sat too high in the water to have anything aboard. She was unarmed and Rackham might have engaged her then and there had not another sail come up over the horizon.

The newcomer was, in the parlance of the pirates, fat; that is, she was wide of beam and sitting squat and low in the water. The first vessel had covered the Rancour and through their glasses the pirates saw the fat vessel quickly lower her Spanish colours and run up the British ensign for safety; 'twas all the pirates needed. She was so rich in plunder she was easily frightened.

Yet Calico Jack did not strike boldly; manoeuvring his vessel about he fiddled away several chances at a telling attack before he threw his first shot across the Spaniard's bow. She did not strike her colours but fled ahead under full sail as if trying to show her heels to the buccaneers. This was not her day and the Rancour quickly ran her down, coming up alongside with the grapples and taking her prize while still under sail; it was a daring feat, but one that was more risky than practicable. She was the Santa Olivia, one of the great Spanish gold ships that should never have travelled save under powerful convoy. Here she was, alone in the Atlantic, and only Jack Rackham to take her in his clumsy way.

She yielded much plunder, more in fact than the feat deserved and much more than ships of her tonnage usually carried. Indeed, so great was her value in gold bullion that Calico Jack suppressed any desire to take the balance of her spice cargo on the chance of disposing of it at a profit. He sent the Spaniards off in their small boats and then fired the vessel, watching her sink, a fragrant cloud of burning spice, into the Atlantic waves.

Four thousand pesos de oro were the share of the meanest man on board the Rancour and Jack issued each man a triple ration of rum in honour of the capture.

The crew were in good spirits when they left La Desirade, but not so their master. Anne was back in her hammock on the quarterdeck and Jack was apparently happy when he was with her though moody when alone. That his jealousy had been aroused was no longer in doubt and even reckless Anne made it a point not to be alone with Buttons, not so much for her own sake as for her lover's and the lad's. But thunders were brewing and suddenly they broke.

Anne Bonney was with child. She had been with Calico Jack for four months; before that she had been with her legal husband and Jack knew not whether he was the father of the child or whether it belonged to the other. That was not alone his worry. The child was his or the husband's and he could do nothing about it. But here jealousy reared its ugly head and asked Calico Jack if it were, by any chance, the spawn of his second in command. There was nothing subtle about Jack Rackham and he came to the point in a characteristic manner. The scene was laid in the master's cabin where Massey had come for a conference, the same reason that had brought Buttons Read. Mrs. Fulworth was there to attend Anne. Buttons and Anne were talking together in low tones when Massey was brusquely and roughly sent back to his station and Mrs. Fulworth packed off to her cabin. Calico Jack turned on Buttons and Anne.

"Nollies together as usual," he ripped out. "Do you know, lad, the wench is with child?" The last words were barked.

Buttons accepted the news in a puzzled manner. What was she so say? Jack went on:

"When you've had your nollies together she's probably told you how I took her from her lawful fellow. That was four months back. Now she informs me she is with child and I know not whether I be the father or t'other. Aye, there's the rub! But it be worse than that, and what I aim to learn here and now is if by any chance the brat be one o' yours?"

Buttons was on her feet at once. She had entered the cabin unarmed and Jack had his pistols and his baldric about him. His hand fell to the hilt of his cutlass and he made as if to draw as Buttons rose.

"Stand back wi' those evil fists o' yours or I'll run you through. But answer me truly, be the child in her belly yours or mine?"

The shrill laugh that came from Anne's throat frightened Buttons and enraged Jack the more and disconcerted both. Anne did not stop laughing but gave herself up to great gusts of it. When she had regained control of herself, she said to her lover:

"Put up your sword, man jack, and grieve not whether the child be yours or the lad's we left behind us. Take it from me this fellow had no part in it, none at all." And with that she started giggling and laughing again.

Jack went over and took her wrist and began to twist it and Buttons wondered whether to take to her heels or go to the assistance of the woman. Jack was in earnest and in a few minutes Anne's laughter had turned to cries of pain.

"Have done! Be you that fox't that you'll not take my word? Have done or I'll ask Buttons to use his fists on you. You want the truth and you'll have it."

Jack released his hold, but Anne's wrath did not bridle her tongue.

"You want the truth, Jack Rackham?" she cried furiously. "Well, the child is none of yours. See? I throw it in your black teeth. It's none of your spawn."

Jack's face was distorted with rage and his sword was out of its scabbard and he was on Buttons like a flash, forcing her to duck from chair to table and back again.

"Stop!" Anne Bonney shouted.

Then, seeing her words were not heeded, she threw herself on Calico Jack's sword arm and bore his weapon to the ground. He struggled to free his arm from her grasp, but her terror had made her strong and the man's struggles were in vain. After a moment both had calmed somewhat.

"I'll have the cheild's blood," panted the man.

"Stop!" said Anne again.

The word served only to infuriate Jack and, suddenly flinging her from him, he was again on Buttons like a fury, pinning the lad to the ground.

"Now," he cried, unlimbering his sword arm and holding the weapon over Buttons' head, "if it's not mine it's yours, and I'll be no man's cuckold."

But once again Anne was on him and this time she grasped the broad blade with her hands and refused to let it go.

"Stop, fool that you are! It's no lad you'll be killing but a wench. She's no man, Jack, but a lass. How could she be the father o' my child?"

"'Tis you who are daft," cried Jack. "Are you that daft? I've known this lad for o'er six months and you're trying to tell me he's a wench. By my bollys, I shall find out for myself."

Buttons had something to say about that. Taking advantage of the pause she toppled Jack from her and leaped to her feet. But once again a torn shirt revealed that which she wished to keep hidden from her fellows and all Jack could do was to stare, goggly-eyed, at the rent in her bosom.

"Beshrewe me eyes, 'tis true. Buttons be a wench if ever there be one." Overcome by surprise as well as his exertions, he fell into a chair, feet extended, cutlass still in hand. "An' a halesome lass if ever there was one."

"It's a fine temper you be after having, me John. You should not have known, for I gave her my word never to discover her sex to you. She had no fear until you thought you were being harried. Nay, the child is none o' yours, but 'tis none the less honourable. I knew when I came to you I was with my belly, but I feared you'd not have me were I to tell you."

"Oh, aye?" was all Jack could ejaculate. "Then all's well."

"'Tis not, Jack Rackham, not by any means. This lass here has chosen to live and work wi' the men and here in the Islands her life would be ruined were this to become known. You'll seal those black lips o' yours or I'll have your heart out in your own bed i' the dark o' night. Do ye understand? No word o' this shall ever pass your lips whilst the lass lives as she is. Wench or no wench, Jack Rackham, she's a better man than you be."

III

No other on board the Rancour learned Mary Read's secret. She went about her duties saluted by some of the crew as "Mr. Buttons" and by others in less complimentary terms, depending on the nature of the man who spoke. Jack Rackham, if he had had his way, would have had a crew made up of men entirely lacking in respect for authority, but withal sensible enough to know they required leadership. He knew that in his crew of a hundred and fifty, a full third were capable of taking his place as master and moreover would attempt it when they no longer believed in him.

Jack was not wholly rapacious, as we have said. He liked a life of ease and comfort and would seek the necessities for it, but he did not stay constantly on the account. And for this Anne Bonney found great fault with him, believing he should raid everything in sight, accumulate a fortune and then retire. She was her father's only heir and his fortune and great estates would come to her on his death. She wanted her man to take his place beside her in position and wealth.

The Rancour made her course on the inside of the Windwards and Leewards, skirting to the south of Puerto Rico and the Spanish Island, but staying clear of the vigilant English fleet at Jamaica; then through the Windward Channel and the Grand Bahama Bank. Here Jack cruised about in seeming idleness, waiting for an opportunity to scuttle into his rendezvous.

This little inlet would shelter four or five vessels from any prying eyes and provided a wide expanse of greensward for recreations. Here, when the ship was at anchor, the men would go ashore and throw up makeshift tents. Supplies would be landed, a kitchen or galley set up, women brought in from the surrounding towns, and, when all were settled, the great division of spoils would take place.

For days the representatives of both watches and the officers had been weighing the gold and valuing it, dividing the jewels and trinkets, and making up the two hundred shares that were to go to crew and deck, each share equalling a two-hundredth part of the entire loot. But before this was done, certain awards were made. Each wounded man received a hundred pounds over and above his share if his wound were not such as to force him to retire from piracy; if he were permanently incapacitated he would receive from five hundred to a thousand pounds and be given the privilege of remaining on board the vessel until it stopped at a port where he might be safely put ashore. Buttons, as mate, would get twice as much as any member of the crew.

At the distribution all the booty was piled high before the captain, who sat in his hammock with pistols cocked. The men sat facing each other in two long rows with their women and natives behind them. A representative from each watch would pick up a share from each classification and, passing down the line, drop it into the lap of a pirate while Calico Jack called out the item being distributed, the amount of that item taken and the value of each share. All went well while the plate and bullion were being distributed, either gold or silver, for this was divided by weight and each man could see that his share was no less than his neighbour's. It was when the jewels, no two of equal value or weight, were being given out that quarrelling and complaints began. Here was a man who received something he neither valued nor cared for and with a gesture of contempt he would hurl it over his shoulder to the native woman behind him. Some exchanged with others and many sulked. They forgot it all, however, when the distribution was complete, for it was then that a rum cask was broached, musicians were called to work, and dancing and singing began.

Often the cooks and galleymen forgot their duties and natives were impressed to do service. At these moments the pirates were generous and, while they made merry, the inhabitants of the country, mostly mestizos and Spaniards would form a great circle about them. A dancing woman from the town would suddenly leap into the centre of the pirate ring and dance a wild fandango to the cheers of the buccaneers who would show their final appreciation by throwing coins and trinkets at her feet. At night a great fire would be built and the drinking and feasting continue unabated. Natives would bring more and more wood, more casks of rum would be broached and it would not be until the last pirates and their ladies of the evening had toppled over drunk that the festivities would halt. Most would awaken when the sun was high-with tongues thick and heads ringing, and seek a cure in the hair of the dog that had bitten them.

Calico Jack Rackham and his crew remained in the rendezvous for a fortnight, awaiting the coming of the Morning Star. No ship had called since their last rendezvous, the natives assured them, and finally the vessel and her crew were given up as lost, taken or forgotten. There was no lamentation or pausing in the festivities; they were gone and so to hell with them.

It was late in May when Calico Jack took his rum-soaked men back to the vessel and set sail. Once more they needed flour and rum, dried meat and other foodstuffs. They were loaded heavily with the fruits and vegetables of the tropics, limes, oranges, bananas and great heaps of coco-nuts. These, with the fish they could take from the Caribbee Sea, would sustain life. Their first call was at Tortuga where they laid in a great supply of boucan, the dried and smoked meats of the Islands; in three months, Calico promised, they would be back.

But all was not well in the cabins of the Rancour, even though Jack's jealousy had been laid and he kept Buttons' secret to himself. She was a fine officer, a sterner disciplinarian than he could ever be; often Jack marvelled at her ability, despite her sex, to stifle complaints and check the threats of uprising that arose periodically. It was inevitable that his appreciation should take a different turn. Anne was now becoming large with child, an infant that Jack could neither love nor claim as his own; too, she was older than the second mate. It came to Jack that Buttons would be a very attractive woman if she could be induced to don the garb of her own sex; together they might go far in the gentle world of piracy.

Jack's interest in Buttons as a woman had not gone far before it was sharply caught up by the quick-witted Irishwoman. Buttons herself was unaware that she was being courted; she accepted her master's compliments as richly deserved. But Anne turned on him like a tigress.

"Tell me, if you dare, that you aren't trying to make the tyke?" she cried to him one day. "Tell me that and I'll cut your white-livered heart out of your guts!"

"Now, my dear," expostulated Jack. But he got no farther.

"Pinching the lad's buttocks you were, faith, and I saw the pass she made at you. I think you might be forewarned about such tricks."

"Listen, bonnie Anne, I love none but you."

"Faith, say it again," she murmured.

"I'll say it a thousand times," he answered softly.

"Nay, I do not trust you, at least not beyond the sight o' me eyes. But I'll warn that wench to do her poaching in other parts of the Rancour."

And Anne pushed Calico Jack aside with such force that a less conceited man might have felt taken aback at having on board his vessel two women who handled him so cavalierly. Catching himself before he fell, he heard his mistress speak to the blackamoor at the door to the cabin.

"Send Muster Buttons Read here an' tell him to waste no time wool-gathering."

Even in her wrath the Irishwoman's sense of honour did not permit her to reveal Buttons' sex.

"Get hither and do not return until I call," she shouted to the black servant when the second mate appeared. Then she turned upon Buttons, demanding stormily:

"Have you the occasion to desire Jack Rackham? Do you intend to take him while I'm large with child? Tell me truly, wench, afore I cut the heart out of you."

Buttons was frightened by the woman's fury and stammered she did not understand what she was driving at.

"Ooo aye! You understand not, methinks I shall have to make it plain to 'ee. Doth desire my Jack? Wouldst like to share command and bed wi' him? Tell me truly afore I put my mark on your face."

"On my honour, mistress, I understand you not. Share command? Bed? You speak in riddles. Tell me plainly your meaning."

"Aye, I'll tell you, innocent. What plan to be rid o' me is stirring in your addled brain? What plan have you and Muster Rackham for the future? He has told me I'm to go ashore in Cuba with Mrs. Fulworth to be brought to bed, leaving him and the Rancour to you."

"'Tis news to me, madame, I know none of such plans."

Buttons could probably have made no reply acceptable to Anne, but, as it was, her words served only to infuriate her farther; the pregnant woman, fury blazing in her eyes, flew at the lad. From her bosom a small poniard came out and the very surprise of the attack was almost Mary Read's undoing. She managed to dodge the sharp blade by a goodly distance, but Anne was flailing away with it and with such speed that there was nothing for Buttons to do but keep moving. By a lucky chance Anne caught hold of her and brought her into a clinch, hoping to stick the knife in her back, but Buttons was a little too fast and squirmed out of reach. She called to Captain Rackham to have the woman off, but that worthy stood grinning at the sight; whatever was going on in his mind, he made no effort to stop the fight.

When Anne came on again Mary was ready for her; she caught the poniard hand by the wrist with a twist that brought a groan of anguish from the Irishwoman and the knife went hurtling into a corner of the cabin.

"I do not wish to harm you, madame," Buttons said calmly, but still holding the woman's wrist. "But either you cease or I'll toss you at your lover's feet and I'll warrant you won't rise without his help. I'd not harm a woman in your condition save to protect myself."

At this Calico Jack came to her aid; taking Anne in his arms he said quietly:

"The lad's at no fault, my own. You've been misinformed or your mind's fox't. It's yet two months before we go to Cuba and much may happen in that time. Quiet, wench, quiet. You'll be harming yourself."

Anne was induced to sit down in one of the comfortable chairs of the cabin and drink a watered rum. Buttons awaited the signal from Rackham to retire to her station, but it did not come. After a long silence, the sullen Irishwoman said:

"It's either her or me. One o' us must go. You must decide, Jack Rackham, and this very night."

"Not so," said Jack. "Both o' you are too valuable to me. Buttons be a fine officer and you a lovely wife. I need ye both on the Rancour."

"I'll not rest while she's here," said Anne and at that she stuck. "I'll kill her while she sleeps or in the lonely watches of the night."

Over Anne's head Jack nodded to Buttons to return to her duties. He winked his eye as he nodded and Mary Read, unversed in the ways of a man with a maid, knew not what he meant.

IV

For a few weeks Anne Bonney's jealousy seemed to be held in control and Mary Read went about her duties with her usual single-mindedness, unaware that Irish temper seldom sleeps. The Rancour's takings were not extraordinary during this time; her master was too concerned about other problems. All pirates, from the beginning of history, have sought to expand their operations by placing the vessels they took under a kind of feudal control, sending them out on the account and taking toll of their prizes. Jack Rackham wanted the easy wealth promised by such means, but of the two or three ships under his command none had ever returned to the rendezvous or given any account of themselves.

As Anne's time for going to Cuba for her confinement drew nearer, her wrath against Jack and Buttons rose to new heights. Jack's laugh, reckless and confident, drove her to the verge of insanity. His glances at Buttons as she went about her duties were wasted on that officer, but they infuriated Anne. In her mind she saw Rackham preparing to put her aside and take up with his second mate and she was determined to circumvent any such plan. But Calico Jack was a patient man and knew his own mind; he let Anne rave as she wished and continued to look at Buttons appraisingly.

The Rancour lay to the south of the Spanish Island to prey on whatever shipping she might chance upon. It was not a good lay, but it was a safe one. The British at Jamaica were ever active and the Spaniards were not so certain now that piracy was at an end. Many ships had been dispatched from Puerto Bello,

Acia and Cartagena that had never arrived in Spain. A few might have been lost in storms, others taken by their own crews, but some must have fallen victim to the freebooters of the Spanish Main. Some of these fell to Calico Jack, that is certain. And it is known that Bart Roberts, Yeates and others were roving the Main on the account.

The final events on the Rancour happened fast and furious.

Night falls fast in the tropics and the dark is ever a lure for love. Buttons on her evening watch was standing close to the wheel when her master came up for her reports. For half an hour they discussed the probabilities of the weather and the chances of taking one of the gold ships if they made for Barranquilla or Maracaibo.

Dark fell while they were talking and Jack's arm went around Buttons' shoulders in a gesture of fellowship, later finding its way to her waist. Jack then lost the train of his thought and brought the mate closer to him in a hug. Buttons knew she could lay him low with a single blow, but she also knew one did not strike his captain with impunity. There was a short scuffle and suddenly the light of a lantern was flashed in the surprised faces of the two. It was held by Anne Bonney and the Irish jade let out a burst of epithets that would have done justice to a male.

Jack went toward the woman.

"Nay, wench, no jobation now. Bridle your damn' tongue and hie you back to your pallet."

"An' leave you wi' this strumpet? Stand back afore I blow the top of your head off."

A long pistol came from her side and covered her lover. Buttons began to circle behind her, but Anne backed to the rail and covered them both.

"Now, me fine Jack, the wenchin' pirate, list to me. I heared you tell Captain Buttons here that you planned to sail to the south'ard. Good and fine. I mind there be some lonely cays and on the first we come upon this wench is to be put ashore. Marooned. D'ye understand me?"

Calico Jack Rackham laughed long and loud.

"Nay, I'll not jettison such a valuable officer, wench. My plan is to sail south and take my chances and then return wi' you to the Cuban Island. This lad here will stay in his post."

Impotence drove the Irish woman to new furies and she cried out loudly:

"She's no lad an' I'm through with this jockeyin'. I'll tell all aboard this vessel that their mate's a wench, and a swyvin' one at that."

That members of the crew were listening became apparent when a laugh came out of the darkness of the deck below. Anne's pistol wavered a bit; her fury made the role she was playing a hard one and Buttons, ever watchful for the advantage, closed in on her and pinioned her arms to her sides. Before she could stifle the woman's words Anne again announced in a loud voice that Buttons was no man but a woman. Lights were flashing on the deck below and Jack went to the rail and ordered the men to return to their quarters. But one man, holding a lantern aloft, came up the ladder to the quarterdeck.

"Wot's this, master, about Muster Buttons bein' a wench?"

"Go below, fool," ordered Rackham. "What goes on here is none of your business."

The man made no move to obey the captain's order.

"'Tis to my mind a vi'lation o' the articles," said the fellow. "We made an exception in the case of Mistress Bonney but we did not give you permission to bring along a seraglio. If Buttons be a woman she must come to us."

"You heard me," stormed Calico Jack. "I ordered you below."

"I heared you, master, but I hain't heared your answer to my declaration. The articles says it plain; the first wench to you, the next to the men. If Buttons be a wench, and she be a halesome one a' that, to my mind, she must be sent down to us."

Buttons Read stepped forward and into the arc of the lanterns. She looked over the fellow from the deck, a chap from the afterwatch, and asked:

"Who is to say where I shall go?"

"'Tis in the articles, master, I mean, mistress, and we'll stand for no more foxing."

He put his hand on the second mate's forearm and immediately wished he had not. Buttons placed a blow on the point of his jaw, a short one that came from nowhere in particular and spent almost no time in travelling to its destination. The man measured his length on the deck, landing in a crumpled heap against the taffrail. Buttons did not follow up her advantage, it was hardly necessary, the man had had all the "sea law" taken out of him and did not intend getting to his feet merely to be blowed down again.

Buttons went to the rail and looked into the dark well. She could hear the mutterings and breathings of the men as they whispered what was in their minds, questionings and wonderings. She listened for a moment and then called:

"Aye, I be a woman an' I be dressed as a man. 'Tis my way o' doing matters an' if there be among you those who do not like it, let him come take his share and say it truly. I'll sarve him as I sarved the cheild on the deck here. A woman I be and say it again and a woman that's a better man nor any o' you. To your quarters! 'T'once!"

She went over to the man she had felled and ordered him, with the aid of her boot, to go below and pipe down. As the fellow limped down the ladder she flashed a lantern to the deck and watched the men as they went to their bunks. Then she turned back to Calico Jack and Anne Bonney and called to the man at the wheel.

"Give your wheel to your master an' go below. I'll hail you when I need you."

Obediently Jack grasped the spokes of the wheel and the man, relieved, went down the ladder.

"Now I'll tell my own story. I've a mind to leave the Rancour, but I love the vessel and 'tis a far better thing than its master or its mistress. Aye, I love it well and I've no wanting to be quit o' it. It's a deal like my going as a man, I've no great respect for my own kind, they're good for little else than giving a man a bit o' pleasure, an' I've no great admiration for the men, for they're a silly lot, what with their wenching and rumming. Too, they're a flock o' cowards an' I want little enough to do wi' 'em. 'Tis no mutiny I plan but 'tis a plan I'll insist upon you accepting. 'Tis that I shall be master o' this vessel from now and that I shall continue master until such a time as we take a vessel more to my liking an' at such time I shall forgo command of the Rancour and I will be allowed to recruit my own crew and go on my own account. 'Tis my plan, Master Rackham, and I'll trow 'tis yours, too. 'Tis Mistress Bonney's plan and it'll be the plan o' every man jack aboard the Rancour!"

"'Tis mutiny," said Jack Rackham meaningly.

"An' be you the man who can deal death?" Buttons looked through the pale light at Calico Jack. "'Tis my mind to sail as you planned this very night. 'Tis my mind to attack every sail we meet, bar none. 'Tis a more aggressive career for the Rancour and not the lazy gadling you favour. Aye, and the crew will hold wi' me in that!

"Mistress Bonney will keep her cabin. If she must come on deck, let her stay below. You may not care muchly for my plan, Master Rackham, but now that I'm known for a woman I must have my say. You'll not have to endure it long for I care little enough for your company. Gi'e me my way and the Rancour'll be yours again within the week."

Buttons blew her pipe and the watch returned to his station.

"Ye ken now that I be a woman," she said to the steersman, "but I be a woman unbeknownst to you. At the first sign o' trouble I'll waste no time but blow down the first man to whimper."

"Go below, master, an' you, too, mistress, an' I'll meet you there." Then Buttons' voice hardened and she added: "An' no treason or, by my bollys, I'll blow you so hard you'll ne'er get over it."

No one who knew him could accuse Calico Jack of cowardice. He was a man of daring, reckless and spectacular, but only in the face of an audience. He would fight any man with a gun or cutlass and let the devil take the loser. But he had felt Buttons' blow and he had seen the crew obey her where it had refused to take orders from him. And besides, he liked the wench.

Buttons looked at the priming of her pistols and arranged her baldric so that her cutlass would be at hand. The gesture was eloquent and Jack and Anne without further ado went below. Mary Read made a final tour of inspection, giving orders to the watch and resigning the quarterdeck to Massey, whose trick was due. She felt very fine. For the first time in her life she had become a definite element, a positive force, and she knew better than anyone on board the Rancour that she was master or mistress of the situation.

Yet as she went to the master's cabin she was cautious and sly. She knocked twice and, when the summons to enter came, she threw open the door and stepped quickly to one side. No pistol shot greeted her and she stepped across the threshold, only to stop and place her hands on her hips and give one of her deep and husky belly laughs.

Master or mistress? Did it matter? The Rancour was hers to do with as she wished and she realized it.

V

When Buttons left the cabin of Calico Jack Rackham she was probably the most amazed person on board the good ship Rancour. She came out boldly, hesitating not at all, and walked fearlessly to her own cabin, which she entered without turning to look back.

She was, without peradventure, master of the Rancour.

Calico Jack Rackham, gallant lover, gentleman of fortune and one of the last Brothers of the Coast, was in an ignominious position, one in which he ceased to be a dashing figure and became merely a subject for pity or sympathy. For the calico-breeked pirate was in irons.

Aye, in irons and he had taken them without a murmur.

Only Anne Bonney's shrill voice had protested. But the pirate's mistress was already locked in her own cabin and her screams meant nothing.

Thrice had Anne been locked in her cabin only to be released each time by her lover. The last time Mary Read had taken advantage of the situation. Calico was just closing in on her when she suddenly pushed out her fist and blowed him down. His head struck the cabin table as he fell—and Mary Read knew full well the penalty for mutiny.

Master of the Rancour, yet she was but a mutineer.

It would be but a matter of time until Calico Jack would be freed from his irons and then she would know his wrath. How long she might keep him prisoner would depend upon many things: the curiosity of the company; a situation requiring the exercise of authority; indeed several other elements. For a few hours she might stem off any investigation by informing the company that the master was ill and confined to his bunk. How long she could maintain the fiction would be a matter of luck.

Needless to say, Buttons did not sleep that night, but paced her cabin or the quarterdeck throughout the dark. As each hour was announced she went to Calico's cabin to see how he fared. She nursed his head, took him water and rum, and assured him with each gesture that she was as unhappy about the situation as he was.

"'S'help me, Calico, 'twas no fault o' mine. Yon wench would 'a stuck me in my sleep. Nor would you have lifted a hand to stop her. You're that fox't wi' your hankering for her."

Jack did not answer Buttons but nodded toward the decanter of rum. When he had sipped from the cup she held to his lips, he said:

"I'll forgi'e you, lass, if you'll release me. I'll say nowt to anyone."

"Nay, Master Calico. I fear you not because o' any love for you. But you are naught but putty i' the wench's hands. Your final decision will be hers an' I know't. Sleep, man, and in the light o' day we'll put our nollies together and devise a plan. Sleep, marster."

She returned to the poop deck, spoke a word to Massey, and returned to her cabin. Mary feared greatly the coming of day. She knew that as long as the crew slept she was master of the situation. Only the coming of dawn would reveal her strength or weakness.

At four bells in the early morning, just before the dawn would spring full-fledged into being, the call came from the lookouts on the crossjack.

"Lights! Lights five points to the starboard!"

The call was repeated by the forward and after watches and, before a further announcement could be made, Mary Read was on the quarterdeck, trying to make out if the vessel were friend or foe. Neither she nor the men could discern her flag, the vessel standing gaunt against the southern skies.

"Hard over," Buttons ordered the helmsman, suiting the words by placing her hands on the spokes and easing the wheel into position.

She brought the Rancour bow on toward the other ship, straining her eyes; she would continue until she learned the stranger's mission. The vessel was yet a mile away when she heard from the forward watch.

"A Spanish Don, armed. Twenty-four guns."

Steadily the Rancour stood and Mary called to her crew:

"Starboard and larboard gunners to your stations. Matches ready! Musketeers aloft! Topmen aloft!"

She could see the silent figures of the men, unaware that a new master was in control of their vessel, hurrying, some still in bare feet, to their guns. The small arms men were priming their muskets preparatory to going up the rigging, getting their equipment arranged and in condition for the precarious work they were about to engage upon. Steadily the Rancour made for the Don, bow on, all hands at their stations and the new master with one hand on the wheel to secure instantaneous response to her commands but calm, bawling her orders in her hoarse, mannish voice.

Instead of bringing the Rancour up along the larboard side of the Spaniard, Buttons cut across his bow, giving the command to her own starboard guns to fire. The twelve guns before her belched their messages of destruction as she cried to wear ship. Her helm at once went to the other side and in a trice she was travelling alongside her quarry. The two commands to fire came simultaneously from each master, but the Spaniard's blast was weak and scattering while that of the Rancour was strong and steady and devastating.

"Stand by to board. Grapplers ready!" called Master Buttons. "Musketeers fire! Boarders forward!"

With the last command she leaped to the deck and, cutlass in hand, was among the first over the rail. She met the Spanish master, golden-hilted sword in hand, at the foot of his companion-way and with her heavier cutlass put him hors de combat instantly. The whole thing was over in ten minutes. De Orozco, master of the Bella Christina, and his crew were her prisoners. It was not entirely the surprise of the attack that had won the victory. The Spaniards only the day before had been attacked by a pirate ship and had captured and fired it. Their elation had been so great and the rum haul so excellent that the night had been given over to celebrating and when the Rancour came up hardly a man was able to walk directly to his post.

The pirate taken by the Bella Christina had been none other than Will Cunningham, master of the vessel on which Boatswain Jones was second officer. What had they done with their prisoners? Buttons asked. They had killed many in the battle; others, the wounded, had been cast overboard; a few had escaped in the ship's longboat; the balance were below in the hatches.

"Time enough for those unfortunates. Now, as to your cargo! What are you and where do you go?"

Captain Orozco had been too long in the service and had had too many encounters with freebooters to feel unduly overwrought by his predicament. He had saved his skin before by not antagonizing the ruffians who had taken his ship and by concealing nothing. If these pirates were after gold alone, he might readily escape without injury; if they wanted everything, only courtesy would serve. He conducted Buttons to his cabin and pointed to the leathern chests stacked against a bulkhead. Twenty of these contained Peruvian gold and four were filled with the semi-precious stones of the same region. There were in the cabin, in addition, several small consignments of pearls from the Gulf of San Miguel. In the hold were many tons of silver ingots, much native produce and twenty captives being taken to Spain for execution.

"We'll attend to that for you, captain," Mary said. "If they're good pirates, that would be no death for them and we'll replace them with twenty Spaniards."

Mary then ordered the Spanish prisoners divided into equal numbers, half to be sent aboard the Rancour and the other half to be confined aboard the Bella Christina; for the time being, the captive pirates could remain below the hatches.

The Bella Christina was a new vessel on the last lap of her maiden voyage; a self-armed treasure ship, a bark, fleet, slender and staunchly built. She had, on her first crossing, justified and betrayed her designers. The men she had taken captive were to have been taken to Spain and exhibited as tokens of what Spanish shipbuilders and gunners could do when properly equipped. The Bella Christina would never again see Spain.

Mary Read, not insensible to the full value of the prize she had taken, politically as well as financially, ordered the treasure brought on deck. A quick estimate showed that it was worth a little over one and a quarter million dollars, which when divided would give the lowliest member of the crew a share valued at sixty-five hundred dollars. Posting guards over the treasure she started for the Rancour's cabin, but before she could reach the deck she was faced by an infuriated Calico Jack Rackham, whom one of his crew had found and released.

"Throw that man in irons," yelled Jack.

But Mary's cutlass was out and she was retreating from the rail.

129

"Place a leg on this deck and your life won't be worth a —," said Mary, evenly and calmly. "Stand from behind me, you fellows, or by my bollys, I'll cleave you head to guts!"

One hand held her cutlass and the other a pistol.

"I took this ship, Jack Rackham, where you'd have turned tail and you know it. I and your men took it while you lolled in your cabin. If you're awake, you can see the prize behind me, ready for honest division as our laws demand. Your shares are there and will be delivered to you, mine with them, if need be. But the Bella Christina's mine, to do with as I see fit, and later I'll tell you my thoughts."

Behind her a man made a false gesture, one that was misunderstood by Mary, and, wheeling quickly, she fired; the ball caught him full between the eyes and before a move could be made her empty pistol was in her belt and another, loaded, in her hand.

"Every man jack o' you know I'm not one to be made a joke of. Stand to your places if you value your nollies. The next will die as did the first."

Slowly and deliberately, but with no confession of defeat, Mary Read retreated in the direction of the poop of the Spanish bark. She backed up the ladder and, when she was at the rail, she called to Jack Rackham:

"Drop your arms and come aboard, milord Calico Jack."

Calico Jack Rackham had rushed on deck without his sash of pistols, armed only with his cutlass; he knew that Buttons, through her courage, had won the respect of his crew and that he could not afford to have the issue put so cavalierly to the test. Unbuckling his baldric and tossing it to the deck, he sprang somewhat gingerly over the rail to the deck of the captured ship.

"Calico alone," called Buttons from the poop. "He'll not be molested unless he asks for it."

On the deck of the Spaniard were the guards of the captured treasure and several other pirates, but, as none made a hostile move, Mary let them stay.

When Calico Jack had made his rounds of the prize and looked upon the treasure, he stopped beneath the poop and looked up. Mary Read untied her sash and threw it on the deck at her feet, calling:

"Come up, Calico, my lad, an' let's gadle a bit. There's much to be said atwixt us."

Calico Jack came up the ladder and stood facing his second officer.

"I have only to summon my men and tell them you be a mutineer an' they'll be on you like a pack o' wolves."

"I know. But I fear you not, only the wench you call mistress. You are a good cheild, Calico, an' I'd like to sarve under you. But atwixt your lust and your wench there's no livin' wi' you. Keep her hence and all will be well."

"What do you? You said the vessel was yours."

"Aye, Calico. The vessel, the Bella Christina, an' those o' your crew who wish to follow its fortunes."

Jack laughed shortly.

"As ye know them, Buttons, how many would sarve under a wench? Hey, now?"

"Were I you I'd not put it to the test, Calico. 'Twould hurt your pride were I to take too many. Hey, now?"

Calico Jack looked at the horizon and remained silent. And Buttons laughed from far down in her belly.

"'Tis funny, by my shirt, 'tis funny, Calico. Here I be a woman fearin' no man in all your crew, not even you, Calico. Hear me, I fear no man I've yet met. The only one of your company I fear is that foul witch, that fishmonger's wife in silk, your mistress. Her do I fear and her alone. Where be she? Still locked in her cabin?"

Jack did not answer directly. Carefully pleating his gay breeks and stretching out his legs, he said:

"Buttons, you and I could go far together. What say you? I'll place you in command of the Bella Christina and together we'll rove far and wide. The wench'll be placed ashore at Puerto Principe an' that'll be an end to her. Make it so, Buttons!"

As if she'd been waiting for this moment, Anne Bonney, slightly dishevelled and very angry, hove into sight.

"How now, Jack Rackham? What's afoot wi' you and that—wench? Plannin' to do away wi' me again!"

Heavy with child as she was, she came over the rails of the two vessels in a single bound and angrily made her way toward the Spanish poop. There was more than fire in her Irish eyes as she made the quarter-deck.

"Popinjay you are, Jack Rackham, macaroni an' a poor cheild, but I'll not let this wench take you."

"Silence, wench," said Jack. "We have business to discuss. Go to your cabin." Unexpectedly he reached down and picked up one of Mary Read's pistols. "Get hence before I do you harm."

Jack had picked up the pistol only as a threatening gesture against his mistress, but once his hand was on the butt Mary Read realized he had become master

131

of the situation. The crew of the captured vessel were all confined below the hatches, the two vessels were locked in the embraces of the grapples, and the crew of the Rancour, anxious to see their booty, were swarming to the deck of the Bella Christina; whether from intent or not, they were boosting Buttons' stock to the skies. One of them, in sheer admiration for the leader who had captured the bark, called for three huzzas for Captain Buttons. It was given with a will, cutlasses out and held aloft toward the poop.

"Huzza! Huzza! Huzza! Captain Buttons!"

If Calico Jack Rackham had had more courage, that was his moment. He should have shot her down, telling the crew that if the Spaniards had not been drunk and asleep they themselves would now be below the hatches like Will Cunningham's men. But he lacked the courage and the wit to take advantage of the situation and his indecision gave Mary her last chance. Springing to the rail she spoke to the men below.

"Men, gallant fellows all, I've a plan to put before ye. Below yon hatch lie twenty buccaneers, captives of the Spaniard who this morning became our prize. Before we release them we will go forward with the distribution of the booty. Then Master Rackham will go to his own poop, taking with him his wench and all who prefer to follow him. Those among ye who have guts and who are not afeared to follow a woman will stay with this vessel, which I will rename the Blackbird, a fitting title for the career I plan for her. Then we will separate and go our own ways. When the division is complete we'll open the hatch and let those poor lads decide who they will join. Say me what you will?"

"I'll take the wench," cried a voice and he was cheered to the echo.

"Ye'll not take me, you're not the man who can do it," laughed the wench. "You can come along of me but there'll be no taking without my consent. Put your nollies to it, think twice, my men, an' those o' you who've the guts to be led by a woman lean against the starboard rail. The rest o' ye get back to the Rancour."

"Gold first," cried another voice. "Then we'll decide who's to be marster."

Mary Read fretted while the distribution was being made. The process was a slow one, for the entire booty had to be divided into two hundred shares and each item counted out in a loud voice so that the slow-witted men could not later claim they had been harried of their rightful share.

"Each share of gold will amount to forty-six pieces. To the captain ten shares or four hundred and sixty pieces. To Captains Massey and Read, five shares each, two hundred and thirty pieces."

Each man as he received his share let it lie before him so that any of his fellows might see he was getting no more than his rightful due. As usual fights broke out when it came time for the distribution of the pearls and gems. These were all mixed together and a blindfolded pirate would pick out the number of stones to which each man was entitled and drop them one by one into the recipient's hands. The silver was divided last; the men had difficulty in carrying their shares back to their bunks and many of the less provident swapped them for a few pieces of the more easily carried gold.

When the division was complete, the men called for their distribution of rum, but in a quick consultation with Calico Jack, the woman pirate insisted that the distribution of the liquor await her recruiting a crew. It would have been decidedly to Jack's advantage to have his men bloody well drunk before the recruiting began, but once again he neglected his opportunity and gave Mary her way. But Anne Bonney was more far-seeing than her mate.

Buttons had scarcely enlisted a dozen men when she saw the woman moving about the deck of the Rancour and rum being distributed to the men. Ordering two of the men who had already joined her to bring Anne before her, she dispatched two others to release the Spaniard's prisoners from confinement under the forward hatch.

Anne was hustled to the Bella Christina's poop and Captain Buttons cried:

"How now, fair Anne, wouldst undo me? I ordered that no rum be sarved to the men until after we parted company."

Anne Bonney broke forth in a line of vituperation that drew looks of admiration from the two men who held her.

"Nay, ye, —— —— —— —— wench. I'll ha'e none o' your fine talk. I'll not be set aside, I tell you, for the likes o' you. If I can't kill you, I'll kill that gay-breeked paramour o' yours and feed 'im to the barrycuda. How d'ye like that, my fine wench?"

Mary Read's attention was distracted from the shrewish screaming of the Irishwoman by the sight of many men emerging from the dark of the hatch into the bright burning sun. For a moment they stood wiping the tears from their eyes, trying to get their bearings on the unfamiliar deck. Two of them limped from wounds in their legs and another had one arm bound in a sling. Through the dazzling rays Mary recognized a familiar face, once well-beloved, and forgetting her antagonist entirely, she called:

"Jones! Boatswain Jones! Come hither."

Boatswain Jones looked aft and saw his wife standing on the poop of what he knew to be a Spanish treasure ship. Hailing her with his good arm, he came toward her.

"Aye, Buttons, lad, 'tis good to see ye again. What do you here?"

"Oh, lad, I be master of this vessel. I be on the account like Morgan and Teach and Roberts. I be my own master and master o' this fancy bark. What say you to that?"

Before he could reply, Anne Bonney put in her oar.

"Be not fox't by 'er gadling, cheild. She's no more a mon than I be. A dirty — — — filthy wench she be, a-tryin' to rob me o' my man."

Jones laughed and Mary with him.

"Aye, wench, I know she's no man, none know it better nor I," said Jones.

"Mistress Bonney,'" said Mary Read, with a great mock at courtesy, "may I present my yokemate, who has no other name than Jones save that of his rating? Seaman Jones he was when I met him and Bosun Jones when I left him. Husband he is to me and if he knows his wench, he knows too he's never been cuckolded. Hey, now, Jones?"

"'Tis the truth, Mistress Bonney, never found I a woman so hard to lay. It takes a fightin' man, and I be that, to mate wi' her."

Jones and Mary laughed again.

"An' to show me love for him," said Mary Read, "an' to show me pride in him, I make him navigator o' this vessel, wi' none but me to answer to. Chief officer he be an' every man jack o' my crew salutes him as master. His name now, I suppose, 'll be Master Jones! An' Mistress Anne Bonney may as well begin the courtesy right now." Anne would have drawn back, but Mary was adamant. "An' then will come the great and gallant Calico Jack and every man jack of the good ship Blackbird."

From her bar-boy days in New Providence Mary recognized others among the released prisoners. The distribution of rum had been stopped and the recruiting of a crew went on. About half the men decided they'd go with the woman pirate and, be it said to Mary's credit, those who joined her from the Rancour were the most ruffianly of its company. Calico Jack's lazy ways had not appealed to these men and the way in which Mary had taken the Spaniard, with never a movement that was not direct, had won their admiration. She captained a loyal and cut-throat crew.

Book Four   The "Black Bird"

I

Mary Read had not won her ship and her crew as easily as the swiftness with which her plans had been executed might indicate. Calico Jack could have denied her the right to enlist among his men, he could have refused her needed supplies, arms and ammunition, even denied her the right to appropriate the vessel for her own purposes. That she had succeeded in her coup was due largely to Anne Bonney's jealousy; the Irish wench was willing to let Mary do almost anything if only she would leave the Rancour, and Calico Jack, lazy and comfort-loving, chose the easiest way to domestic peace.

But he still showed himself something of a business man. In a last conference with Mary he insisted upon a share of all the Blackbird's takings, beginning with a fifty per cent demand, and gradually coming down to a more equitable fifteen; even then he made Mary pay heavily from her own prize money and savings for the victualling of her vessel. The new pirate captain was glad enough to accept almost any conditions to be off on her own. She made a hurried survey of the ship and its stores and ordered the carpenter to paint out its name and home port and substitute Blackbird, Bristol. The sailmaker was instructed to make a flag that would make the Blackbird's mission known to all beholders. Instead of the traditional Black Peter with red or white skull and bones Buttons decided upon a red field on which was mounted a vulture in black, dining upon a human skull; there would be, she argued, no misunderstanding its meaning.

The next day the grapples that still held the prize to the Rancour's side were cast off and the new pirate ship, the first and quite likely the last ever to be wholly commanded by a white woman, began her career. She was to sail up and down the Islands of the Caribbees, roving and raiding, burning and killing, causing havoc in the shipping of the world, becoming a terror to honest seafarers and the hunted of nations. At this moment she was mastered and captained by a very frightened, indeed an almost timid girl.

But whatever qualms she may have felt did not last long.

Mary Read, standing alone on her own quarterdeck save for the man at the wheel and with some eighty brawny ruffians to obey her commands, was timid only by courtesy. She was engaged on a heavier venture than she had ever known before and she knew she had to make good from the beginning or have her own men, even to her husband, turn on her and deal her death—or marooning, which was worse. Her strength lay in the way she had captured and was handling the ship she sailed. True, the crew of the Spaniard had been in no condition to fight, but she had not known that and she had her mates' word for it that she had executed a fine piece of piratical seamanship in her attack by not bringing her ship broadside to the enemy until she was ready to meet him broadside for broadside. Even had the Spaniard's broadside been more effective, it would not have prevented her manoeuvre, since the ships were too close for effective work with the heavier guns and the pirate had used hers merely to clear the enemy's decks, leaving them free for her boarders.

On her first raiding attack she had been successful, that was that. On her second and further attacks she must also be successful or there would be another story to tell and a sorry tale it would be.

Buttons put her vessel about and made for the Yucatan Strait, keeping as far south of the Island of Jamaica as possible. Her plans called for careening at Dry Tortuga, a quay off the west coast of Florida, after stopping en route at the Isla de Piños where, she had heard, a bloody band of cut-throats had made their headquarters. She needed a bigger crew, perhaps twenty to forty more men, and on the Island were the runagates of all nations, ready for anything that would put gold in their pockets and booze in their gullets. They lived there on the produce of the natives and what they could take from the waters surrounding the Island. Many had taken native girls to wife or as mistresses. Most of them had been pirates at one time or another; their ships had been lost or taken, some had been marooned, others were just gadlers who were waiting for the main chance. They would welcome a berth on such a ship as the Blackbird, a vessel that openly flaunted its determination on its stern.

Mary found it good to be back with her husband, and from him she learned the story of Will Cunningham's last ventures on the account. Will had, it seemed, travelled in too great fear of the Royal vessels to make a success of piracy. Woodes Rogers and the Governor of Jamaica had commandeered all the ships in their waters that could carry a cannon; disguised as merchantmen, these ships would stop at the command of any pirate, even going so far as to strike their colours. It was when they were about to be boarded, when their attacker had become careless, that their crews would go into action, often badly damaging the pirate vessel before they were driven off. Even those pirate ships that escaped injury suffered from such encounters when the captains were recognized or the ship's characteristics were determined and word was sent out that such and such were operating in such and such waters. Will Cunningham had let half a dozen good prizes slip from his grasp because he could not determine their origin or nature; then he had come upon the Bella Christina, a Spaniard by her cut and design. But who was to say she was not actually a disguised British vessel out on a pirate hunt? When the Don showed fight Will felt that his worst fears had been confirmed; while his men were putting up a brave fight under the first officer on the quarterdeck, he and a few others had lowered a cockboat and made good their escape. Later, at the Isla de Piños, Jones would learn that Cunningham and his companions had won to Jamaica, only to be recognized as pirates and hanged forthwith.

"Sarves him right," muttered the pirate wench. "No man should ever leave his ship on deep water; only the ship may leave the man without dishonour."

Arrived at the Isla de Piños, Mary was too wise in the ways of men to leave her ship. Sticking to her quarterdeck and maintaining a double watch, she sent her husband and four others ashore to spread the news that good and brave pirates might find berth on the Blackbird; it would not be necessary, she instructed her emissaries, to inform the recruits the master was a woman. A dozen new men were won to Mary's crew, as sorry-looking a crowd of runagates as could be found. Three had lost their ears for crime; another's nose had gone in a fight, and four were branded on the forehead: KT, King's traitor; T, Thief, and M, Murderer. These men had been branded or mutilated in England and then transported, their markings making it impossible for them ever again to enter any part of the King's Realm. But the very marks that set them apart from the rest of the world made them ideal for Mary Read's venture; here were men who would not hesitate to attack even a British ship, for they had no love for their homeland nor anything to hope for from it. Two of the new recruits were Spaniards, another a Frenchman, and all were renegades and ready for any desperate deed.

The Blackbird arrived at Dry Tortugas with a crew of ninety-two men, none of whom had yet signed any articles. Buttons saw her vessel careened, preparatory to having the hull cleaned, and then retreated to her improvised shelter where, after much thumb-sucking and puckering of her brows, she produced the most fantastic document ever read to or by any pirate of any sea. It was, as will be seen, a curious mixture of feminine and masculine demands, beginning with interdictions and ending with rewards for service and courage.

ARTICLES OF AGREEMENT entered into at the Dry Tortugas, an Island in the Seven Seas and known to all signers thereof and made on this day of the first careening of the vessel, the Blackbird.

That Captain Read will be of the last command and that every man will obey a civil order.

That any man who shall offer to run away, desert, or keep a secret from his master shall be marooned.

That if any man shall steal anything from any other man or from
the ship's stores he shall be marooned or shot at the discretion of the captain.

That any man who attacks another shall receive the Law of Moses.

That any man who smokes his pipe or snaps his arms or carries a
lighted candle without a lanthorn shall receive the Law of
Moses.

That any man who fails to keep his arms clean and fit for an
engagement, or neglects his business, shall be cut off from his
share and suffer such other punishment as the master and
company may think fit.

That any man who meets with a prudent woman and offers to
meddle with her, without her consent, shall suffer death at the
yardarm.

That no man may invade the master's cabin without a summons
from the master or suffer the Law of Moses.

That in any engagement any man who shall take it upon himself to
consort with the enemy, or show the white flag, or offer other
consolation to our quarry, shall suffer death without trial.

That any man who shall suffer the loss of a leg shall receive five
shares.

That any man who shall suffer the loss of a right arm shall receive
six shares.

That any man who shall suffer the loss of a left arm shall receive
four shares.

For the loss of one eye, four shares.

For the loss of both eyes, ten shares and be assured he shall be set
down upon a friendly town.

That the captain shall receive ten shares.

That the master shall receive five shares.

That each mate shall receive three shares.

That the carpenter and sailmaker shall receive each two shares.

That all other members of the company shall receive one full
share of all prizes.

That for any outstanding act of courage a man may, at the captain's
discretion, receive one or more extra shares.

Understanding fully all the conditions mentioned above the
undersigned do fully offer their lives and their loyalty to their
master.

The conditions were read to the pirates three or four times to the accompaniment of much head-wagging and lip-twisting, as each sought to give the impression that his great mind was wrestling with the possibility that some joker had been inserted or some loophole left open for his final humiliation. A few of the company were able to sign, but most had to mark an X and let their names be writ beside their marks.

The Dry Tortugas offered nothing in the way of amusement for the pirates and, when the careening was completed and the ship swung at her moorings, there arose a movement among the crew to visit the rendezvous of Calico Jack, but the pirate wench vetoed that: not until we take a prize and a good one at that, was her decision. Cruising alertly down the Grand Bahama Bank, the Blackbird held up several small traders from whose cargoes Mary replenished her stores and took some clothing and rum but very little specie. She realized her dependence on her men and, not liking to thwart too long their desire for a debauch, hoped for a prize before they arrived off Puerto Principe. And fortunately she found it, literally picking off as beautiful a prize as a pirate could hope to find in a year's roving.

She was a big, cumbersome old-fashioned galleon, slow-moving and unwieldy, a relic of days long passed and newly returned to service only because of the lack of bottoms. Her master had hoped that by clinging to the coasts he would succeed in keeping out of the lanes frequented by pirates and his very strategy had proved his undoing. She was not so rich a haul as the Bella Christina yet well worth the taking. The final division gave each man a greater share of gold plate and silver marcas than the earlier prize.

What to do with the ancient galleon gave Mary some thought. Her first mind was to destroy it but she could not take the men captive, there were too many of them, and if she ordered them to the boats they would make for the nearest coast and report her whereabouts too soon. She ended, after the booty had been completely transhipped, by giving the master food and water enough to get him to the Spanish Island, holding him overnight and the next morning ordering him on; he was to have a two-hour start in a chase which, should she catch up with him, would result in her sinking the galleon with all hands on board. It was a good threat and the pirate wench did give him a chase, a half-hearted one that ended just before dark by her firing several shots after him. Then, as night fell, she turned the Blackbird about and made for the rendezvous.

When the men were debarked at Puerto Principe, as they called the spot, because it was the nearest shore to the city of that name, Mary found she did not care to go ashore; she could not leave her ship. It was not that she feared mutiny but that she was happy on the Blackbird and unhappy at the thought of leaving her. In her cabin, with her husband at her side and all the wine and rum they cared to drink, she would have as much fun as any member of the crew.

Mary Read was a saving soul and wanted to keep her prizes for the time when there would be no more roving for her or for any man.

Happy though she was to have found Jones, Mary's married life was not without its rifts. For one thing, it irked her that Jones' knowledge of navigation should so far excel her own. He could take a ship anywhere, a true master of navigation, whilst the best she could do was to hold the helm true to a given compass point. Yet, when it came to manoeuvring into a favourable position, she, with one hand on the wheel, could bring her ship into position more smartly than her slower-witted spouse.

The wench's very ignorance of the limitations of a vessel made her the more daring, the more successful of the two. Jones would yell that she could not do this or that, and she would retort with a shout that she could and then she would. Jones was cautious, she was impetuous; Jones obeyed laws and she did not even know laws existed; Jones was a second man and as such fitted nicely into the scheme of things; she was a natural leader and she knew it.

Jones, too, was a bit daft from the riding sometimes given him.

"What sort o' mon be you to take sarvice in your wench's vessel? Tell us thot, mon, if mon ye be!"

These gibes infuriated the husband and, like all husbands in history he vented his spite upon his wife. Mary took it all more or less good-humouredly; she needed Jones not only conjugally but professionally and she could afford to put up with his temper. Indeed, she admitted to herself, the whole affair of the Bella Christina had been most fortunate; first the taking of the ship and then finding her own personal navigator in the hold. Without such luck where would she have been? Whom could she have taken? Anne Bonney, if she had not been convinced the boatswain was really Mary's husband, would surely have betrayed her in one way or another. Let the boatswain make his moan; he was for the time being her lucky charm. Again, it had been at his insistence that the crew could be put off no longer that she had been setting her course for Puerto Principe when she had happened upon the ancient galleon which had proved worth no less than one hundred thousand pesos of gold to her and her husband; had it not been for him, she surely would have missed it. Aye, she thought, the boatswain's a valuable man, so let him have his bloody whims.

The men had rum enough for a week's festivities, and Mary knew that while they were carousing it would be policy for her to make one trip ashore and join them in drinking toasts to those who had acted heroically in the taking of the galleon, toasts to future successes, to herself and to her ship, to this and to that until she should be as fox't as the next one. She went, managed to keep her head on her shoulders, and got back to the ship to conduct her daily inspection before the fall of night. It was bad business to leave the vessel with so few hands on board, she thought; any marauding gang could surprise the handful of men and make off with everything. While the Blackbird was at anchor it was her custom to spend most of the nights standing guard on her quarterdeck, alert to every noise or whisper. Captain Mary Read was happy when the first man of her crew came aboard, sick and belchy and fit for little else than being stowed in his bunk, there to sleep for a couple of days until once more he was fit for duty. When half her men had returned voluntarily she sent the call for the rest, firing a single shot as warning she was about to sail.

II

Mary Read's only recreation was with dice and cards, but, much as she loved gambling, she did not let it interfere with her premier interests, her vessel and its mission. She maintained a discipline which, if it had not been for her aggressive and profitable leadership, might have led to mutiny. The easy-going pirates, heartless and merciless, liked to take prisoners to do their work while they prodded the poor wretches with their cutlasses to greater activity. Only a master could know that a ship could carry only so much provisions and that every extra mouth made heavy inroads upon the stores. Mary declined to take prisoners except when it was necessary to destroy the prize vessel, and then only in order to land them on the nearest shore. If her crew made the temporary captives toil, that was their business; a rebel could always jump overboard if he liked not the treatment. Nor would she permit heavy drinking on board, but reduced the usual rum ration to a small pannikin each night. The rule against one man attacking another was broadened to include all personal quarrels that might lead to cutlass work. Differences, Mary ordered, must be settled with fists; if the two disputants were too enraged to be satisfied with pummelling each other, they were placed in separate watches until a convenient strand was found on which to permit the bloody play of swords.

But the pirate wench never relished losing her men in civil strife. In her own days before the mast she had been compelled to dig a grave for the vanquished in a quarrel in which she had no part or interest, and she saw no sense in continuing a custom like that. Two of her men one day averring they could not resolve their quarrel without the death of one or both, she ordered them ashore to settle it. What the dispute was about she neither asked nor cared; what she did care about was that the two foes were valuable men and that the loss of either would be irreparable. Appointing herself and one man from each watch as judges, she went ashore with them. And there were two long-handled shovels in the boat.

The two fighters spent their time on the short trip examining the priming of their pistols and whetting the edges of their cutlasses; each had the customary two firearms, a cutlass sharpened to a razor edge and a light broad-axe hanging

141

at his belt. Once ashore, according to the usual procedure, they would face each other at twenty or twenty-five paces and at a command fire their pistols, charging forward as they fired. As each pistol was discharged it would be thrown aside, and when the men came together they would be at each other with their heavy blades; should one of these be broken, the axe would be brought into play, and with such weapons they would fight to a finish until the victor, if able, returned to the ship and the vanquished was left to rot in the sun, the vessel being the only real loser in the end. Looking forward to such a contest neither of the battlers seemed to notice the shovels in the stern.

But when they had gained the shore and were examining their weapons with even keener interest, their attention was sharply diverted. The captain snapped an order to them both to begin digging a grave for the one who lost. Standing with pistols cocked and arms crossed, she was not to be ignored, yet there were protests, each man claiming the other was hardly worth the honour of burial.

"Aye, I believe you both. But dig and be damned to you. Dig!"

The sun shone down hard on the strand, and digging for a pirate was an onerous task. Each man began tossing aside small portions of the sand.

"Nay, m'lads, heavy on those spades. It must be wide and deep, that hole, for I may have to lay both o' ye in it. Wide and deep, down near the water line. Such hot-blooded corpses will need the cooling influence of sea water. Dig!"

The two men took a firmer hold on their implements and added a little speed to their movements; soon the perspiration was running down their bodies. When they were down a scant eighteen inches they paused for a rest, hopeful that the pirate wench would consider that deep enough.

"Nay, lads," said Mary, divining their intent. "It must be above a fathom deep, you scuttlebums. Deeply, I say!"

Two feet! Thirty inches! Three feet! The men were already down to the tide line, and as each shovelful came up another slid into the hole. It would have been the devil's own job for an agriculturist; for a pirate it was hell's labour. The two combatants, muttering against each other, turned on the captain and, before long, they were consoling each other with having taken service on such a vessel. The cold water, now up to their knees, cooled their passions and, as if by mutual consent, they laid down their shovels and refused either to dig or to fight.

Mary Read, still standing with feet wide apart, her arms crossed on her breast, laughed loud and long from the belly. The two would-be fighters, humiliated and contrite, stood together apart from the others, wiping the sweat from their brows. There was no fight left in them.

One thing Mary Read had learned from Jones that caused her some concern: Will Cunningham had been recognized by some of his victims even though separated from his vessel and in a smallboat rowing to safety. It had been chance, of course, but it was a chance all had to take. She herself, unless she adopted a woman's attire ashore, might be pointed out as the terrible Captain Read and summarily hanged. Even the dress of her sex might not protect her. The news was going about the Carib Islands that there was a woman afloat, a woman pirate more terrible than Morgan, Misson and La Bousse, more terrible indeed than Blackbeard, one who styled herself and her ship the Blackbird.

It sounded fanciful to the landlubbers. A woman pirate, forsooth! They had known that type of man and they were not to be fooled, not they. But the story persisted. Men came ashore in smallboats who told of how their ships had been taken by a vessel, a brig, known as the Blackbird, and of how on the quarterdeck had stood a person shouting orders through cupped hands who might have been a woman or might have been a man. A well-packed piece of femininity perhaps; a face not unpleasant to the eye, hair cut short in front and worn in a pigtail behind. Aye, she might have been a woman.

"An' tell me more, mate!"

The pirate wench gave the danger of recognition a great deal of thought and laid her plans to avoid it. It was seldom that members of the crew were recognized; the ordinary pirate, washed and clothed in clean garments, might easily pass ashore for an honest sailorman. It was the features of those in command that made the deepest impression on their captives, and many a man was hanged on no better evidence than the testimony of a witness who was certain he recognized a pirate. Mary Read ordered her officers to blacken their faces before going into action against any vessel, no matter how small, and little pots of lamp-black were placed where a man might easily and quickly swab his face and hands.

Now, at last, she was a real blackbird when she attacked.

Mary Read's frequent declaration that she would never stretch a rope was no idle boast. She had seen the men at New Providence hanged and she was determined that she would never die that way. Two of her men, the carpenter and the sailmaker, and her husband were the only ones aboard the Blackbeard who knew her plans if the vessel ever suffered defeat. Chips had bored two large holes forward and aft along the keel, stopping them up with plugs; in case of defeat, he was to knock out the plugs and make his escape as best he could. The sailmaker, in addition, was to lay a powder train to the nearest companionway and then strike off. Either device would preclude capture; all hands would go down with their ship, saving the hangman that much work.

About her personal heroism, Mary had no illusions. She feared that a small remaining trace of feminine indecision might take her in the middle of an engagement, that seeing her men about to be killed she might order them to retire and take their chances on cheating the gallows. This was only a fear; anyone who knew her, who had seen her in action, knew she would a thousand times rather go down with her ship than accept the humiliation of capture. Yet when another vessel was challenged, some womanly quirk made the pirate wench toss her whistle overboard lest, in her excitement, she pipe all hands to retreat; deliberately walking to the taffail she would drop the pipe into the sea and then go on with her attack.

It was said on board the Blackbird that all the carpenter had to do was to whittle pipes for his captain. At any rate, he made more than the number required by any other pirate chief.

Captain Mary's growing success did little to ease the tense situation created by her peculiar relationship to Boatswain Jones. Jones was a man among men, a good fellow when among his kind, a leal shipmate and a bit of a martinet. In an army he would have made a corking corporal yet a poor sergeant; no fighter, he aspired to leadership over men whose very lives depended upon fighting, and his chief weakness was that he was unable to take orders from the one who, in his order of things, should have been his servant, that is, his captain, his wife.

Mary, a natural leader, did what she could to alleviate her husband's lot. She consulted him whenever possible, accepted his decisions, and made him navigator with authority over the men at the wheel and the two officers while they were on watch. But when he placed his foot on the ladder leading to the waist he was a man without authority and his wife's consideration for him worked both for good and ill. It made Boatswain Jones, who for all his rank as navigator could not be rid of his former title, conscious of his worth, even a bit fox't with power, and it fanned an inner ambition to some day command the Blackbird as captain. Once a sail was sighted, his opinions no longer had any weight. Mary would mount the poop and with one hand on the wheel give all orders until the ship was taken; it meant hurting Jones, but that could not be helped. And, while the Blackbird swooped down upon her prey, her husband would sit sulking in his cabin, his mind full of plans for taking command of her beloved ship.

Jones knew well that any night whilst he lay beside her a knife in her heart would settle the question of who was master for all time; a pillow across her face, a poniard between her ribs and the heaving of her body out of the cabin window. It would have to be done quietly and quickly and on a night without a moon. A surprise. It could be done. He alone had access to the cabin and he could explain she had been taken with remorse for her evil life and had committed suicide. That would be a hard pill to make the men swallow, but they

144

were accustomed to accepting sudden and curious deaths as part of their daily routine.

Hearing the carronading above the deck, the shouts of the Blackbird's crew, and the cries of the wounded, he would sometimes hope a lucky shot would wipe his woman off the poop. There would be more shouts, commands, cries, a bumping as if two ships had come together and were letting the tide play with them. Then after a pause the door would burst open and his wife would stalk in, out of breath, excited and triumphant.

"On deck, Jonesy, and look after the family's interests. She's a West Indiaman and she sat so low in the water she'd hardly answer her wheel. Run her over and tell me what she's worth and whether we should sink her or keep her. Promptly, now!"

At times Jones was able to carry off this duty as if he and not his wife had taken the prize. He would carefully inspect the whole vessel, order all goods of value brought on deck, estimate its value and return to his wife to report. Rested after her terrific exertions, she would come on deck and approve or disapprove his value. When the crew of the prize ship had any clothes of value on their persons, there was one duty she always left to Jones; after the cargo of the prize had been transhipped and she had given orders as to the destiny of the vessel, she would retire to her cabin whilst the captives were stripped to the buff.

When the ship with the naked crew had veered off so that her eyes would not be shocked by the sight of so many nude men, she would come on deck, order a couple of shots fired at the retreating quarry to speed him on his way and then superintend the division of the spoils.

O modest pirate wench!

III

Despite the efforts Governor Woodes Rogers and the British Admiralty put forth in the sending of numerous vessels and men-of-war after her, the Black-bird remained free and her ill-fame penetrated into the furthermost corners of the white man's world, striking terror into the hearts of sailors and merchants alike. Captains of trading vessels, returning with naked and starving crews, a single sail on each harried ship, told highly coloured tales of passing a peaceful-looking island and being surprised by a bark sailing out of some hidden inlet and taking them before they could so much as man their guns. The pirates, said the survivors, were a fearsome and rapacious lot, taking their purchases with shouting and cursing, leaving nothing of value in their wake.

Looking for a scapegoat and seeking to gain the attention of their listeners, they would say they had been taken by the pirate wench. The only thing that served to identify her was the blackened faces of the officers and the terrible red flag with the black vulture dining upon a human skull in its centre. When it was pointed out to the victims that any pirate might blacken his face and make for himself a similar flag, they sought to identify their captor as a woman, dressed in the clothes of her sex, amorous, voluptuous and bedizened with gems. Fantastic word pictures of a woman with hands bloodied, more rapacious than any man, were heard in the inns and taverns of Charleston, in Jamaica, even in Philadelphia, Boston and New York. Men walked the streets, telling of their experiences with the female pirate, cadging drinks as gullible landsmen listened to their yarning and thanked their stars they were not sailormen.

Many of these tales would have sounded strange and romantic to the ears of the company of the Blackbird. They would have expressed virtuous indignation at many of the crimes they were charged with and would have blowed down the narrator for traducing the fair name of their leader. True, they were capable of almost any crime, only the imaginations of their traducers were greater than their own.

The articles of agreement which Captain Read had copied and posted in prominent places on her vessel were kept in active force. Every attempt at evasion was met with drastic action, but the only penalty ever inflicted was the Law of Moses, which was forty lashes less one on the bare back. This punishment was meted out often enough, as the division of spoils nearly always brought quarrels among the men.

Ships of the Gold Fleet were scarce enough at any time. A pirate coming upon one of these vessels could call that day blessed; yet it was not a bad day's business when he had to be content with an ordinary merchant or trading ship. Except when she carried a cargo of rum, the equable division of spoils from such a vessel was much more difficult than from a treasure ship. A general cargo of merchandise, for instance, consigned to a merchant in Jamaica and comprising household goods, dry goods, farming implements and the general goods shipped from English merchants to their agents in the colonies, was not easily divided between a hundred and odd men. In the older days a pirate chief, taking such a vessel, would let his wrath get the best of him and destroy both ship and cargo and inflict upon the crew untold indignities for daring to use the seas for transporting such junk. Mary Read's men were inclined to deal in much the same way.

Indeed, one of them used to tell a story of sailing with another master, who, after a stiff fight, had taken just such a vessel. In their fury the pirates had thrown everything overboard, stripped the crew of its clothing, the captain's cabin of its instruments and sent the denuded vessel on her way. Early the next morning they came upon a sail and went after and took it without any trouble, only to find it was the vessel they had looted the day before. This indignity was unendurable, and the outraged pirates loaded the naked crew into the smallboats and sunk their vessel, probably as a lesson to all skippers not to be taken twice on the same voyage.

Mary Read's Bristol soul sickened at the thought of such waste and she set about making plans to cash in on these apparently worthless cargoes. She pondered the possibility of taking such material to some place where she might cache and later sell it, but who would do business with a pirate? There were "fences," dealers in stolen goods, who would pay good gold for such cargoes, whatever their nature, but to deal with them would mean keeping in touch with them at various points and towing the prize to them. With all the naval activity, such a practice would be impossible; it would advertise the Blackbird's business and whereabouts, in addition to slowing the vessel's progress. Mary gave the problem much thought and decided that a rendezvous, that at Puerto Principe perhaps, would make an ideal cache. She could place some of her own crew in command of the prize vessel, order them to take the ship thither and unload it. They could then destroy the vessel or, if it was marketable, hold it at anchor until a purchaser came along. It was a thrifty plan, but there were many difficulties.

For instance, whom could she trust? Not Calico Jack Rackham nor, for that matter, any man in her crew or out of it. If the Blackbird should be on the account when a customer arrived and a sale was made, who would take the purchase money? Indeed, who would be the purchaser who would think of dealing with pirates?

The whole plan seemed ridiculous. She could trust no one and she could think of none who would trust a pirate.

The Blackbird was cruising east of Puerto Rico when she sighted a likely looking quarry. Mary ordered a shot fired across the vessel's bow which brought her promptly about, and she almost stood still until the pirate ship came up to her. With every man at his station, every eye alert for possible treachery, the woman pirate was bringing her ship up to hail the stranger when her nostrils, accustomed as they were to the stench of unwashed pirate bodies, were further insulted by the stench of human effluvia. A man more versed in the ways of shipping than was his captain called out that the vessel was a slaver.

Mary Read ordered the grapples out, and when the filthy vessel was secure she went aboard. It was, indeed a slave ship with one hundred and twenty blackamoors beneath her hatches, stinking and sick. Mary would not go below to inspect the cargo, preferring to examine the master's books. He had accommodations for upwards of two hundred slaves, but trading had been poor; he still had many casks of rum, a goodly amount of gold coin, some ivory and other material. The slaves, Mary learned from her crew, were worth twenty guineas a piece and could be sold in several ports not dominated by the British. There would be great difficulty in realizing on these blackamoors, but she was reluctant to let them go. The rum and ivory were transhipped, the captain and mates of the slaver were brought aboard the Blackbird and men from the crew sent aboard the prize. Then Mary called the deck officers, the navigator and the two boatswains, and told them her plans.

"This is a daft business. Here we have a prize that'll reckon up to four and twenty hundred guineas and we have no way of realizing on it. 'Tis my plan to take these blacks to Mariaguana or the Gran' Caicos and put 'em ashore. I' the future we'll do this with all our prizes. Then we'll find a way to dispose of 'em to the Yankees. Could we but get word to Boston and New York we have goods for sale cheap, we might turn an honest penny 'ere and there."

Boatswain Jones didn't think much of the plan, but his objections were silenced by a gleam from his wife's eyes. The two representatives of the crew were all for anything that might bring more rum and money to their men.

Mary went on.

"We can take the mahogany ships from Campeche and the aromatic ships carrying pepper, spices, and what not. 'Ere, where we go, we shall have a Rogue's Bazaar, where honest traders can come with money or goods and strike a bargain that'll be favourable to both o' us."

"Aye, captain, an' who'll be the fool to do business wi' a pirate that will first trade wi' him and then take back 'is purchase? Answer me that."

"There's a rub to it, I know. But i' the back o' my mind a plan is brewing. There must be a gentleman's agreement, a sign to be given that we'll recognize. Honour bound we'll be to harm no vessel privy to the signal."

"Aye," objected Jones, "an' 'ave all the King's men down upon us in an hour."

"Bridle your tongue, Mister Jones. I'll ha'e me way until I'm proven wrong. Then you may be marster o' the Blackbird. Aye, but a marster that'll have to step high to get over my body."

To the others she said,

"Mind us not. 'Tis only a family squabble; it gives m' thoughts a rush. An' I think I have it. Send me the sailmaker at once." This last to Jones.

"I'll ha'e him make us a lot of ensigns. To any marchant who is privy to our rendezvous one o' these ensigns will be given. He may display it only when coming up to our port and we will immediately lay to beside him, all hands alert and at their stations. If he truly be what the ensign shows, well and good; if otherwise, we'll blow the barstard out o' the waters. 'Tis done!"

The slaver was taken to a lonely spot on the island of Grand Caicos, one of the south-easterly Bahamas. Little of the soil was tillable and no fugitives from justice or escaped slaves had settled there; no inns or taverns had been set up and the only available food supply came from a few coco-nut trees and from the seas. There were numerous indentations in the coast, hardly any of them large enough to be called bays or harbours, yet many capable of shielding a ship from the view of casual passers-by. These were so numerous that several prize ships could be distributed along the shore and not be seen from the open sea. The long narrow island itself offered opportunities not to be found elsewhere. There were bluffs of trees, literally oases, springs of fresh water and also dunes behind which stolen goods might be sheltered. With the slave ship to begin with, the slaves themselves as labourers, and the great quantities of merchandise in the hold of the Blackbird, a settlement was started. Tents made of sails were set up, a house was constructed of the timber from the slaver, cookhouses and larders were built. Some of the slaves were put to fishing and digging for shellfish, others were sent under white men to scour the island for any kind of food.

Within a week every slave was housed, a form of government had been set up and the pirate wench declared a grand holiday, a short one because she was enthusiastic about her settlement and wanted to add to it in people and goods. Leaving ten heavily armed whites in charge of the blacks, she took the Blackbird back to foraging. Before she left she ordered that none of the whites should meddle with the slave women and she announced that she would visit some port still open to freebooters and enlist women and merchants to come and set up shop on Grand Caicos. The ten men left behind were assured that their shares in any prizes would be honoured and brought to them on the return of the vessel.

The settlement sponsored by the pirate wench, fated to rise and fall without a name, was almost a success from its beginning. From her experience with other corsairs, Mary had abandoned any desire to be an admiral, to have other ships subject to her, rendering tribute or perhaps betraying her. When she came upon other freebooters she would offer them the facilities of her port, but would not divulge its location; they might take their prizes to Turks' Island, south of Caicos, she would say, and there await her coming. This meant the Blackbird had always to carry a store of gold and powder, rum and such other goods as pirates needed to exchange for their prizes. Unknown to her own crew, Mary carried her entire fortune in her cabin, hers and her husband's. In leathern chests she had over a hundred thousand guineas, to say nothing of much plate, both gold and silver, and many jewels. Other trunks and chests contained rich raiment she was saving for the time when piracy would not longer prove profitable and she must go ashore for good.

The thought of that day obsessed her. She still hungered for a quiet home with Boatswain Jones, a place far away from strife and the danger of her trade. She cared not where the place should be, whether in America or in the Islands.

She was sure it would not be England, even her beloved Bristol, for England and Bristol, since she had accepted the King's Pardon and then betrayed His Majesty, would forever be closed to her. She had thought much of Puerto Principe and even of the Isla de Piños as places where she might settle. She did not see that her settlement on Grand Caicos was the result of this same impulse, this desire for a home; her thought did not carry her that far. To say she craved consciously for a home and children would be laughable; it is highly probable that after she rose to command she never saw herself as a woman, that is, as a wife with dresses and underkirts, herding a brood of squally brats out of danger. Yet there is much that went on in her subconscious that neither we nor she could tell. We do know that she, womanlike, craved the comfort and the safety of a hearthside. Mary herself would have admitted that much, and indignantly denied all the other implications of her desire.

When a passenger vessel was taken, and these were not many for such vessels clung too closely to the coasts for corsair safety, Mary Read would take entire charge of transhipping the goods. With her guard of six, the two boatswains and four men-at-arms, she would make her inspection of the prize. Such goods in the cargo as could be disposed of were sent aboard the Blackbird and stowed on deck; the trunks and chests were sent directly to Mary's cabin. A rule she insisted upon, and one which the pirates felt deprived them of tremendous fun, was that, when there were women on board a prize, the passengers and crew should not be stripped, not even the sailors. If one of these had on some garment a pirate craved, he must substitute some other piece.

If there were women on board the captured ship, there were always left enough provisions to see them to the nearest port of the vessel's nationality. Their sails were not taken but they were stripped of all arms, powder and cannon.

When the passenger vessel was sent on its way the pirate wench would retreat to her cabin alone, not even permitting Jones access, while she went through the chests. Later she would call the men and have the chests taken on deck for an equable division of the spoils. There was much talk among the crew about this strange procedure, but as none of the contents ever seemed to have been disturbed, all the chests rendering full tribute in jewels and gold coin, the most desirable loot to pirates, they accepted it as a silly quirk of their leader and let it go at that. Sometimes when a fine trunk was emptied, Mary would ask that it be made a part of her share and it would take its place with the others in her cabin. Only Jones, the one male privy to the captain's cabin, saw the ever mounting pile of trunks and wondered at them.

The obtuse Jones did not realize that few if any of the trunks were empty and that those that were would not long stay that way.

Things were growing no easier between Mary and Jones. It cannot be said there is evidence she had tired of him as a husband yet indisputably she had begun to look upon him as a bore. He dared not give her orders on deck, but once in the privacy of their cabin he sought by devious and canny ways to become the dominating male. It was there the two took their meals and, after the slave ship was taken, Mary Read kept two black boys to serve her. Jones protested that these blackamoors received more consideration than he and justifiably. The pirate wench in becoming master of her own vessel had tasted power. She had a hundred and more men in her suzerainty. She was a queen in the king's clothes. In the great chair at the head of her table she sat as master of her own board—a position that her husband felt belonged to him. The two black boys were her servants and would seldom obey his orders. If he wished another helping of a dish, he was compelled to ask his wife who in turn would send one of her boys to the galley for it. Jones' demand for a servant of his own was ignored and when he became too demanding, Mary would deny him admission to her cabin, compelling him to take his meals with the under officers. For days he would suffer banishment, living in his own cabin, forced to bribe an ordinary seaman for any service he felt should have been his by right of marriage. He grumbled and complained but was always careful not to be overheard by his spouse. Times enough he had gone to her cabin and, as her husband, sought unobstructed entrance, only to find the door barred. Humiliated, he would knock and say who he was and still be denied entrance. This might continue for days and days.

Then, just when his wrath against his wife and his lot was at its height, some midnight his cabin would be invaded and a hand would shake his shoulder and drag him from the depths of sleep. He would ask who 'twas and what was wanted and the only answer he would get would be a single word, spoken by his wife and captain.

"Come!" she would say and, barefooted and with only his long shirt flapping about his knees, Jones would follow Mary to her cabin and for a short time he would be his wife's master and his master's companion.

IV

In the pothouses of Boston and Philadelphia there were tales told of the cruelty of the Female Pirate, tales brewed in the wicked liquors the tellers imbibed at the expense of their listeners; tales of such cruelty, of such inhuman deeds that men raised their eyes to the heavens as if to protest the taking down of woman from her high pedestal. There was much cruelty, indeed. There were invasion and violation, there was inhumanity in stripping men of their clothes and turning then naked into the hot tropical sun, in taking all but barely enough food and water, in reducing captives to so low a state that they could not

151

turn upon their oppressors and smite them. But there was no wanton cruelty, only vengeance and revenge.

There was, for instance, the Frenchman who, having been brought about by a shot across his bow, had quickly pulled up his white flag of surrender. The ship sat so high in the water that Captain Read felt certain he carried nothing of value. Wearing her ship, she sent a longboat out in command of one of the quartermasters. Six men sat at the oars and pulled for the prize of questionable value while Mary watched them from the quarterdeck. When the longboat was half the distance to the quarry she saw a small puff of smoke from one of the cannons and a shot dropped into the centre of the long boat, sinking it almost at once. Promptly Mary called for a broadside from her larboard guns, brought her ship about and pulled up under the Frenchman's starboard. Again she raked him with a broadside and then ordered the grapples out. Jumping to the waist of her own ship, cutlass in hand, she led her men over the rails and on to the deck of the prize.

"You —— —— —— Frenchy! What do you mean by firing on honourable men such as mine?" she cried.

"There be no honour among such as you," the captain declared in English.

"Say you. If honour be lacking in our ranks, it is well made up in loyalty, aye, and in vengeance. I say ye shall pay by two for each o' my men. There be a smallboat out now to pick up those who survive and for each lost I shall take the lives of two o' yours."

The captain made a scurrilous remark.

"By three," amended Mary. "Nor does that include your head. I shall decide your fate later and make myself your executioner. But I be a fair man and I shall let you select those who are to accompany you to hell. Choose, and quickly."

"Nay, you'll do your own killing and choosing too, my fine pirate."

For a moment Mary was nonplussed. She looked about at the blanched faces of the crew of the prize ship and ordered her men to disarm them at once and line them up against the rail; there was not a man among them who did not believe his end had come.

"Aye," said Mary slowly, "I'll do my own killing and it will be a joy to kill such a craven as you." Pushing her pistol sash to one side, she drew her cutlass and cried: "Defend yourself, if you be man enough."

The man drew his heavy sword, not bothering to answer his opponent's salute. Their blades crossed, slid downward toward the hilt, were withdrawn and clashed again, steel upon steel. The Frenchman was a swordsman and, no doubt of it, he was quicker than his female antagonist but not enough to pierce her shirt. Around they went, the man warily balancing, the pirate swinging and

152

sawing in the manner of her kind; once he drew blood from her arm but she paid no attention to it, pressing the fight to him. Again he pinked her but could not follow up his advantage. Lithely he evaded her heavy blade and then, in making a grand thrust, was caught by its downward swing. It tore his arm from shoulder to elbow and the man lost his fine control and began battling in earnest for his life. This was more to Mary's liking; again her sword came down and, as it passed to his shoulder, blood spurted from where his ear had been. He grasped his blade with both hands and began sawing the air, hoping against hope to split his opponent's head; he came very near doing it but Mary's blade landed first, cleaving his forehead open and plunging him to the bloody pool on his own deck. Then she tossed her sabre aside and, taking a pistol from her sash, gave him the coup de grâce.

The woman's wounds were slight. She suffered her husband to bind them up and went about her business of inspecting the ship. Its cargo was more valuable than she had expected. The ship was one of the semi-piratical ventures of the time, a vessel with honest papers and apparently honest intent whose chief officer was not above killing off an unarmed merchant when the opportunity presented.

The Frenchman's ill-advised action in sinking Mary Read's longboat made it imperative for her to take full vengeance. If he had shown his true colours, breaking out the ensign of piracy, he might have gone on unmolested, but whatever peculiar quirk had made him attack the unarmed tender cost him his life and his crew their ship. They refused to tell who the man was who had fired the shot, sticking together thick as thieves, so Captain Read ordered their cargo transhipped, the men stripped of their clothes and sent to the smallboats, allowing only a single cask of water to each one. Then she ordered the vessel scuttled and fired, making his own ship a funeral pyre for the captain's body.

Cruelty, if you will; cruelty whether you will or no, but justifiable vengeance in the eyes of Mary and her men.

V

Each prize taken by the Blackbird meant additions to the new settlement on Grand Caicos. One of the crew had offered a substantial sum for the tavern concession and the crew had voted him permission to set up his casks and tables and to do business. A curious aspect of the transaction was that the concessionaire had to purchase his first stock of rum from the very men he expected to sell it to later on; an amiable arrangement all round and one completely within the comprehension of all moderns. The new tavern keeper engaged a small prize ketch and with one other for a crew sailed to the Spanish Island and Tortuga to engage women for bar and tavern maids and to secure such equipment as he was unable to obtain from the stores of the settlement;

before leaving he was placed on honour not to reveal the location of the rendezvous.

But news of the settlement inevitably got about and half-castes from the neighbouring islands, liking full well the companionship of the open-handed corsairs, came with all their goods. Within three months there was a substantial house for the Captain and her husband, a tavern, and several cabanas occupied by trulls and filles de joie. A single Jew came, pack aback, and before the first evening was ready for business. Others would come, some would attain riches, most would be no better off than before, but all would prosper to the degree worthy of their talents.

Mary Read was lord of all she surveyed whether she was on land or sea. She liked well her little house on the shore and she moved her trunks thither and took up life as chatelaine of her own town, forgetting the while to give it a name. To say she was beloved by all her people would not be the truth; she was, say, feared and admired. Few men cared for service under a woman, but those who had accepted Mary's leadership were compelled to admit her courage and daring. And of those she called subjects, many aspired to her and her bed; none of these believed in her marriage to Boatswain Jones nor did they consider his prerogatives important enough to warrant his destruction. He was, to put it baldly, only their captain's consort, a small man who might be displaced by any aggressive lover.

Boatswain Jones had not changed, he was, in essence, the same man Mary had met on the Sparrowhawk; what change had come had taken place in his spouse. She wanted a man worthy of herself. She had fought her way to the top, had made herself as much feared as any buccaneer of her time, and there was no man within her horizon worthy of her favours. Boatswain Jones, who held the second highest position on the Blackbird, could never rise above the station from which he took his name. It is certain that if his wife, in a burst of generosity or compassion, had made him master of a prize he would still have been called Boatswain instead of Captain and very certain he would never have been called Master. Mary was a lonely woman and, though her husband was a frequent visitor at the house on the shore, he spent most of his nights at his station on the Blackbird. His star was not waning, it was his wife's that was rising and, poor chap, he could not rise with it.

This pirate captain put on some airs. When she went abroad, she must needs be followed by her two blackamoors, now dressed in livery taken from some prize. The wench herself wore silk breeches and satin brocaded waistcoats and a crimson silk shirt. A gallant hat with an enormous feather completed her garb. About her waist was a great sash of green and into it were thrust her pistols, silver-butted, and her gold-hilted poniard. These arms were merely for decoration, she needed no weapons on her own strand.

Mary now made no pretences about being a man; she was a woman who preferred man's garb and man's ways, a man's life instead of the one she had been born to. Sometimes as she rejoiced in the high estate she had won, she let her thoughts take her back to Bristol Town and the night she had won from the drunken sailor the means to take a station on the snow Cadogan. What, she wondered, would have been her fate if it had not been for that? Mary shuddered at the thought and shut the picture from her mind. Better a life with the stupid Jones than that.

She was contented with her lot. Her position gave her certain pleasant prerogatives; for instance, in rifling a prize it was an accepted custom that everything in the captain's cabin, save treasure, went to the pirate captain. Many skippers would stock their personal larders with choice delicacies, preserved fruits, confitures, dried figs and dates, cheeses and other morsels to delight their palates. These upon capture became the wench's share and the Blackbird carried the stores of many prizes. Mary's wealth, divorced from that of her husband, was now well over a quarter of a million pesos de oro, more than one hundred thousand guineas. Most of this stayed aboard the vessel, since she had sworn her wealth would go down with her if she was ever taken. When the time came to settle down, then she would take it from her cabin and put it in a safe place near her hearth.

Contented yet unhappy. With wealth, position and power, she yet yearned for more. She could not tell what it was she desired: probably the companionship of persons as strong as herself. She wished to move in other circles than those of Grand Caicos and the Blackbird. She thought of London and Paris and sighed, knowing that both these capitals where her wealth would open most doors to her were for ever out of bounds; too, the thought of dressing as her sex demanded frightened her more than the interdictions of kings and chancelleries.

A lonely woman, contented and yet discontented. She became nervous and overwrought and, though the rainy season had come and her men were happy in their drunkenness, she suddenly gave orders to make ready for sea. One of the blackamoors carried the word to the tavern where her men spent their idle hours. The carpenter hurried to her quarters and saluted.

"But marster, the Blackbird's careening on this evening's tide. Her bottom's that foul."

"Aye, let her stand. Clean her well, man, and forget the command."

"Thankee, marster, thankee. 'Twill be good news to the men."

Mary dismissed him with a wave of her hand almost queenly. But before he had regained his seat in the tavern she was sorry she had not ordered him to forgo careening and prepare for sailing. The shore life had staled after a fortnight and she craved action. Behind the settlement was a high hill and she clambered to the top; it lacked three hours to darkness and she preferred not to see Jones, yet did not wish to leave him to the mercies of the women at the pothouse. She still wore her fine clothes as, forgetting a mild rain, she scrambled through brambles to the top. For an instant she stood there scanning the skies, hoping for a clear day, hoping, too, for a speedy cleaning of the Blackbird and a quick return to freebooting. From where she stood she could see her beloved vessel, her keel already in the sand and lanyards to her masts so that she would careen to the larboard. Even in her off-centre stand she was a thing of beauty and Mary Read for the moment forgot her desire for more power, for a wider life. There was beauty she could understand, a life she wanted above all others, the life that had given her life.

Then, without warning, there drifted around the westerly point a gallant ship and one of greater size than the Blackbird; a bigger and better ship but never a more beautiful one. Less than a mile off shore she was, a West Indiaman, cruising and trading among the island colonies of Great Britain; an English ship, rich, well-manned and armed to the teeth. Aye, a fine prize if there were the men who could take the proud beauty. Mary was glad the Blackbird was careened for she might be tempted to attack the vessel. She watched it slowly drift into full sight, becalmed in the light evening air, a thing of power yet almost powerless here in lee of the Bahaman lulls. Two hours yet to dark, but that vessel could not drift far in that short time.

Mary was galvanized into action. She hurried down the steep hill, tearing her fine clothes again and again, ruining the silken hose that had been made for a marquis at least, forgetting everything but that she was a corsair. A corsair without a ship but nevertheless a corsair on the account.

She stopped at her house, called her blackamoors.

"Send Mister Jones, Mister Doone and the quartermasters and bosuns to me. Hurry, you —— —— ——."

VI

The settlement and all its activities had been so located that nothing was visible from the open sea. If the lookout on the drifting vessel had seen any movement on the island, it would have been only the lone figure on the hill-top. Within a few minutes after she began her descent she was again out of sight. Once on the beach she ordered all the Blackbird's smallboats to be taken to the tide line, the men to be ready with full equipment, the fox't to be left behind. There were eight boats and each was placed under the command of one officer or under-officer. These she called to one side and told her plans. Two protested; to attack such a vessel from open boats was unthinkable. The two were deposed and replaced with men who would do her bidding.

Long before dark the eight boats with fifty-four men and one woman were already masked behind the eastern point of the little harbour. The lookout could still see the Britisher drifting along with the ebb. The pirates would have to wait until night fell and then be guided by the lights of the vessel. The orders called for an attack from every quarter, each man scrambling to the deck as best he might and beginning to fight as soon as his feet struck the deck. The wench herself, with the crew of a longboat, would take care of the men on the quarter-deck.

"'Tis none to my liking, captain, to be attackin' one o' His Majesty's vessels," protested Jones.

"An' 'tis little enough that's to your liking these days. Stay behind then and cozen one o' the pothouse wenches. I'll ha'e none o' you in this venture," said Mary brusquely. "Be gone, Mister Jones, an' should you pass one not too fox't, send him i' your place."

As Jones turned to obey, another asked, "Do you mean to take yon vessel from the sea, master? I' the dark o' night? 'Tis a daft idea an' one that'll send us all to Davy Jones."

Mary Read looked upon the man, not without impatience.

"'Tis a fool's errand, I agree, an' it may be the end to us all. What of it? She'll be a rich prize an' I've set my mind on't. All right, captains, shove off. See that all faces are sooted an' remember, silence until we make the deck. Onward."

The eight small boats pushed off from the shore and with muffled oars turned the point. Mary's longboat led and she was the first to see the lights of the West Indiaman less than a mile off shore. Indian file the boats made their way toward the quarry, not a fathom separating each boat from its follower. Mary had counselled silence and no man spoke, even though his heart beat with unsual force. Most of them had misgivings; this was a vessel directly under the King's protection and if it were taken by pirates it would loose upon the waters of the Caribbees every man-of-war in His Majesty's hands.

The night was a black one and Captain Read had ordered four of the boats to larboard of the British vessel and four to the starboard. It would be all of four bells and most of the crew asleep; the officers, through with complaints at being on such a lonely tour of duty, would be tossing off their nightcaps and getting ready to turn in and dream on pretty faces left in Liverpool and London. The attack was to begin when the lookout called the hour.

"Four bells," called the man at the wheel of the West Indiaman, "and all's well."

He struck the ship's bell four strong thumps and the forward watch called, "Four bells and all lights are burning brightly."

The lookout in the crow's nest, the afterwatch and the men between the decks repeated the call, but before they had finished the entire vessel was thrown into a turmoil by the most outlandish screaming and shouting. Dark and almost silent figures scurried about the decks, the man at the wheel felt the hard barrel of a pistol at his ribs and the soft-spoken command to "put her over," which he promptly obeyed. The captain's adjutant hurriedly buckling his sword of authority rushed out to find himself covered by pistols held in the hands of a stranger whose silken breeches were torn and soiled and whose brocaded waistcoat and silk shirt looked as if their wearer had come through some terrible battle. Over the man's shoulder he could see four other figures and, as his fellow-officers opened their doors, they, too, were met by men with pistols levelled at their heads.

"The master o' this vessel," said a hoarse voice. "Bring him out."

Behind her Mary heard shots which sounded as if they came from the bow of the vessel and then silence. There was a slamming as if companion-ways and hatches were being closed. The captain, in his small clothes, appeared and grasped the situation in a glance. His hands went above his head and he demanded:

"What means this? Who are you?"

"It means you've been ta'en, sir, an' it'll do you little good to protest. My men are in possession o' your vessel and naught will happen if you'll take it easy."

"Easy, sir. You're a pirate or I'll be damned. An' an English pirate at that. This is an English ship."

"Aye, I've always wanted a big one and now I have it. What now, master?"

Mary Read laughed her long, loud laugh and called to one of her men to locate the ship's irons.

"They're below decks, sir, and the 'atches are battened down."

"Very well, go through these men and disarm them. You, Gregory, look into yon cabin and see that there are no small arms concealed. We'll use it for a lazareet for the time."

"Your name, sir!" thundered the captain of the West Indiaman. "Your name and your vessel!"

"Sure now, I'll tell you that just to make ye happy. My vessel's not wi' me. You've not only to face the humiliation of being taken from smallboats i' the open sea, but to admit ye've been taken by the female pirate. Forsooth, 'tis an odd fate for a likely marster such as you be."

Again the long and hearty laugh rolled from her lips.

One man stripped the officers of their arms and tossed them at the feet of another, then one by one they were led into the officers' galley and placed under a double guard. Next the pirate captain, with but a single man-at-arms, went about her tour of inspection. She found the vessel had been but half-taken; her men were in possession of the officers and the decks, but there were almost two hundred men below, barricaded and armed and unwilling to surrender without a fight.

"Take it easy," she counselled. "'Tis a dark night and anything can happen."

On the forecastle head she found those of the crew who had been on deck at the time of the attack herded together by her men, all of them disarmed and ready to accept the worst that could befall them.

"Aye, a fine lot o' cowards," she jeered. "Th' King's fancy."

One of her men she bade locate an empty cabin and confine in it the men on the forecastle and place a guard over them. When she had distributed the rest of her men so that any attempt at an attack from below decks could be met, she went to the captain's cabin. It was but a second's work to locate his papers, ship's manifest, accounts and all. She was King's Courier, out of Plymouth, and the haul was a rich one, not Mary's greatest, but one that would mean the ultimate success of her settlement if she could safely land the vessel's great cargo.

The problem that faced her was not one to be solved in a minute.

Mary had a white elephant on her hands. A mistake had been made. The vessel, with its great company, would be difficult to dispose of. To kill the entire company was more than she was willing to undertake. To set them adrift in boats would mean that they would make for the nearest land; to transfer its solid wealth to the smallboats, her own having been set adrift, would leave the Englishmen in possession of their vessel and of the knowledge that attack had come from a certain quarter. Any real search would reveal her rendezvous. She might keep the company below decks for days, sail to the Spanish Island, put them ashore at night and then beat her retreat. The winds would have to be her friends.

Or she might maroon them. On Turk's Island they would find water and some food, hardly enough for over one hundred Britishers, but under the stern rules governing British ships, they might be made to do.

As long as they lived, as long as a single man of the West Indiaman remained alive to tell of the attack, Mary Read knew that the admiralty would search the seas for her. She had revealed her identity, the point at which she had taken the ship would be remembered, and the powerful forces at the call of His Majesty would relentlessly track her to her doom.

"'Twas a fool's feat," she muttered, then cast regret behind her and resolved to make the most of the situation.

Mary paced the deck and then retreated to the cabin again. A long table whereon the master studied his charts was now covered with the ship's papers. Studying them by the light of a lantern, she saw that there were some fourteen passengers, all men, on board besides thirteen officers and two hundred and ten men, including one company of marines. In the cabin was a fine armoury of officers' pistols and swords and the master's strongbox held a large quantity of gold coin, some documents of interest, commissions for various men elevating them to deputy-governorships, passports and other papers. Mary had the gold coin, the arms and the vessel's plate taken on deck, the ship's boats lowered and the swag placed in the three largest. Then she ordered the officers on deck, also the men who had been taken in their last futile stand on the forecastle, and led them to one of the hatches. This was opened with caution and several stench bombs dropped to the deck below. When there was no show of resistance, Mary ordered the officers, one by one, down the ladder. Then the sailors were sent down and the hatches double battened.

"All's well," she muttered.

"Not so, marster," whispered the man at her elbow. "There be a cheild i' the crow's nest."

With a curse she answered:

"Bring 'im down or silence 'is tongue for ever. You! Speedy now. We've no time to lose."

The man hurried up the ratlines, pistols in both hands, and soon she saw two figures descending. The prisoner was brought to her.

"It seems a pity to open up these hatches just for one man. Mayhap you'd care to join us, lad? 'Tis a grand life an' one for a man o' bowels. Be you he?"

"Not I, master. I'll have no part i' piracy."

"Aye, but we might take you as, say, a hostage. But forsooth, your life's o' no value to you or to your sovereign. Hi, an idea. Wait a mo, you men. 'Tis a device that will beat the best the King can do."

"You," to the man from the crow's nest, "lead us at once to the passengers' quarters. Or your head will pay the price."

To her escort she said.

"Bring them all on deck, in whatever state they're in. I'll be in the master's cabin."

Hostages! There was a name on the ship's roll that she had read. Where was it? Aye, there it was. She read aloud—

"Honourable Edwin Brangwin, son of a former Governor for the Lords Proprietors of the Carolinas. Boarded the vessel at Falmouth for passage to Charleston, Carolina. With all honours from the Admiralty and commending him to the care of all the King's Governor-Generals."

"'Tis honours he shall have," smiled the wench. "He'll give the settlement the tone it needs."

Then she went on deck to find the fourteen passengers, some in their small clothes and others in their night garments, standing against the larboard rail.

"The one known as Master Brangwin will step forward."

Into the arc of light cast by the lanthorn held at her right a slim, pale youth of twenty stepped. In his small clothes, his shirt opened at the throat, he looked a fine specimen of British young manhood. He wore a small wig, the nightwig of the macaroni, and the soft velvet breeches favoured by such dandies while at their ease. He stepped forward and in a soft, almost careless voice said:

"That is my name. What would you of me?"

There was nothing brazen in his manner nor was there fear. Unarmed and in the face of men he knew for cut-throats and desperadoes he did not flinch. Captain Read ordered the lanthorn held closer to his face. It was not an unpleasing one, showing some promise of strength, and the jaw was resolute.

"'Tis my thought to hold you as hostage against the violence of the master o' this vessel an' others o' the King's men. You may return to your cabin and prepare to leave the vessel. Ten minutes should be enough. Gregory, you accompany his lordship."

Mary turned on her heel and went again to the captain's cabin. There she took a piece of paper and a quill and wrote a note telling the master what she had done with his passenger. Then she ordered the man from the lookout locked in the passengers' quarters and the wheel of the West Indiaman lashed at a point south by south-east and went to the boats. Prayerfully hoping for a breeze that would carry the British vessel far off its course before dawn, before the men battened under the hatches could effect their escape, she bade her men lean on the oars. At two bells of the first morning watch she saw the last gleam of light from the West Indiaman as it slid into the darkness.

It was dawn before the pirates made the settlement and Mary's first order was to abandon the careening, to board the Blackbird and be off before the alarm could be given. The hostage was given a small cabin and placed in leg irons to cheat any attempt at escape. Two men were left as guards and at eight bells of the morning watch the Blackbird weighed anchor and made for Tortuga. The thought occurred to Buttons as she set her course that no matter where the West Indiaman made for, Jamaica, St. Kitts or even New Providence, it would be a month before a ship could come from one of those ports. In the note she had left behind her she had stated in no uncertain terms that at the first hostile sign the life of the Honourable Edwin Brangwin would be forfeit. The threat would only serve to delay the final moment, she knew. No one in the colonies would take it upon himself to condemn such a personage to death; that order, however inevitable, must come from the Admiralty, but it would come as sure as death and taxes. The majesty of the British Crown would offer up a thousand such lives to wipe out an affront such as she had offered it.

She might possibly evade the issue but, if so, it would be due entirely to her own quick thinking and her courage.

VII

The Honourable Edwin Brangwin took his capture as pretty much of a lark. He jollied his guard when that worthy came to take him to the master's cabin for his meal.

"But two pistols, man? And a single cutlass. 'Tis danger for you surely and your head would be forfeit should I escape. Better hold your pistols against my kidneys. An' be sure they're cocked." He laughed easily. "I hear your master's a wench, the Blackbird they call her. What manner o' men be you to accept service under a trollop?"

"Hold your tongue, sir. The master's word is to report to 'er all you say."

"Indeed? Then my compliments to madame and inform her that his lordship requires wine with his dinner. Will you now?"

"Aye, worship, every last word."

"And tell her, man," Brangwin whispered, "that I like not the interdiction placed upon my tongue at table. A civilized man talks while he satisfies the inner man. Tell her, too, that I think she is a very beautiful wench, but no, better I should mention that. A silence upon you."

The sailor did not reply but gently guided the young man to the door. He was one of four detailed to watch over the former Governor's son and he knew his life would be forfeit, not to the pirate wench but to the wrath of his fellows, should anything go wrong with their prisoner. In his safety they saw their one chance of escape. With him they might again take the King's Pardon, forgo piracy and settle down to the enjoyment of their constantly increasing wealth; the Grand Caicos could, in time, become a haven for such as they and every man jack of them wanted to make it a permanent home.

That evening, when the hostage was brought to the table, Mary Read was quick to question him:

"You care not for the silence imposed upon you."

"Nay, mistress. 'Tis a hardship for such as I."

"And," Mary's voice dropped but there was no trace of a blush, "you think I be a beautiful wench?"

"Aye, only beauty such as yours, madame, could inspire loyalty in your crew, cut-throats all."

"And you require wine at table?"

"If you please, madame."

Mary clapped her hands and ordered one of her black boys to bring several bottles of wine. She liked this youth, liked his easy grace and lack of fear. He had bowed low as he had entered her cabin, had helped her be seated and was now watching her every need and seeing that each was filled before she herself quite realized it. Mary grew a little self-conscious and tried to recall how her mistress had acted at table in the days when she had been a boy-in-waiting to the Frenchwoman. Putting together what she could remember of her childhood days with what her sharp eyes could gain from her prisoner, she made a better appearance than she had hoped for.

When dinner was finished, she asked that another bottle of wine be opened and she learned then that it is the duty of the man to entertain the woman; and she was rejoiced that her prisoner knew her for a woman. He poured the wine, was ever watchful that her cup was never empty; so when the watch called eight bells, the time for her evening inspection, she was reluctant to let him go back to his cabin. Also she felt giddy, and ascribed it to the wine. She must be strong, this way lay danger; in the future she would let him drink the wine whilst she listened to his pretty talk.

When her prisoner's guards had taken him away, she called her negro servant, and ordered a plentiful supply of wine sent to his cabin, then went on deck.

The effects of wine are short-lived; Mary had not taken enough to make her fox't in the morning but when she next saw the Honourable Edwin the giddiness reasserted itself, so it even came about that she was compelled to admit she felt more than a passing interest in her young prisoner.

The class from which the Governor's son had sprung, the semi-aristocracy, was a class which to Mary Read had always seemed slightly effeminate and lacking in courage. She had had the lower classes' suspicion of and distaste for men of his kidney; they were not men, rather something precious and fragile, to be left in the parlour when men went out to fight and love. They were, in a word, the privileged; she and her kind were those who battled and won.

If his wife had not been such a forthright woman it is doubtful if the obtuse Jones would ever have known of her growing fondness for their prisoner. As second in command, he had the cabin next to Mary's and the hostage had one which might have been assigned to a boatswain or a quartermaster. On the third day out of Grand Caicos Jones was summarily dismissed from his cabin and saw it given to the young aristocrat; the same day his wife threatened to banish him from her table because "thy manners would irk the very swine." The outraged husband debated as to whether he should take his quarrel to the crew or settle it himself—and chose the latter plan.

The wench's next concession to her prisoner was to remove all constraint; he was permitted to go and come as he pleased, even to sitting with the captain in the hammock on the deck. Whether Jones chose his time or simply took advantage of a spark that set the flame is impossible to say, but the inevitable outbreak came over a question of the handling of the vessel. It was four bells in the mid-morning, the time when the crew were accustomed to come aft with their pannikins for their ration of rum. Mary was on deck, chatting with the prisoner. The vessel was becalmed and the lookout had reported land dead ahead. Tortuga it was, and with any kind of a breeze they could make the port within a few hours. Tortuga was a clearing-house for all piratical gossip and it was the captain's intention to send ashore for news of the West Indiaman.

The Honourable Edwin was quite as anxious for news as Mary Read or her husband, though on a different score.

"Were you to clew up your top-gallants and reef your jib, the Blackbird would make Tortuga even in this calm," said the prisoner to the first officer.

"Aye, so say you," said Jones truculently. "And who be the navigator o' the Blackbird? Answer me that, sor."

Edwin laughed.

"You are most assuredly the navigator but that does not mean you are a good one. As a matter of fact, I'd say the Blackbird is a badly handled ship."

This was more than Jones could stand and he passed the blow to the prisoner who, knocked off his balance, had difficulty in drawing his sword. In a trice the men were at each other and only the intervention of Mary Read who thrust her body between the swords of the combatants, and cried out the rule that prohibited fighting on shipboard, kept blood from being spilled upon the deck. Still the two were not to be put off; honour had been questioned and the issue could be settled only with swords. Mary Read pointed to the shore far ahead and the men agreed they would settle the matter during the dog watch when Jones would be off duty.

The men on the deck cheered. Here would be a fight worth witnessing and all were for going ashore at two bells. Their loyalty went to Jones but some voices were raised in protest against endangering their hostage, the one person whose safety could save them from official wrath. On the quarterdeck the officers were with Jones to a man; only the captain remained silent, yet her inclinations were shown when she gave an order to clew the top-gallants and reef the jib, as the prisoner had suggested. Jones protested, but his wife told him she considered the Honourable Edwin's advice better than his.

"He's had his training with the Royal Navy. 'Tis plain he knows the more for that. Too, I like not your thought of fighting him."

"'Tis no question for a wench to decide," he answered shortly.

"Wench or not, I be the captain and with another word from you, I'll send you to the lazareet to cool off."

Then Mary went to her cabin and ordered the prisoner brought to her.

"I like not you fighting with Mister Jones," she said. She felt his sword arm. "'Tis little enough meat to that arm o' yours."

"Madame, have no fear of the outcome. I shall kill him or pink him as you direct."

Mary bade him draw his sword and defend himself, and she could not suppress a smile when she again saw his slender, needlelike rapier drawn from its sheath. Her own wide cutlass passed to and fro before his eyes and, with a gesture of contempt more for the sword than for the man, she struck his blade a blow with her cutlass that broke it off at the hilt.

"Take this, 'tis a man's weapon." She passed her cutlass to him and took another from the rack.

Edwin Brangwin tried to handle the heavy weapon as he had his rapier and the woman was able to pink him at will.

"'Tis no go," she said. "I'll have to forbid the fight."

"Pray, madame, do no such thing," he beseeched her. "I must fight e'en though it means death to me. Honour demands it."

"Honour, forsooth. That Jones will cleave you to your bowels. He's a rough one, that man."

"Were he not your husband, madame, I should have cut him down then and there upon the deck. Indeed, were he not madame's husband, there would be another tale entirely."

"What mean you, sir?"

Bowing, he placed his hand above his heart.

"I mean only, madame, that for the first time in my life I have met a woman I could love, a woman who would be more than wife, more, aye, than mistress. One who might be a companion so that the friendship of men would be unnecessary. 'Tis my misfortune that I've found you only to know you already married to another. But then, 'tis my good fortune to be able to remove the obstacle and I mean to do it."

Mary Read blushed for the first time in her life. She looked narrowly at the man, not knowing whether he was jollying her or not.

"Be you serious, my lord?" She almost trembled.

"Madame, I care not for jesting in such matters. I come from a race of warriors and in the New World, in Carolina, we have fought side by side with our women. 'Twas necessary. With a woman like you at my side I could open new lands to the glory of His Majesty." He paused to smile into her eyes. "'Twould be no great task to make you both widow and bride before the sun sets. Have I your permission to do so?"

Again Buttons blushed; for once she was out of her element. In matters of the heart she was accustomed to take what she wanted, by force if necessary, but never had she been courted before. Aye, let this man kill Jones if he could.

"Go to your quarters, sir. You are yet my prisoner."

Mary busied herself with her log to hide her embarrassment. The Governor's son stood for a moment and then went to the door; turning he bowed low and went to his own cabin. Once he was gone the log did not hold her attention long. There was much to be done before the two men could meet on what was called the field of honour. That her new love had little chance was evident; the men in the crew would not even wager on the result for it was unanimously conceded that Boatswain Jones would emerge the victor; Brangwin's nearest approach to support came from those sane members of the crew who deplored endangering their hostage.

As Mary sat at the noon meal with the prisoner on her right and her husband on her left, these last sent a delegation to her to protest the coming fight. The Honourable Edwin rose, asking permission to withdraw; his honour could not brook such interference with his personal affairs; therefore, regardless of the value of his person to his captors, the duel would take place.

"There will be no duel, men," Mary Read said quietly to the spokesman of the group.

"Thank'ee, captain," and the men withdrew.

"Madame," protested Brangwin, "I must request you not to concern yourself. I will not permit myself to be made ridiculous and contemptible. Better to die on Tortuga's beach than that."

Jones sneered.

"There's no doubt you'll die, my noble lord. You'll have your fine wish, come two bells."

"Bridle your tongue, Mister Jones," said his wife. "'Twill be my decision and you'll abide by it. I've said there'll be no duel and there's an end on't."

Mary applied herself to her food, wondering how she was going to make her statement good. Boatswain Jones, his mouth full of food, persisted in insulting the governor's son.

"Methinks the noble lord has aspirations to fill me boots. 'Twould do 'is 'eart good to ave me out of the w'y, so that he might take my station and aye, I'll say it, my bed and my wench. 'Tis a neatly clever trick, but one that I'll fox wi' me trusty blade. Fear not, my noble lord. Yon bed's mine and mine alone. The wench here, I trow, does not look upon your silken breeks with any loathing, but I'll put an end to it all, never fear."

"Take your plate elsewhere, Mister Jones! I'll have none o' your talk in my cabin. The bed's mine and who sleeps in it will be there at my asking. Get thee gone, an' in a trice!"

The boatswain did not tarry; he felt himself to be the master of the situation and was sure that before dusk could settle over the Caribbees the noble lord would be eliminated.

"I beseech you, madame, a thousand times not to meddle with this matter," the young man said. "I am certain I shall come out the victor and if I should not, death would be far preferable. May I leave, madame? I wish to prepare myself for the coming duel."

"Aye, sir."

Mary inclined her head toward him and smiled. She admired his courage, his eagerness for a fight that could end only in disaster. Such courage was worthy of a stronger body. He came to her and she rose as he took her hand to his lips. A chair toppled and fell over with a crash but they heard it not. His lips found hers and for a moment they stood holding each other tightly. A woman and a man, loved and loving.

"With this I cannot fail," the man said simply. Holding her hand to his lips, he kissed it and went to the door. "Worry not, lass, the duel's as good as won."

But worry Mary did, and in a most unpiratical fashion. She moped about the cabin for above an hour, half-hoping, half-praying for a prize to appear that the men might forget their differences in the common cause. But there would be few vessels save others of her own stripe that would dare the Tortuga shore. At six bells in the afternoon she went on deck to select an anchorage for the Blackbird. She found her husband arguing and disputing with the very men who had come to the cabin at noon. The men were urging him only to pink the noble lord and not to destroy him entirely, but Jones was unwilling to forgo his final drop of blood.

"Mister Jones," called Mary Read. "Mister Jones, how many times have I warned you against arguing wi' the company? If you've such a fondness for their company, by gar, you shall become one o' them. Come hither, 't'once."

But Jones went on with his defence of his intentions; the noble lord, he contended, was worth nothing as a hostage, there was danger that when they were taking a prize he might betray them all. He was, was he not, a navigator, and if his word was to be ta'en above that of the rightful navigator of the vessel, what was to stop him from delivering the Blackbird right into the Crown's hands?

"Answer me that!"

The men could not answer without betraying what was in their secret minds. They were by now rich men; they had all that for which they had come on the account, for the meanest pirate in the crew could claim ownership to as much as two thousand pounds. They wanted only to go ashore and enjoy themselves and the fear that they might stretch a rope before they could achieve their desires was making them uneasy. Too, they were getting fat and lazy.

"I'll spit him like a pig," Jones averred. "I'll have his heart's blood reddening Tortuga's sand, that's what I will."

From the poop came the shrill pipe of the master's whistle. The men rushed on deck to find the cause and Captain Read ordered the first two to bring Mister Jones to the quarterdeck. There was a short, sharp struggle and Jones, kicking and shouting, was carried to his wife.

"Mister Jones, I gave you an order, a civil order, and you did not obey. 'Tis in the articles of agreement, the Law of Moses is the penalty, forty stripes on the bare back less one. Do you understand, Mister Jones?"

"These laws be for the men. I am an officer of the deck."

"Aye, 'twould be bad for discipline to permit a high officer like yourself to be seen triced to the ratlines and I'd have to do the flogging myself an' I be in no mood for it. Release him, my men. But Mister Jones must be punished and I've a mind to see what manner o' man he be wi' the sword. Defend yourself!"

The last words were snapped out and Mary's cutlass was in her hand and waggling before her husband's nose. He was reluctant to cross arms with his wife but she was insistent.

"It's the lash, man, or this. The choice be thine."

"I've no mind to be fighting a wench," he said and the crew, watching from below, saw their captain deliver the navigator an insulting blow across the head with the flat side of her sword.

This stung Jones to the quick and as he drew he cursed his wife.

168

"It's a lesson I've been meaning to give a long time now," and the two were at it, pirate fashion.

The boatswain drew first blood, inflicting a slight wound on the captain's sword arm which only served to make her attack the more furious. The clashing of steel, the heavy, gusty sighing as each lunged or parried, the very ferocity of their attack meant they would weary quickly; if one did get the advantage there was danger he would be too weak to use it.

"I'll kill thee, damn wench, and make mysel' master o' this wessel. I'll kill thee deader'n a herring. Oop!"

The woman's sword had flashed up, down and across and then was pushed forward, and Jones' last exclamation came from his lips as her cutlass found a space between his ribs. He lay on the deck, his lungs pierced and the blood gasping from the wound with each breath.

"Ye begged for it, Jones, me lad," was all she said to him, turning on her heel and going to dress her own wound.

At the companion-way she ordered his body, "when he was finished wi' his dying," to be taken ashore and buried.

At eight bells Mary sent for the Governor's son and informed him there would be no duel.

"But madame, I cannot accept your decision. My honour demands that I fight Mister Jones."

"Then you'll be doing it with a spade. He's been buried this last hour. He disobeyed orders and was given his choice of punishment. He was a sturdy chap and——"

"Madame, you did this for me. 'Tis humiliating to have a woman fight one's battles. I am mortified."

"Nay, lad. You said you loved me, did you not? And I love you, I could never risk your heart to Jones' cutlass. You be a gentleman, you fight wi' honour, to the rules, but Jones knew no rules; he fought for blood and I'd be a poor master who'd permit my captive, aye, my love to be murthered."

"I am convinced I would have mastered him," he said.

"Forget it, lad. Did you not suggest marriage would be possible if it were not for him? Or did my ears deceive me?"

"Nay, lass, there was no deception. Be there a dominie on Tortuga?"

"Aye, if you need one. 'Tis the law of our kind that a master of a vessel may do in place of a dominie." Mary laughed. "Sure, now, couldn't I be marrying myself to you? I be the master o' this vessel. We'll ha'e our wedding here with the officers and others to witness it. How now, m'lad?"

169

Within a few hours the late boatswain was well-forgotten; the bride said she was a very happy woman—but when she sat down to supper she still sat at the head of the table and her hostage-husband was at her right.

Happy Pirate Wench!

Book Five - Gallows Cheat

I

A more curious mesalliance than this had probably never been consummated on land or sea, yet it was justified by the passionate love for each other of the principals. The Honourable Edwin Brangwin took to a pirate's life with surprising readiness. His wife had not insisted that he go with her on the account but he had offered and, where previously the pirates had been a bit reluctant to attack British vessels, Brangwin now insisted they were far more legitimate prey than the vessels of other nations. Also, he urged his bride not to be content with piracy alone but to raid small and unprotected colonies, the Barbadoes and other plantations.

"Nay, lover, I care not for such wantonness. A fat West Indiaman now and then, but no campaign against our own people. The King would be down on us 't' once."

"I see not the difference. We are all common sea-robbers and the wealth of any nation is our prize."

But Mary was adamant, reminding him that though he was master of her heart she was still master of the Blackbird. Later she learned the reason for her husband's hatred of the Crown. The Bahamas had been feudatory to the Carolinas and his father, one of the Lords Proprietors, and a former Governor of the colony had offered the son the governorship, had sent him to England for training and experience. The youngster had been about to go to his post when the Admiralty, wearying of the piracy in the Indies, had sent out Woodes Rogers. Thus the Islands had been taken away from the Lords Proprietors and made a Crown colony.

The reputation of Woodes Rogers was unsavoury enough and it looked to the Brangwins, father and son, as if they were being jobbed out of a very valuable colony. Young Brangwin had been at pains to have the new Governor withdrawn, but without success, and he was now only too happy to cripple Rogers in his efforts at reform. His one desire was to harass the colonial government at every possible point and it was only Mary Read's unwillingness to stick her head into a noose that kept her from doing his bidding.

Love held the pirate wench in its sway; she did all she could to please her lover, even making him navigator against some grumblings from her crew. The Honourable Edwin could handle the Blackbird better than his wife and now she no longer went to the wheel when she was about to attack; she could leave all that to her husband with confidence.

The pair continued their work of depredation and such was the fame of the pirate wench that all she had to do was to fire a warning shot and unfurl her ensign. Only ships with cannon and manned to repel pirates would stand against her once the terrible red and black ensign was broken out. She liked to fight, she cared more for matching her wits and courage against a male than for anything else. First came her ship, then her husband.

The men of the crew were of two minds regarding her marriage to their hostage. It was all of a month since the West Indiaman had been turned adrift and not even in Tortuga had the news gotten about. It seemed to the men on board the Blackbird that the crew of the prize were ashamed to admit that two hundred and odd men on a well-armed vessel had been taken by fifty pirates led by a woman and from open boats. There would be laughter for the crew in the offices of the Admiralty, loud, contemptuous laughter and a court-martial for the officers. There would be hell to pay and some of it would be visited upon the innocent head of Governor Woodes Rogers.

If there were any change in Buttons after her marriage to the high-born lad, it was only in the degree of intensity with which she attacked her prizes. Since the day of her first prize she had realized that surprise and daring were her best weapons. With her there was no cruising about a quarry looking for an opening, no parrying and seeking a strategical advantage. None of that. As soon as a quarry was sighted, the man at the wheel turned his vessel and then called out the news. The officers on the quarterdeck would apply their glasses and before they arrived at the scene of the coming conflict they knew pretty nearly all there was to be known of the enemy. Every man was at his station, every gunner was armed; in the rigging were the musketeers ready for the command to fire. Mary Read knew the terror of the average seaman for her flag but she did not relax her vigilance; there was no way of telling when a vessel might play the part of a decoy and seemingly accept her command to stand to so it might better destroy her.

The Honourable Edwin marvelled at the completeness of her preparation and work. Not even aboard the vessels of the Royal Navy, he told her, had he seen anything that could surpass it. She went into action like a shot from her own guns and her attack was as devastating as a complete broadside from her vessel.

Mary sought her husband's encomiums and increased her energy in attacking vessels far larger than her own.

"I trow you'd go against one of the King's eighty-fours without two thoughts on the matter," Edwin said.

But stories of a change in the woman captain went through the crew. It was said that in the privacy of her cabin she would don for her husband the clothes of her sex and let him teach her to be the lady. The trunks that had mystified Boatswain Jones now gave up rich garments of brocade, silks and satins, silken hose and jewelled shoes and slippers. One of the crew, coming to her cabin in the night to report lights on the starboard bow, had returned to his post to tell his fellows of a strange wench on board.

"A bedizened wench, the likes o' which you'd never before seen. Painted, she was, like a bloody whore, wi' her hair in a peruke and hanging wi' jewels.

"A lady she thinks she is and far too good for the likes o' us. 'Tis the pirate wench, our master, and I said no good'd come from 'er taking up wi' the macaroni."

Another came in from the deck and announced that no attention was to be paid to the lights, that the Blackbird was to stick to her course which would take them back to Grand Caicos.

The settlement had grown in the absence of the Blackbird, not alone from the captured slavers Mary Read had been sending there, but from the human flotsam and jetsam that drifted hither and yon seeking the easy money the pirates had so hardly won. These worthies set up shops and cabanas, games and other devices to take the pirates' wealth as easily and quickly as possible. The single street, at the head of which the wench had built her own house, was now crowded with various types of buildings, from those built with timber from captured prizes to the thatched huts of the negroes. There was some legitimate business done but it was small in comparison with the amount of money that daily changed hands.

The Governor's son was installed in the mistress' home and daily he went in silks and brocades for his promenade. He could not mingle with the pirates; they would have none of him and his high-born manners. If he wanted to drink, he must do it in the company of his wife or his fellow-officers whose social standing was no greater than that of the men beneath them. The Honourable Edwin was the loneliest man in the settlement and he was constantly urging his wife to return to the high seas. She knew her men and never forgot that her high position was held only through them, that they would depose her and replace her with another as soon as they lost confidence in her.

Among the runagates that came to the Grand Caicos hoping to find another Port Royal or New Providence, a Rogue's Harbour, was one who had real news. The French, it was said, were founding a new city on the Louisiana Plantations and were in need of goods and slaves, both commodities of which

173

Mary Read had more than enough. She had heard of this other colony, indeed two of her recent prizes had been vessels consigned to the new port. New Orleans it was called and within the first year of its founding it had almost five hundred citizens, including slaves. It was, it was said, a bustling community, trading furs and pelts for food and tools. Too, there was some gold for trading.

Mary's settlement had too many slaves on hand; a score could do the menial labour and, as there were about three hundred of them, they made serious inroads upon the food supply. Many of them had been put to work at gardening and raising their own food, others to fishing and hunting. Men from other islands, buccaneers, came to trade their produce for rum and other necessities, finding an industrious village and a happy one for all the lack of law and order.

The pirate wench cared not for the company of her own sex, of whom there were in her settlement about a score of whites, English, Spanish and French. She dressed as of yore when she went abroad, saving her feminine appearances for her husband. The decision as to what to do about the new French colony was to be hers. She would, she determined, load what she could upon the Blackbird, take it to Louisiana and trade with the Frenchmen; she would drive a hard bargain for their gold, their furs held little interest. Then, her trading complete, she would revert to piracy.

But she was not to go on the honourable trading bout. One morning the lookout on the hill reported a sail coming into the harbour. The pirates assembled for the attack but the stranger sailed directly toward the settlement and dropped his anchor. His vessel was a three-masted fore-and-after and sat so high in the water that almost any pirate would have ignored her. A smallboat put out from the shore and Mary, who was watching from her house, saw her own flag broken out at the foremast of the vessel, a signal that here, indeed, was a customer.

The ship was a Yankee, out of Boston, and her captain had heard that on Grand Caicos goods were to be had cheaply for cash. He was a bluff chap who showed no fear of the pirates' double-dealing. He could use some fifty slaves, he said, and would take a look at the stores. He found much he wanted, but the pirates balked at his prices, so low were his offers. Ten pounds a head for slaves in good health, the same as he would pay for them in Sierra Leone, and the pirates could take it or leave it, as they pleased.

"You've such a chest of gold," suggested Mary, "that it might be of interest to us without your purchases."

"Nay, man, I've come prepared for that. Ten thousand pounds I've got for trading but none of it is to be spent until my safety's assured."

"My men could take your vessel and your gold." ventured the wench. "What then?"

"You may take my vessel and my life but you'll find no gold on board. I took care o' that."

"I'll wager you did," said Mary Read.

"That I did," the Yankee leered. "I buried it back on an island known only to mysel'. When my purchase is complete I'll take two o' your men hence with a sma' boat to return wi' the gold."

"But how am I to know you are to be trusted? What'd it boot us were you to show us a clean pair o' heels and a merry laugh?"

The Yankee bridled.

"I be a man of honour and such trickery be below me."

And so it proved. A bargain finally agreed upon, he took with him two pirates in his own vessel and permitted himself to be followed by half a dozen more in a small ketch, leading them to a small cay, just north of the Caicos, where he revealed the spot where he had buried his gold. The amount was found to be correct, so the money was taken aboard the ketch, together with the two men from the Yankee vessel, and the sale was consummated.

For his ten thousand pounds the Yankee sailed away with a handsome cargo of Staffordshire ware, Lyons silks, Manchester metal wares and almost one hundred healthy slaves. He would put in at Philadelphia and New York, he said, and sell what he could and both the pirates and the trader knew that even with poor business his wealth would increase fivefold and perhaps more.

Taking leave of the men who had come for the gold, the skipper sent a message to the pirate chief, that he would return in the fall and hoped for another successful business deal.

With the Yankee's ten thousand pounds divided Mary Read took counsel of her husband regarding New Orleans. She had heard of Biloxi and its prosperity but she knew little or nothing of the Gulf ports and she went about the settlement asking questions of all newcomers. Much of her information was false but all of it inclined her to the idea of raiding rather than trading with the new town. She heard of a John Law and his schemes for great riches, that the French were pouring gold into his coffers, but she also learned that little of this gold was going through to Louisiana. The English and Dutch were sending adventurers thither with the intention of getting as large a share as possible for themselves and their nationals; these men, to further their interests, were known to be plentifully supplied with gold coin and it was these fellows on whom she had designs.

II

What with marriage and love, her settlement and a hundred other matters, the year 1720 had arrived before Mary Read was able to outfit for New Orleans. Her illegal cache on Grand Caicos had become well-known and many American and Colonial merchants had made profitable purchases. Two other pirates had been using the port for the sale and distribution of their prizes; these were Bart Roberts and Charles Vane. Calico Jack Rackham had visited Mary Read but had not been asked to participate in her business because the wench did not trust him.

When Mary announced her intention of sacking the new port in Louisiana and called for volunteers, she found that but fifty of her men responded, the others deciding against the venture because of the danger and the possibility of little profit. She herself felt it would be little more than an adventure but there was more than she told in the back of her mind. The ill-fame of the Caicos was spreading and it might be but a few months before Woodes Rogers would learn of the place and send his vessels to storm it. In a colony such as Louisiana, Mary had an idea that with her husband and a few select souls she might find a harbour where she could swallow the anchor and settle down for a life of comfort.

The Honourable Edwin was still second in her thoughts, only the Blackbird taking precedence. Piracy was again in bad straits, only Vane and Rackham and Roberts and a few lesser lights still being active. Captain Yeates had gone and taken a belated Pardon, the others had stretched their last lanyards. Her own fate had taken far too many chances and she was too wealthy now to take many risks. With the money she had taken, plus Jones' and Edwin's shares, the couple were worth a quarter of a million pounds; enough to keep them in luxury for the balance of their lives.

Mary Read would this year celebrate her nineteenth birthday, still the youngest member of her company if the two slave boys were excepted. For three years she had been on the account, having begun with a distinct distaste for the life but by now craving it and unwilling to admit that the end of piracy was in sight. It was not that the merchants were not as fat and fatter than ever before, not that there were not more of them. Ports like New Orleans were opening up all along the American coasts, the British Crown was shipping more colonists than ever to the wide-flung empire, food and goods were following these movements of people and the ships carrying these necessities were the prizes the pirates sought. But Woodes Rogers, in whose bailiwick Mary Read had set up her rendezvous, was more determined than ever to wipe buccaneering from the waters of his province. Every vessel not needed in commerce, from ketches to brigs, was armed and sent after the marauders; the smaller vessels trading between the islands were armed and instructed to shoot to kill and to destroy. One by one the great pirates fell or were driven to other seas. Bartholomew Roberts was off for Madagascar; Vane was to be hanged shortly in Port Royal; Frank Spriggs had been ingloriously chased across the seas and had taken refuge on land, in the woods, where he still languished. Others had gone to the Pacific and far South Atlantic, but most had stretched the ropes from gallows trees.

The pirate wench's men felt strongly the urge to settle down. On more than one occasion now armed merchantmen had turned upon them; twice such results had driven them off, not ignominiously yet decisively enough to permit the quarry to get into a port.

Mary knew she could barely handle her vessel with fifty men and she planned to stop at Tortuga and at Calico Jack's rendezvous for recruits; indeed, if she failed at those ports she would go to the Isla de Piños and pick up as filthy a bunch of ruffians as she could find. At Tortuga she got fifteen and at Puerto Principe she found Calico Jack Rackham unwilling to go so far afield and his men mostly of the same temper as he; she did, however, manage to induce five of his scoundrels to join her company.

Calico Jack was jubilant for more reasons than one. His mistress had given birth to a child, the one whose paternity had been open to question, and then, less than a year later, had presented him with a pair of sons who needed only gaily coloured breeks to make them the living spits of their sire. Anne Bonney took Mary Read to see her brood, now in charge of Mrs. Fulworth, and slyly confessed to Buttons that she was again with child. She and Calico Jack had practically come to an agreement to abandon piracy and to return to Carolina to claim the woman's inheritance.

Another reason for the pirate's happiness was that he had settled his long-standing feud with Captain Dick Turnley, a pirate himself who posed as one of the King's men and who had informed Woodes Rogers on many occasions of Calico's whereabouts. The two pirates had met off Tortuga and Calico had sunk Turnley's sloop, driving the man ashore and taking what remained of his company as recruits for his own.

Jack's natural laziness and his new responsibilities as a family man made "the main account" too hazardous an undertaking and he was now awaiting only an opportunity to be through with it all.

Supremely contemptuous of Rackham, Mary Read, with her husband and seventy-five in her company, sailed not for the Isla de Piños but direct for New Orleans. She would assault the port with her small company even though the Honourable Edwin was opposed to it.

"If it is a fat port you are seeking, lass," he said, "why not one of the Spanish towns, or better still, New Providence itself? 'Twould please me mightily to come to grips with that cheild, Woodes Rogers, his honour, the King's Governor. I've a long-standing grudge to settle with the upstart. After that, we can take New Orleans."

"Nay, lover. My plans first and then yours," and Mary called the course to the man on the poop-deck and went to her cabin.

There was one in her crew, a man she had taken on at Tortuga, who had been to New Orleans within the year, and she had him in the cabin to tell her of the town. She got from him only that there seemed to be much money in circulation, and that the population had grown from a few hundred to five times that number, almost two thousand souls, within the past year. One Jean Baptiste Le Moyne, Sieur de Bienville, was the Governor, and, taking advantage of the Mississippi scheme of John Law, he had won many important concessions from the French Crown. Money and goods were pouring in, as many as three ships a week arriving with slaves and merchandise.

It was late in the summer when the Blackbird came to the mouth of the great river, the Mississippi. She stood off in the Gulf, the British ensign flying, and took in the lay of the land. It was not entirely prepossessing. The little islands that made up the delta were verdant green and the man who had been to New Orleans told her it was a matter of six or eight leagues to the new settlement. To the pirate wench the place looked like a trap and she felt an unwillingness to put her head into a noose, especially one made of French rope. Mary still believed that she would evade the fate of so many pirates; still boasted that she'd cheat the gallows in the end.

On the vessel two men were placed at the bow with leads to sound and she sailed under the barest canvas. Mary's caution and her fear of French trickery led her to keep every man at his station but without any show of arms. It required two and a half days to make the town and when she saw it she gave one of her harsh laughs. It was hardly worth the taking.

She was immediately visited by the Sieur de Bienville who asked her mission and cargo and to see her vessel's papers.

"Indeed, I came but to purchase, milord. What 'ave ye for sale or barter?" There was a canny leer in the pirate wench's eyes.

"English, heh!" said De Bienville. "Some of your men look to me like the veriest of buccaroons. I beseech you, sir, to give but a portion of them shore leave at the one time. Our accommodations are limited."

"Aye, few enough will be needed for my purpose," said the wench. "Say, but a score."

"Merci, m'sieu. If you will but set your time I shall be happy to show you through our stores," the Governor said.

"Now's as good a time as any," Mary suggested. "I shall bring but a small escort."

"And your papers?" This politely.

"Oh, aye, my papers. This way, milord Governor."

Mary led him to her cabin, calling two of her huskiest men to follow, offered De Bienville a seat and called for wine, the finest on board. Then she introduced her navigating officer and sat herself at the table.

"Bring me," she said to one of the huskies, "that chest. Lift it carefully to the table."

When the heavy trunk was on the table she loosed the catch and, tilting it forward, spewed its contents over the table top, a flood of golden louis that rolled to the floor, clinking and ringing. De Bienville, a rich man by birth, had never seen so much money at one time. Mary Read bowed low and said, smiling:

"Aye, milord, I see you and I speak the same language. 'Tis the only papers men o' our stripe need."

De Bienville's eyes sparkled. He forgot the formalities of papers, forgot his sense of danger. He had much to sell this vessel of questionable origin but whose wealth was that of his own land.

"If m'sieur will but make use of my smallboat, we can be to our business at once."

The pirate wench called for her husband and two of her most likely-looking musketeers. Bidding the men wait for her on the deck, she dressed herself in her finest clothes. Then she entered De Bienville's tender and was rowed to the town.

Mary found a settlement better situated than her place at Grand Caicos, more substantial buildings and warehouses far too large for the merchants' present needs. The levee, on the west side of the river, had tables under palm trees. Here the wench was seated and the traders of the town, almost as villain-ous-looking as her own company, brought their goods to her, principally furs and fresh water pearls. She was served with French wine and little frosted cakes. Mary asked many questions of each trader before dismissing him, not-ing that De Bienville always prefaced his introduction with remarks as to "the master's great wealth of louis d'ors." In what little French she could muster she informed the merchants that her tastes were catholic, that all she wished was an opportunity to strike a good bargain in goods that she might sell in England and the Colonies. They assured her that their prices would be just and she asked for the night to decide on her choice. That would, for one with such great wealth, be granted happily; as many nights as she chose.

"I would see your town, milord Governor. I, too, have a settlement but not one so grand as yours. Mine is in the Bahamas where milord Woodes Rogers plays at being Governor."

"Indeed, m'sieur, we'll be that happy to show New Orleans to you."

There were several taverns, a bank, shops, bazaars, warehouses, and the ever-present cabanas of the women of the town.

"My good men will enjoy their liberty here. But twenty will be granted leave for this night. They may prove a rough lot but 'twill be mostly noise. Pay no 'tention to their merry-making, milord."

"We've many of that kind of our own," said De Bienville with meaning. "I've no fear but that our civil guard will be able to care for even the roughest."

Mary Read carefully noted every place of interest and value in the town, the location of the bank, the better bazaars and shops. Her half-formed plan was to send as many men ashore as would be permitted and at a given signal to attack, the guns on the Blackbird reducing all resistance in a surprise. She picked out the Spaniards and Portuguese in her company, deciding their natural enmity for all things French would make them the most aggressive. There were a couple of bazaars rich in clothing that she had decided to take, the bank and a slave barracoon. Except for the fur warehouses there was little else in the town of value to pirates.

Back on the Blackbird Mary explained her plans, pointing out from the deck the various points of attack, also where the men on shore would begin and where, at the other end, they would wait for boats from the vessel to bring them back.

Just before dark two men rowed to the Blackbird and came on deck. They asked for the master and, having been shown to her cabin, informed Mary Read that they were representatives of the Sieur de Bienville, who had sent them to say that all prohibitions as to the number of the company to come ashore had been removed.

"We find," said one, "that we will be able to entertain the entire company. In fact, we wish it; we desire to entertain our good friends in a manner befitting their important mission. You are, sire, our first English customer. M'sieur Le Moyne wished us to lay aside our own concerns and welcome our English friends. You yourself are to meet the Governor at La Belle de Joie to dine."

The speaker bowed low and retreated a step. At this point, and Mary Read could bless her husband for it, the Honourable Edwin stepped forward and suggested the entertainment be postponed until the following night, that is, as far as the master was concerned. General leave would be accorded as many of the company as was possible but many of the men would be required on the ship.

The ambassadors retired after informing the master that couriers had been sent out to bring in as many adventurers as possible. Most of these could remain only the one evening and would have to return to their traps and plantations at dawn but, since it would not be possible to entertain the master, they would do their best by the crew. At the rail, before they entered their tender, they delivered what was expected to be their telling shot.

"There will be many French girls who, we know, have a very high regard for English seamen."

"Look ye, lass," said Edwin when the ambassadors had left the vessel, "what make you of this invitation?"

"Nothing, lover, save that the Frenchmen have seen the colour o' our gold. They are stretching themselves to be nice to us."

"You're right, lass. They have seen the colour of our money and I bid you be on your guard. I shall stay by the ship. I scent danger."

"Toosh! What danger can come from a lot o' land-locked Frenchies? But as you stay on board, so do I."

The party of leave was increased to forty and all were given the same instructions. They would foregather at one of the commons at the upper end of the town and, when the signal was given, they would go forth to take New Orleans. Smallboats would later go out and return them to the Blackbird.

Darkness fell and the men detailed for land duty took to the smallboats and were rowed ashore. They were greeted by citizens who held torches high that they might see the way. Mary and Edwin watched and were not troubled when they saw nothing of the Governor; it was hardly within his province to greet men of the company. They did recognize the ambassadors of that afternoon and other leading men of the new town.

At two bells, which to the people of the town was nine in the evening, one of the starboard guns of the Blackbird fired a shot at the town. It was but a signal, no shell raked any building, and from the poop the wench could see her men emerge from the ordinary. But it must also have been another kind of signal. From forward came a cry, the cry of a man taken by surprise and cut down before he could defend himself. Another cry, "Repel boarders!" and Mary piped all hands to their stations. Too many were ashore and the fight was too fast for the small company. Unsheathing her cutlass and ordering her husband and the man at the wheel to follow, Mary flew to the deck and entered the mêlée. To the right and left her cutlass flew, swiping a head here, cutting another there. In the dim lights of the ship's lanterns, it was impossible to distinguish friend from foe.

"Larboard cannoneers to your stations! Load and fire at will!"

Half a dozen men detached themselves and went to the cannon to obey the captain's orders. In a minute Mary heard the cannon, a staccato firing as her few gunners raked the little town. But her cutlass took no relief; she went on, driving before her friend or foe, caring little which he was so long as he faced her. At her side she heard a familiar voice say:

"Good work, lass. Another such attack and we'll have them in the muddy waters."

"Forward!" she screamed. And suited her actions to the word.

Someone of the settlement Frenchmen had heard of the pirate wench and shouted the knowledge to his fellows.

"La Femme Inconnue! La Boucanierre!"

The cry was enough for all who heard and they forthwith leaped over the railing and into the Mississippi. The cry was repeated ashore, cannon mounted on the levee began dropping shells about the Blackbird.

"Weigh anchor," cried Mary Read and hurried aft to lift the one anchor the Blackbird had out to steady her position.

The capstan groaned and creaked and in another minute the vessel was floating with the tide downstream. Without a pilot she drifted for less than ten minutes before she ran aground. But she was around the bend; the mêlée had subsided, the Blackbird was out of range. New lights were brought and the dead on the deck, both friend and foe, were heaved overboard. A check-up of the crew revealed that of the forty men on board at the time of the attack, twelve were missing and eight were so badly wounded they were useless. Mary Read, believing that the town's booty was hardly worth the effort of further attack, sat on her poop awaiting the dawn.

The pirate wench's frenzy was too great to be endured. She blamed herself for bringing her men to such a dangerous spot, for attacking the town without sufficient knowledge of the people: yet the truth of what had happened she did not guess. The pirates had not been double-crossed nor had they, as they now thought, run upon a den of thieves incorporated into a legal township. They had merely been the victims of a band of thieves who had used the planned celebration as a cover for a grand attack upon a rich merchant. They had called in men of questionable repute, among them one who had recognized the wench and some of her men. The call for voyageurs had brought to the town almost a hundred men, little better than pirates, who were willing to give the pirate a taste of his own medicine.

De Bienville, an honourable man, was no party to this counter-raid; he had been confined to his own plantation by men from the conspirators' army. But indeed, if Mary had known this, it would not have changed her desire for revenge.

The Blackbird rested on the mudbar and from her position it seemed she might stay there until she rotted. Calling to a sailor to throw a lanyard over the bow, Mary lowered herself, hand over hand, to the bar and saw that the vessel could be poled back into the stream. It took above an hour to accomplish this and the wench's temper increased with every passing minute.

When light came, Mary peered through the mist for a sight of the men who had gone ashore. None came and she was for manning a smallboat and going in search of them when Edwin pointed to a man on shore, waving his hands to attract their attention. A smallboat was sent to bring him aboard. He was one of Calico Jack Rackham's men and he had a sad story to tell.

The forty men who had gone ashore had been killed or taken prisoner, all save himself. They had followed orders and at the signal had gone directly to the bank and broken down the door; if there had ever been any gold in the building, it had been removed. They had then gone to the bazaars that had been indicated for ravaging and these, too, were found to be empty. Then, as the men had approached La Belle de Joie they had been overwhelmed by the trappers called voyageurs, numbering over a hundred and fifty, who had cut them down like reeds. The speaker alone, so far as he could know, had managed to escape. It had been hell for half an hour and he had learned what fighting could be.

The Honourable Edwin dismissed the man after giving him a large beaker of straight rum. They had, he informed his wife, but twenty-odd men left on board; they could hardly be expected to repel any concerted attack. But Mary was hardly listening to him.

The pirate wench had foreseen the time when she would have to admit defeat; she was too much of a gambler not to know that she could not make a win every time she cast her dice. But defeat at the hands of a lot of scurvy Frenchies, dirty thieves who were too cowardly to go boldly on the account, who sat and waited for their prey and then sneaked upon them under cover of darkness, was too much. She had no illusions as to the nature of her own enterprise; she was a thief and so were her men, but in their law-breaking they added something of gallantry and daring to the act. They came out fighting, showing their guns and giving their quarry to understand their business.

Mary lay to the south of the new city and awaited the reorganization of her forces. Her original intention had been to raid the settlement, to take anything of value to herself and her company. Now she would do just that but she would also revenge the scabrous death of her men; in addition to pillaging, there would be raping and destroying. She would fire the town.

To Edwin she said:

"They moved their gold from the bank for security. Now that they've driven us off, they'll move it back. Do you see, man?"

The Honourable Edwin did see. And he set about reorganizing the shattered company. Twenty effectives! Twenty whole men against a population of five hundred. It couldn't be done. Not even with the most extraordinary surprise. But, if his wife wanted it, she should have it.

Mary brought the Blackbird about in the wide waters and took her to within half a mile of the settlement, hidden from sight. Leaving the vessel in command of her husband and taking but fifteen men with her, she landed on the muddy shore. Then she took her little troop around the town and before sunset they were north of the place. The wench knew her men and, before sending them out on their tour of ravaging the settlement, she passed out triple rum rations to all.

"Forty men good and true gave their lives to these Frenchies. First we'll hack our way to the bank, take their gilt, and then back to the ship. Spare no one who attempts to thwart our designs. Kill any daft enough to come within sword's length o' ye. Forward with the Black Peter."

Quickly the pirates descended upon the now dark town. There were few citizens afoot, the voyageurs having returned to their traps or to the woods, and most of these were at La Belle de Joie. The wench's men used their cutlasses on the first to object to their passage. The bank, they found, was still empty, and so were most of the bazaars. Only the taverns were open.

Thwarted, Mary said to the men:

"We can't spend the time to root out their gold, no one can understand a Frenchman's mind when its dealing wi' money, so we'll go from barracoon to slave-house and drive every blackamoor before us. That'll bring them to terms."

There were at that time over two hundred blacks in New Orleans and three-quarters of the total, men, women and children, were routed from their huts and barracks and driven ahead of the pirates. The French offered some resistance but were afraid, eventually, to fire into the group for fear of killing their own people. As each hostile man or woman appeared he was pounced upon, disarmed and made to carry as much loot as he was able. Along the bank they were driven until they came upon the Blackbird at anchor. The whites were sent aboard the vessel, the blacks kept on shore under guard.

When dawn came Mary Read sent food ashore for her captives. Then she had her white prisoners, a mere ten men and six women, brought on deck for

184

inspection. The women, save one, were filles de joie and these already had made the most of their opportunities. The lone chaste woman was the wife of one of the men taken, a German who looked as if he might have some standing in the community. Briefly the pirate wench stated the facts to him.

She had come for gold and wanted it. The wary French had hidden it in the woods and her time was too limited to go in an extended search for it. She would sell them the captured slaves at ten louis d'or a head, the whites at a hundred louis, and trading could begin at once. The husband was to go ashore to open negotiations, Mary being assured that in his effort to redeem his frau, he would gain the better terms.

"But, mein Herr," declared the emissary. "Truly there is not that much money in the town."

"You've heard my terms. Go hence and tell your Governor what they are and that I am in great haste. For each day lost in waiting for his action a louis will be added to the price of the blackamoors and ten louis to that of the white hostages. Go, quickly. My hand that no man o' my company meddles wi' your wife."

"Ja, mein Herr! I hurry."

"One minute. If there is a single false move or any attempt to take my prisoners by force I'll blow blacks and whites to pieces wi' my cannon. Get thee gone."

The man clambered over the side, dropped into a smallboat and rowed himself ashore.

"Lover," Mary Read said to her husband, "you speak the language o' these people so I leave the negotiations to you. Make as good a deal as possible. Any blackamoors they cannot purchase are to be sent aboard to help work the vessel. Come here, into these shadows, an' gi'e me a buss."

The Honourable Edwin did as he was bid.

"'Tis a rough woman you picked for yourself and a woman who needs a lot o' lovin'."

"Aye to all that, my own. I would not exchange you for the most exquisite wench in all England. You are a woman among women and 'tis glad I am I got you." He kissed her again and she pushed him away roughly.

"You disturb me greatly, though I dislike it not. Hurry wi' the deal an' come to me in the cabin."

By noon several individuals from the settlement had appeared upon the bank but De Bienville was not among them. Edwin went ashore and briefly stated the pirates' demands. He pointed to the Blackbird and called attention to the guns on the starboard side, each manned and ready for action.

"Beware treachery, my friends. Captain Read is sore put to it for the loss of his men and he would just as lief return and blow the town from its piles."

The whole episode, which has been considered unimportant by historians, ended by Mary Read's sailing down the delta with eleven thousand louis d'ors and some score black men and women to handle the Blackbird.

III

Calico Jack Rackham greeted Mary Read with a laugh. All that the pirate wench returned of the men he had loaned to her was the one who had saved himself in the shore fight.

"'Twas a brave sally, lass, but piracy's done for. Far better it be to go ashore and put your money out to work for ye. There be the Rancour, ready to sail, and I thought to try for your rendezvous. The Spaniards hereabouts have joined wi' the English an' 'twill be all we can do to get away."

"I think you're yellow, Calico. I intend recruiting a new company and taking a look about. There's many a fat merchant left an' I'm not through yet."

"What of your boast to cheat the gallows? To my mind you're putting your head i' a noose that's already knotted."

"Nay, I stretch no hemp. I be after a company o' men. Do I get them here or do I go to the Isla de Piños?"

"Take whom you will, lass. 'Twill be the less to feed from our stores, so slender they be getting."

But the pirate wench could not recruit a new company at Puerto Principe. Calico's men had made themselves comfortable, taking mestizo women as wives, setting up little homes and raising families.

"'Tis a soft crew you boast, Calico, an' I be off for Piños."

There was mutiny in her own crew at the news, not downright rebellion but muttering and grumbling. The men wanted first to go to Grand Caicos and not turn on their tracks. They had no desire to give the runagates at Piños a majority in their company. First, they demanded, let us get our own men at Caicos. This the pirate wench consented to on condition they leave her at Puerto Principe. She had no mind to appear at the settlement with the disaster at New Orleans hanging over her. She must return in triumph or not at all. She packed her things in a single trunk, the gaudy leathern one with copper bindings. In it she put her best clothes, and a sum of money for any necessary expenditures; then she turned the Blackbird and its treasure over to the Honourable Edwin and, moving aboard the Rancour, was given a cabin next to that of Anne Bonney. Anne's jealousy had subsided; she was in the fifth month of her pregnancy and was now assured of her lover's devotion. Mary stood on the poop deck of her old ship and watched the beloved Blackbird put out to sea.

Almost before she was out of sight some mestizos came out in a canoe and informed Calico Jack that a British frigate was cruising along the coast to the westward. Rackham was safe if the enemy had not learned of the rendezvous; his vessel might remain where it was and not be discovered by the most curious. If the rendezvous were known, he was in a trap from which there could be no escape save on the land—and too many pirates had died in the Cuban jungles to make that haven attractive. In consultation with Mary Read, Calico decided to make a run for it. The Rancour, always a speedy vessel, had been recently careened; with all sails set she might make Cocos Point before the frigate could come up.

All sails were crowded on, every man at his post alert and ready for any eventuality. Whatever happened, the Rancour would not surrender. It was five leagues to the Point; there they might anchor inside and wait for the morning, and at dawn make a long, clean run of it, swinging up the Bahama Bank, through the Florida Channel and then around the Islands and down to Caicos. As night fell their plan had worked as they had laid it out. Extra lookouts were posted to report any lights but no calls were heard in the night.

When the Caribbean dawn came, a dawn terrible to behold, there was an added terror. There, blocking the passage of the Rancour, stood an eighty-four gun ship of the line, her larboard cannon trained upon the pirate vessel, every man of her company on the alert. A single gun spoke, a shot flew across the deck of the pirate and no gun answered. After a conference, Calico ordered his anchors up, every sail set; he would, he averred, yet make a run for it. It would be either death or deep water. He looked at the two women and ordered Anne Bonney to her cabin.

"I'll call you, lass, if we have to take to the boats." he told her.

To Mary Read, he said: "On yon yardarm hangs your rope. Take command of the gunners and let them not relax. We'll go down wi' our vessel first." He smiled but it was not a smile that encouraged.

If it was the Rancour's intention to run for it, it was the H.M.S. Fearless's plan not to permit it. Calico sent his Black Peter to the top and went himself to the wheel. This move was greeted by a broadside from the enemy who was manoeuvring to come to the grapples; the Royal captain wanted to take both the vessel and the pirates back as trophies. The Rancour's cannons spoke and were answered with another broadside, a withering one to the pirate. Mary Read urged her gunners to greater speed, but the accuracy of the warship's fire had taken all the fight out of them.

"Come, load, fire! Faster! Are ye daft you let a few shells make you fox't wi' fear? Load! Fire!"

She screamed her commands, seeking to urge her men on with frenzy. Yet each broadside from the warship silenced one or more of her cannon.

Looking up to see if Calico had further commands, Mary was surprised to see the Black Peter come tumbling to the deck. Not until later did she learn that it had not been lowered but that its lanyard had been cut away by a shot.

"Prepare to repel boarders," she cried, drawing one of her pistols and her cutlass.

Where was Rackham? He was no longer on his own poop deck and Mary, believing he had been cut down, retreated there to take his place, all the time crying her orders to the men on deck. When she got to her point she found Anne Bonney there, a sash of pistols about her, a cutlass in her hand.

"Aye, lass, we'll give them the good fight." The two women would have shaken hands but for the fact that they held weapons in both. "Shoulder to shoulder and we'll not be ta'en."

But the Rancour's company offered no resistance to the boarders. The King's men swarmed over the pirate's decks and up the ladder to the poop. Mary and Anne fired their pistols and tossed them aside to take others, making all their shots pay for themselves; then with cutlasses bared in their right hands they met the next men. Thrust, parry and thrust again. Mary made every stroke count. Here was a man any woman in her right mind might love, a handsome chap, a gentleman and a swordsman—but 'tis no time for meeting or loving. Down he goes, his forehead gashed and here is another, looking for trouble. Before he could have said "halloo" his chest gushed red and he sank over the pirate wench's cutlass, his ribs holding it tight. Before she could withdraw it the others were upon her, bearing her to the deck, disarming her.

"'Tis a lass," cried her captor, holding her about the shoulders and from the rear. "By my trow, 'tis a woman."

"Aye," said another. "The pirate wench, Captain Buttons Read o' the Black-bird. I'd a-knowed her i' the dark. Where's the other, the one in the wench's clothes?"

"Zonder, 'neath the tender. Bring her out! 'Tis a haul to delight the Governor's heart. Where's Calico Jack, the master?"

"Below decks. We'll be needing stench bombs to bring him out."

Mary and Anne were held by strong hands while the men on the deck below sought to oust Calico and his company. Mary remained silent, looking for an opportunity to escape to the rails; Anne hurled invective and vituperation on all and sundry.

"Oooee, what brive men, ye be! Indeed, I can see that ye be a fine lot of — —
— —. Ooh, aye. A fine — — —, indeed. You there, wi' your gold lace, you
must be an admiral or a captain o' the head, by the cut o' your — — clothes!"

It took but a half a dozen stench bombs to bring the company of the Rancour
on deck, hands aloft. They were herded together and Anne's insults were now
no longer directed at the victors but at her cowardly lover.

"Brive Jack Rackham, the 'ero of a thousand battles, aye, battles fought in bed
wi' wenches. Oooee, my brive Calico. 'Ere's where your bloody neck takes a
new ruffle, one that was made to your order, I trow."

The captives were taken aboard the Fearless and before the commander.
Mary Read, recognized as a pirate chief, Anne Bonney and Calico Jack Rackham
were ordered to be taken to Port Royal, Jamaica, for trial. The others of the
company, found guilty on the spot, all sixty-four of them, were hanged to the
yardarms in batches and their mestizo wives and children sent helter-skelter
ashore.

"'Tis the true reward o' scoundrels," said an officer as he led the remaining
captives to the lazareet. "Yours be awaiting you at Port Royal."

"Say you," said Mary. "'Tis been my boast I'll cheat the gallows an' I've seen
naught to change my word."

IV

At Port Royal the three captives were paraded the length of the town and back
to the little gaol beside the water-front where Anne and Mary were placed in
one cell and Calico Jack in another. From where she sat Mary could see both
the sea and the gallows upon which she and her friends were to be hanged.
British justice must prevail; they would be tried before a Crown-appointed
judge, so already they knew their fate; he was a hanging judge, without pity or
mercy. Reports did get to London and, if it were learned he had freed one
accused of piracy, no matter how innocent of the crime charged, his own official
head would have been demanded and he would have been compelled to yield
his court to one less merciful.

There was an examination. Jack Rackham answered all the questions put to
him, confessing his guilt but gallantly insisting that both the women were merely
his wenches and mistresses. Only in the case of Anne Bonney was the plea
even considered. The King's Prosecutor had before him the famed pirate
wench and no such defence could be tolerated in her case. Mary Read was
questioned but she refused to answer.

"Very fine, madame," said the King's Counsel suavely, "but we shall find a way to loosen your tongue, never fear. I'll hang the others first; we'll return to you apace."

Mary Read was taken to court and heard Calico Jack's confession convict him; with him Anne Bonney was to go to the gallows after all. The judge, bewigged and red-faced, had them before his bench and from his height he looked down upon them and roared his verdict.

"You roved together and you laid together and now by the God above us, you will swing together. I sentence you both to be hanged by the neck until you are dead, dead, dead. And may the Lord have mercy on your souls."

But Anne Bonney pleaded her belly and was given a stay.

As she was parting for the last time from her lover, he besought her, for a moment, for a word to take him on his last journey.

"Nay, Calico. Not a word. For if you had fought like a man you'd not be dying like a dog."

The next morning the gaoler came to Mary Read and brought her a message from the man who was about to hang. All he asked was a crown, a coin to have in his pocket for his hangman. From her pouch in the leathern trunk she sent him two, three, and word that she was sorry he should die.

"But," she added, "'tis a gallant death befitting a gallant man."

Later she saw the small cart go past her window with Jack, his gaoler and a dominie standing upright. He was dressed in his best, knowing that all he possessed when he was cut down would become his executioner's perquisite. The little cart hurried to the head of the wharf to Gallows Point, where it stopped under the gibbet. The gaoler slipped the noose over the man's head, for a moment the man of God stood in prayer and then stepped down. The executioner, satisfied that all was ready, struck the horse a sharp blow causing him to leap forward, thus leaving the coloured breeks and their owner dangling at the end of the rope; the body twitched once or twice and then hung awkwardly.

Mary Read turned away from the sight, not with any sensation of sickness or even nausea. Her silly bluff that she would cheat the gallows was about to be called. Two hours later through the same window she saw the hangman, now dressed in the clothes of Calico Jack, breeks and all, on his way to a tavern. There he would recount the story of the great pirate's hanging for a drink or two, repeating it until he was as fox't as man could be. In a few days he might be wearing her old leathern breeks, swaggering about e'en drunker, for 'twas not every day he had a female pirate to hang. But, if she could not cheat the gallows, she might yet baffle her executioner.

Anne Bonney was not returned to the gaol. It was quite the custom in those days for women criminals, even without just cause, to plead pregnancy to escape transportation and the rope. But Anne was with child and there was an end on't.

Did the King's Counsel think he might provide a holiday for the people of Port Royal that he wished to hang Mary Read alone? 'Tis not known, but the delay may have been due to the fact that she refused to plead either guilty or not guilty nor would she plead her belly, though she was given an opportunity to do the last.

V

Mary made a friend of her gaoler's wife, a woman of good parts, sympathetically understanding, eager to be of help to her distinguished prisoner. All during the day citizens of Port Royal would come to the window of the prison and peer in at the female pirate, commenting upon her youth, her garb and what not, holding their babies aloft so that they, too, might in later years boast that they had seen the infamous pirate wench in gaol. There was more than usual interest in the hanging of this pirate, and the King's Prosecutor, depending upon the spectacular for some reward or promotion, intended making the most of it.

The only actual testimony available against Mary Read was that of the crew of the Fearless who would tell how she had fought, killing and injuring so many of their fellows before she was taken. And there was Anne Bonney, equally guilty and escaping by pleading her belly. On Mary's side was Calico Jack's sworn statement that Mary Read was one of his two mistresses, and certainly it would be hard to hang a woman for being in love with such a gallant rogue.

Usually in Port Royal a prisoner was permitted to have a witness present during all interrogations, but Bartholomew Lumley, K.C., was not going to have anyone take from him the credit for the conviction. Daily he came alone to Mary Read's cell and tried to wring from her a confession, almost going so far as to promise her a lighter sentence if she would but admit to being a pirate, confessing that she had taken a vessel by force upon the high seas.

The wench refused to plead, refused even to talk about her past. All she desired in this world was news of the Blackbird and its navigator, her husband. There was no news of either; so far as anyone in Port Royal could say both the vessel and its crew had been swallowed by the waves.

Master Lumley, almost despairing of a conviction e'en though he knew the judge for a hangman, ordered Mary Read to the torture chamber. She took the command stoically, knowing only from hearsay the misery of being pressed and stretched upon the rack. The King's Counsel, however, had more than these in store for her.

In the chamber above her cell the girl was thrown to the floor and her limbs were stretched to their utmost and lashed in ringbolts set in the floor. Then a board was placed on her body and weights, each of two stone, were successively piled upon the board. As each additional weight was added to her burden she was given another opportunity to plead. When the burden became insufferable she lapsed into unconsciousness; she did not come to herself until she had been returned to her cell.

The following day the King's Counsel came and explained to her the working of the rack; when his finely drawn description of the torture of this instrument failed to move the wench's tongue, she was again taken to the upper chamber and racked until outraged nature once more sought relief in unconsciousness. Still Mr. Lumley was not satisfied and he had brought out from its dusty corner "the scavenger's daughter," a device in which a cruelty opposite to that of the rack was practised. In this spherical instrument Mary was rolled like a ball; then its component parts, quartered like those of an orange peel, were tightened. Thus her sore body was compressed until she screamed with pain.

There was no confession wrung from her lips, no admission that she was the female pirate, even any kind of a pirate. It took her three days to recover from "the scavenger's daughter" and then she was with fever.

Seeking to raise her spirits, the gaoler's wife came with news of the Blackbird. The vessel and its crew had been taken by Woodes Rogers, the crew hanged at the yardarms—all save the captain who, pleading that he had been pressed into service after being taken as hostage, was in gaol awaiting corroboration of his story from the company of the West Indiaman.

That was that, thought the pirate wench. Her husband, as piratical and vengeful a man as any she had met in her short life, had in his extremity pled his belly and through his high-born family would save his neck. Too, said the gaoler's wife, he had demanded one-half the treasure, claiming he had affected the capture of the vessel, the Blackbird. Later, though Buttons would not be there to know it, he was to lead an expedition against the settlement at Grand Caicos.

The pirate wench's fever was high when she was led before the Court and her temper was short. She stood erect before the bench and answered his honour's questions jerkily.

"Why, wench, did ye take to pirating?" demanded the judge.

"I've not said I was a pirate," she retorted.

"You know that piracy's a hanging offence."

"As to hanging, I think that it be no great hardship. 'Tis fearsome an' rightly, or every cowardly fellow would turn pirate and so unfit the seas that men o' courage must starve."

His Honour took another tack. Sternly, almost fiercely he demanded, "Why come you here, a woman confessed, in the clothes of a man? It is an insult to this honourable Court."

"'Tis no offence intended. These be the only clothes I ken."

"I think I shall order you back to your confinement to don clothes more suitable to the decorum of this Court."

It may have been the steadily rising fever or the shortness of her temper.

"Have done wi' your jobation and get on wi' your hanging, milord."

Mary rasped the words out and the judge's temper went out of bounds. Forgetting how the record would look, he blurted out that she was to be hanged by the neck until dead, her body dried in the sun, and "may God damn your lecherous soul."

The pirate wench still did not flinch. Turning on her heel, she faced her gaoler who, at a nod from the Court led her back to her cell.

There she was greeted with tears by the gaoler's wife.

"Aye, my bonny, you're to hang. Tch! Tch! 'Tis too bad," and she let go a fresh batch of sobbing.

When the gaoler had gone the wife said: "Now, bonny, list to me. 'Tis easy enough to plead your belly. 'Tis something I'll do for you. They will ask me to decide if you be wi' child or no and I'll say them yes. What say? Those petty golden guineas you ha'e in your pouch would go a long way to saving your pretty neck."

"Nay, woman, if I be wi' child, let him die wi' me. 'Tis a beggars' world the King would make of it."

Then Mary fainted. The gaoler's wife put her on her cot and left her to regain consciousness. At noon the woman became worried about the prisoner; when she returned with the evening meal, destined to be the last Mary Read would eat in this world, and found her no better, she summoned the physician.

He diagnosed the trouble as distemper, that which the Italians called influenza. He dosed Mary Read with great quantities of English salts and left her to her fate. But when the hangman came in the morning he was unable to arouse the pirate wench; the physician was summoned again and this time he bled her and ordered her to remain in bed. For three days Mary hovered between life and death, wasting away from fever and weakening steadily through her inability to take nourishment. The gaoler's wife acted as nurse, staying night and day at Mary's call.

On the night of December 3rd, 1720, the leech again visited his patient and gave it as his considered opinion that he had saved her life and that she would be fit at sunrise to mount the gallows and give up that life in payment for her sins.

Mary Read accepted his verdict and when he had left she asked that her chest be brought to the side of her cot. Then she asked to be left alone.

With great difficulty she rose from her cot and opened the precious chest. There was her little pouch holding a hundred golden guineas, less the three she had given to Calico Jack Rackham, that his hangman might be able to refresh himself after his trying task. There on the top lay many expensive garments, silken breeches and hose, brocaded waistcoats and other rich pieces fit for the finest macaroni in London; the choice of many rich ships. These the pirate wench put aside and digging deeper, brought to light dresses and petticoats, more silken stockings and embroidered slippers. From the very bottom she brought forth rouge and paint and cosmetics, perfumes of great rarity and laid them all at the foot of her cot. It was the clothing of a lady of quality taken from countless prizes and assembled with loving care.

Then she removed the leathern breeks, the coarse sailcloth shirt, the cotton hose and the rough boots.

In the morning came again the executioner, together with a chaplain and the Crown officials, to claim the person of Mary Read who was to be "hanged by the neck until dead and her body dried in the sun," her soul consigned by her judge to the hell of his fathers. Instead they found the dead body of the one they sought, clothed not in the habiliments of her sex but in her old leathern breeks, her old shirt and cotton hose, a gay bandanna about her head.

At the foot of her bed there was a pile of ladies' garments surmounted by a small pouch of golden guineas, now less by three more, a note pinned to the last:

"To my gaoler's wife: I had thought to die as a woman but better judgment prevailed and I die as I lived. Mary Read."

THE END